# MYSTERY CATS

MORE FELINE FELONIES BY
**LILIAN JACKSON BRAUN**
**PATRICIA HIGHSMITH**
**EDWARD D. HOCH**
And Fourteen Other Modern Masters of Mystery

SIGNET ☆ 451-AE8293 ☆ (CANADA $5.99) ☆ **U.S. $4.99**

# FUR YOUR INFORMATION ...

**"THE CALLER"** by Hugh B. Cave
A stray feline falls asleep in a cemetery, then goes calling on an elderly couple with a message about murder in this riveting tale that plays on the cat's traditional role as a medium for spirits.

**"WHO KILLED WEE WINKY?"**
by Barbara Owens
When a big orange tomcat sneaks out of its owner's apartment and doesn't come back, an aging widow goes hunting for a cat killer as Barbara Owens creates a chilling portrait of madness and obsession.

**"THE ALEXANDRIAN CAT"**
by Steven Saylor
A Roman detective tries to save an innocent man from execution in ancient Egypt where killing a cat is punishable by death and motives for murder are timeless in a fascinating story steeped in the mysteries of the past.

**"THE CAT IN THE BAG"**
by Charles Peterson
Kit, the Cat Burglar, gets hired for an unusual heist: to steal a cat made famous by a TV cat-food commercial. But a double cross may leave Kit holding the bag instead of the kitty in this high-spirited caper.

**AND A DOZEN OTHER TALES THAT COME IN ON LITTLE CAT'S FEET ... AND BRING YOU THE LION'S SHARE OF MYSTERY FUN.**

# MYSTERY CATS III
## More Feline Felonies

### EDITED BY
### Cynthia Manson

A SIGNET BOOK

SIGNET
Published by the Penguin Group
Penguin Books USA Inc., 375 Hudson Street,
New York, New York 10014, U.S.A.
Penguin Books Ltd, 27 Wrights Lane,
London W8 5TZ, England
Penguin Books Australia Ltd, Ringwood,
Victoria, Australia
Penguin Books Canada Ltd, 10 Alcorn Avenue,
Toronto, Ontario, Canada M4V 3B2
Penguin Books (N.Z.) Ltd, 182–190 Wairau Road,
Auckland 10, New Zealand

Penguin Books Ltd, Registered Offices:
Harmondsworth, Middlesex, England

Published by Signet, an imprint of Dutton Signet,
a division of Penguin Books USA Inc.

First Signet Printing, February, 1995
10  9  8  7  6  5  4  3  2  1

We are grateful to the following for permission to use their copyrighted
material:

"Phut Phat Concentrates" by Lilian Jackson Braun, copyright © 1963 by
Davis Publications, Inc., reprinted by permission of Blanche C. Gregory, Inc.;
"The Empty Birdhouse" by Patricia Highsmith, copyright © 1968 by Patricia
Highsmith, reprinted by permission of the Gotham Art & Literary Agency;
"The Nile Cat" by Edward D. Hoch, copyright © 1969 by Davis Publications,
Inc., reprinted by permission of the author; "A Feline Felony" by Lael J.
Littke, copyright © 1967 by Davis Publications, Inc., reprinted by permission
of the author; "The Searching Cats" by Frances and Richard Lockridge,
copyright © 1956 by Frances and Richard Lockridge, reprinted by permission
of Curtis Brown, Ltd.; "Chocolate" by Leslie Meier, copyright © 1992 by
Bantam Doubleday Dell Magazines, reprinted by permission of the author;
"Who Killed Wee Winky?" by Barbara Owens, copyright © 1993 by Bantam
Doubleday Dell Magazines, reprinted by permission of the author; "Mrrrar!"
by Edgar Pangborn, copyright © 1953 by Mercury Publications, Inc., © re-
newed 1980 by Davis Publications, Inc., reprinted by permission of Richard

(The following page constitutes an extension of this copyright page.)

REGISTERED TRADEMARK—MARCA REGISTRADA

Printed in the United States of America

# Contents

# Introduction

You have before you the third book in the ever popular *Mystery Cats* series. Mystery fans and cat lovers alike cannot seem to get enough of reading mysteries that feature cats in starring roles. In this particular collection of stories, you will be asked to make a leap of faith when reading "A Feline Felony" by Lael J. Littke, and "Professor Kreller's Secret" by Ingram Meyer. In these stories appearances *are* what they appear to be, so you will have to trust your own instincts (your human instincts). As always, black cats are associated with the supernatural and bad luck, but three stories in this book will change your prejudice against black cats. In "The Caller" by Hugh B. Cave, "The Black Cat" by Lee Somerville, and "The Witch's Cat" by Manly Wade Wellman, you will be witness to black cats acting in heroic capacities. These cats put their supernatural powers to work in order to capture a common criminal or a murderer.

We have also included several traditional whodunits which feature cats in a wide range of roles. Stories by Edward D. Hoch, Frances and Richard Lockridge, and Barbara Owens interweave cats into their mysteries with ease—and considerable suspense. For example, "The Alexandrian Cat" by Steven Saylor, concerns a sacred cat murdered in Ancient Egypt, a crime punishable by death. A wealthy Roman is wrongfully accused and Gordianus (the detective or rather "The Finder") discovers the true cat killer.

Finally, no cat anthology is complete without a story by the Queen of Cats, Lilian Jackson Braun. In her amusing story "Phut Phat Concentrates," a cat tries to communicate with his live-in owners, but with little success. And if cats *could* talk, I'm not sure we would be pleased at what they'd say as demonstrated in a most unusual story, "Helix the Cat," by Theodore Sturgeon. . . .

We hope you enjoy this entertaining and diverse collection of feline fables.

—Cynthia Manson

# THE CALLER

## by Hugh B. Cave

Sarah Pritchard is my name. At any rate, it's the one I'm going to use in telling you what happened. That's because I want it told *my* way, not by a crowd of prying TV people and whoever writes the crazy stuff in those supermarket tabloids.

It began one summer day in the year of Our Lord '92. I was in the kitchen fixing us a supper of vegetable stew—we neither of us eat meat, I want you to know—when all at once I heard this peculiar scratching noise at the back door. Jabed heard it, too. He was sitting there at the kitchen table reading our smalltown weekly newspaper—July the eighth, it was, a Wednesday—and he looked up with a frown.

The scratching sound came again, like a raccoon or something was out there trying to claw the door open. Jabed got up and shuffled over to turn the knob. And there on the stoop outside, staring in at us, was a cat, a little old black cat with yellow eyes and one white front paw. It walked right in as if it owned the place.

Well, now, we don't dislike cats. In the sixty-two years we've been together as man and wife we must have had a dozen or more. So I put some water in a dish for this one—you shouldn't give a stray cat milk, you know; some of them can get sick on it—and I opened a can of tuna and put that down as well. Then we just stood there, Jabed and me, watching our caller till she finished filling herself.

And then—I know you're not going to believe this right off, but bear with me, please, and you'll learn to—then that little black cat looked up at us and said, plain as day, "Thank you, Sarah and Jabed. That was real neighborly of you."

*And I knew that voice. Both of us did.*

Where we live, I have to tell you, is out in the country, and our nearest neighbors are the folks buried in the town cemetery, just down the road a piece. I'm not going to name the town or even the state it's in, for the same reason I didn't tell you our real names. All you need to know is that the town is small enough for us to have personally known a good many of the people *in* that cemetery. And the voice coming out of the cat that day belonged unmistakably to our friend Edna Clifton, whose funeral we'd attended two years and five months before, when she passed away at age seventy-seven after a heart attack.

"How are you, anyway?" Edna or the cat said then.

We stammered some kind of reply, or at last I did— Jabed just stood there looking like he'd been turned into a pillar of salt. Then that yellow-eyed little animal asked, as natural as you please, "Have you see my Andrew lately?"

"Why, yes," I managed to answer. "He was in church last Sunday."

"Did he look well?"

"About the same," I stammered. "Though he still walks with a limp." Just before she died her husband Andrew had broke his hip, falling on an icy sidewalk when he stepped out of the town barbershop.

"Did he mention me?" asked little old Blackie with

the white paw, gazing up at me as if asking questions in a human voice is a thing cats do all the time.

"Well, now, Edna, as a matter of fact he did," I heard myself saying back. "Yes, he certainly did. Jabed here asked him how he was, and he distinctly said—I remember his exact words—he distinctly said, 'Not so good as when my Edna was alive.'" Then I thought of something and hastened to add, "Why don't you go and talk to him? Unless it's too far, and you'd like us to drive you there."

"I don't have time," Edna said.

"What?"

"My little cat friend here is new at this sort of thing. She wouldn't be able to help me that long. In fact, I'm surprised she—"

Then suddenly a strange thing happened. That little black cat stopped talking right in the middle of a sentence and meowed instead. I mean, all at once she was *only* a cat, with only a cat's natural voice. And for the next hour or so, until she went to the door and meowed to be let out, all she did was snoop around the house, upstairs and down, the way you'd expect any normal stray cat to do.

We let her out then—or, to be exact, Jabed did before I had sense enough to stop him—and that was the last we saw of Blackie for twenty-four hours. We talked about her during that time, of course. I expect you would have, too, unless you're accustomed to being called on by cats that speak like people. But we talked about her only to each other. Not for all the tea in China would we have told anyone else about her. Not at that time, anyway.

"What I think," Jabed said, "is that she may have been hanging around the cemetery, and the spirit of Edna Clifton somehow got into her. Ghosts or spirits are able to possess *people,* aren't they? So why couldn't one take possession of a cat for a time?"

"Maybe she was just sort of hanging around Edna's grave," I said. "Or sleeping there by her tombstone."

Whatever, twenty-four days after her first visit—on the first day of August, that is—Miss Blackie came scratching at our door a second time, and again we let her in. And this time after she'd been fed, she thanked us in a *different* voice.

It was a man's voice this time. It belonged to Odell Osgood, who had died more than four years before at age eighty-six, of pneumonia which he got when caught in a spell of terrible weather while out deer hunting.

Odell was buried in the town cemetery, too, of course. His wife Clara was there with him. They had a married daughter who lived in the next county with her husband and two children.

We fed Blackie same as before, this time giving her some leftover canned salmon we happened to have. After she'd eaten every last morsel, she took time to clean her mouth with that pretty white front paw of hers before turning around to look at us. By which time Jabed and I had both got over the shock of seeing her again and seated ourselves at the kitchen table.

"You two are looking real fit," said Blackie in the rusty baritone voice of old Odell. "You must be doin' somethin' right." And he—or Blackie—laughed at his own joke like he'd always used to when he was alive. In fact, if it had really been him instead of a cat there in front of us, he most likely would have slapped his big right thigh along with the hooting. Odell weighed well over two hundred fifty pounds before the pneumonia wasted him away and always made me think of a Santa Claus in overalls.

"We try to eat right and take care of ourselves," I told him.

"Good for you, both of you," he said. "Keep at it long as you can, because layin' there in the graveyard under a blanket of earth ain't much fun, I can tell you." The voice laughed again—sort of like a bullfrog croaking. And then he said, "You seen any of my kin lately, by any chance?"

We told him—Jabed did—that we'd seen Beulah and her husband Derwin *and* the two children only a week or so before, at the county fair. "All of them looked just fine," Jabed said.

"Derwin still on the wagon, would you say?"

"Yep, he was cold sober. Whyn't you—er—trot over there and pay them a visit?"

"Can't," said Odell. "I wouldn't have time."

"Like it was with Edna Clifton?" I said. "This—whatever it is—only lasts a short while?"

"What you mean, Edna Clifton?"

"Well, the last time you called on us—I mean the last time Blackie here called on us—she was Edna. You didn't know about that, hey?"

"Nope. All I know is—" And like before, though maybe not so soon, Blackie's people voice sort of faded away to a meow, and our caller was again just a little old black cat with yellow eyes, sitting there with a sad look on her face. And after going to her dish and meowing for some more of the canned salmon and being given some and taking her own good time eating it, she wandered off to explore the house again, just like any ordinary cat might have done.

I said to Jabed, after she left that time, that we

should have put her on a leash of some sort and gone with her to see if she actually did go to the cemetery like we suspected. And if she did, to find out what happened when she got there.

Well, it went on and on. In September, Blackie came a third time and was yet another person in the cemetery, this time Thelma Goodis, who died of cancer at age sixty-three in the year of Our Lord '88. We talked with Thelma for quite a while, mostly about her husband and children. Then in October Blackie returned as Avery Chatwin, the town undertaker, who, if you can believe it, actually died *in* the cemetery of a stroke while burying his own mother. He'd left a wife and three children, and we talked with him even longer. Blackie was learning to hold on better each time she came, it seemed.

Meanwhile, of course—what else would you expect?—my Jabed and I had gone to the cemetery to investigate. Twice, in fact. The first time was a nice bright day and we walked, thinking we needed the exercise. It tired us out pretty much, though, so the next time we went, we drove there in our old Buick.

On each occasion we strolled about among the grave markers for an hour or more, reading off names to each other and looking for signs that Blackie had been there.

And she had.

We didn't actually see her, I have to admit, but we found more than a few places where the grass was matted down the way outdoor cats do when they make themselves a bed, and each one of those depressions had some black fur in it. One such was by Edna Clifton's grave. Others were on or close to the graves of Odell Osgood, Thelma Goodis, and Avery Chatwin.

There were three other such bedding-down spots,

too. But, as I've remarked, we didn't actually see Blackie herself. Evidently she slept there in the cemetery but spent her days hunting food to keep from starving.

"Food such as field mice," Jabed suggested with a grimace. Like I said, we neither of us eat meat any more.

But then, soon after Blackie called on us as Avery Chatwin, we had a visit of a more ordinary kind. Nothing mysterious this time. No yellow-eyed black cat speaking with the voices of dead people. This caller was only Jabed's nephew, Arnold Pritchard, who drove into our yard one day without a word of warning and asked could he stay with us awhile to do a little hunting.

Arnold was thirty-two years old at this time and still single, though handsome enough if you like your men real pretty. He lived sixty-odd miles away in the state capital, where he worked at selling used cars. We'd never liked him much.

Jabed and I grudgingly said all right, we'd put him up, but he had to promise to behave himself.

"What do you mean by that?" Arnold challenged with a grin.

"The last time you came here to hunt, you played fast and loose with that nice Mary Wharton at the drugstore," Jabed reminded him. "The townsfolk talked about it for weeks and for some reason blamed *us*. So this time, if it's hunting you want, we'll thank you to hunt things that have four legs."

Both of us knew, I suspect, that talking to the grandfather clock in the hall would have been more productive. Handsome Arnold couldn't even look at a girl without making a pass at her. And before he'd been with us a week, he'd forgot all about wanting to take home a deer.

She worked as a waitress at a restaurant in town, this girl. Her name was Nina Petrillo and her father had run off years ago and she lived with her mother in a cottage on Swamp Hollow Road. She was twenty-six, Arnold told us the first time he brought her to our house.

Later the town paper said she was only twenty.

Anyhow, she was real nice looking, with glossy black hair and a quick, bright smile and sparkly dark eyes. And with Arnold being about as handsome as a man can be, as I've said already, they made a fine-looking pair.

He saw her most every day, and the whole town was soon aware of it because he took her just about everywhere a man could take a woman in our little neck of the woods. He took her to the moving picture theater, and dancing at the Red Barn out on the highway, and even to a church supper one time. One evening when he came in late and we were still up watching television, but really waiting to lock up because we could never be sure Arnold would remember to, Jabed asked him, "Now where did you and Nina go this evening, Arnold?"

"Oh, nowhere in particular," said he with a grin.

"Just riding around, you mean?"

"That's it. Just ridin' around."

"What about the deer hunting? You give that up, have you?"

"No, no. I still want a deer to take home when I go."

"When you go," said Jabed, shaking his head. "And when will that be, do you suppose?"

"Oh, pretty soon," says Arnold, grinning again. "Why? Are you that anxious to be rid of me?"

So it went, until one morning Arnold got up from the breakfast table after eating hardly any breakfast and announced he *was* going hunting again. And took his rifle when he left the house.

About ten o'clock that morning our telephone rang and it was Claudia Petrillo, Nina's mother, calling to ask if her daughter was at our house. I was the one answered the call, and I said, "At our house, Mrs. Petrillo? What do you mean?"

"I mean she was out with your Arnold again last night and hasn't come home," said Claudia in a truly distraught voice. "Did Arnold come home?"

"Well, of course," I said.

"Then let me talk to him."

"Mrs. Petrillo," I said, "you can't talk to him now. He went hunting right after breakfast."

"Well, when will he be home?"

"I can't answer that. I just don't know."

She hung up, but called again about twelve thirty and said the restaurant where Nina worked had called to ask where the girl was, because Nina hadn't showed up for work at eleven as she was supposed to. And so it went all through that day, with our phone ringing every hour or so and the poor woman becoming more and more distraught.

About five thirty, when it was getting dark outside, Arnold finally turned up—without any deer, I might add—and we asked him where Nina was.

He was dog-tired and dirty from being in the woods all day, and sort of just stared at us for a few seconds. Then, "What do you mean, where's Nina?" he said.

"Just that," said Jabed. "Her mother's been calling all day. Says the girl didn't come home last night and didn't show up for work today, and no one knows where she is."

Arnold gave his head a shake and stared at us some more. "I don't understand," he said. "I drove her home last night same as always."

"You drove her home," I said. "Does that mean you walked her to her door?"

"Well, no," he admitted. "I guess I just—well, I waved goodnight and drove off after she reached the porch steps."

"And what time was that?"

"What time was it? I don't know. Eleven thirty. Maybe a little later."

"And you haven't seen or heard from her since?"

"Uh-uh." He wagged his head. "I been in the woods all day."

"Then you better call her mother right now," Jabed said, "and tell her everything you know. Because the girl's disappeared, and you're the one she's been going out with for the past ten days."

That began it. Arnold called the girl's mother and she called the police, and pretty soon the whole town was talking about Nina Petrillo's mysterious vanishment. And not only talking about it but searching high and low for the girl. Nothing like that had ever happened before in our little town.

And the girl stayed missing.

Well. Arnold didn't go back to the city like he'd planned to. He stayed on and took part in the search along with every other able-bodied man in town. Even some of the younger women joined in. For days and days, teams of searchers scoured the woods for miles around. Our little town had never seen such goings on before.

The police questioned practically everyone, even

asking for help over the TV and radio and flashing appeals on the screen at the moving picture theater. But Nina Petrillo stayed missing.

Our little Blackie came around only once during those terrible days. We'd just finished a late supper one evening, and Arnold had gone up to his room to rest after being out searching all day, when there came that familiar scratching sound at the back door. "I wonder if *she's* seen Nina by any chance," Jabed said as he went to open it.

Little old yellow-eyes came trotting in and said hello as usual, and this time the voice belonged to someone younger than we'd come to expect. This time it was the voice of Charley Stimson, who had died only two years before when one of those big trailer trucks tipped over his car at Dead Man's Curve, and him only eighteen at the time.

Speaking with his voice, Blackie asked if we'd seen his mom and dad lately, and I fibbed and told him they were fine, which I didn't know was true because they'd moved away soon after he died, saying they couldn't bear living so near to where it happened. Then Jabed said, "Did you know Nina Petrillo is missing, Charley?" Being near the same age, Charley and Nina had known each other, of course. In fact, they'd been sweet on each other.

"Missing?" said Blackie, peering up at us. "No, I hadn't heard. You mean she ran away for some reason?"

"Well, we don't know. That's a possibility, of course.'

"Tell me about it," Blackie said, twitching her whiskers.

It took quite a while for us to tell her the whole story, and she continued to be Charley the whole time, but she couldn't help us any. When her Charley voice finally changed to a meow, we gave her some canned catfood we'd bought for her and she did her usual tour of the house and departed.

A minute or so later Arnold came downstairs with a scowl on his face.

"Heard you talking to someone," he said. "Someone I know, was it?"

"Nope," said Jabed. We hadn't told his nephew about the visits from our little four-legged friend. In fact, we hadn't told anyone, being afraid they might think we were coming down with that Alazaheim disease or whatever it's called.

"Talking about Nina, were you?" Arnold persisted.

"Well, yes, we were talking about Nina. What else does anyone talk about these days? But she didn't have anything new to tell us."

"She?" said Arnold, really scowling now. "It was a man's voice I heard."

"Probably sounds like one," said Jabed with a warning glance at me. "It was old Mrs. Black—you've never met her—and she has a voice deeper'n mine."

With that, Arnold turned to go back upstairs, seemingly satisfied, but at the foot of the staircase he stopped. "I been thinking things over," he said. "This is Friday and I'll stay through the weekend, but then I really have to get back to work or I could lose my job. I'm truly sorry, but if Nina has just up and left town—and that's what it looks like, you have to admit—there isn't much anyone can do about it, is there?" He stood there shaking his head at us. "You know," he said, "I was fond of that girl. I truly was. If she hadn't run away, I might even have asked her to marry me."

He went trudging up the stairs then, and we heard

the door of his room shut behind him. And Jabed looked at me the way he had when we talked about Blackie eating field mice.

"Marry him?" Jabed snorted. "That girl marry Arnold? I'll bet."

Which brings me—at last, you'll probably say—to the end of what I'm trying to tell you.

The weather was bad that weekend—cold and rainy the whole time—but the search for Nina Petrillo went on all the same. Still there was no trace of the missing girl, and on Sunday evening at supper Arnold informed us he'd be leaving in the morning. "I've done all I can," he said. "Even though I was the last person to see her, I don't have any inside track on where to look for her. Like I've told you and everyone else, I left her safe at home that night."

I couldn't think what to say to that, and neither could Jabed apparently. We just looked at him.

"I suppose it'll seem suspicious, me leaving before she's found," he said, "but I have to. Me losing my job over this won't help anyone."

"What time will you want breakfast?" I asked.

"About seven, maybe?"

"All right," I said.

He said goodnight and went up to bed about nine thirty, I remember. That was kind of early for him, but the three of us had been sitting in the living room, still talking about Nina and what could have happened to her, and it seemed to upset him more than usual. No doubt he was truly weary by this time, too. He'd searched for the missing girl as hard as anyone.

We heard him shut his door. Then Jabed picked up a book he was reading—one about cats that I'd borrowed from Abigail Watson, who had at least a dozen of them. Cats, I mean, notebooks. And feeling like I wanted a cup of tea to settle my nerves, I went into the kitchen to put the kettle on.

And while I was at the sink, filling the kettle, I heard that familiar scratching sound at the back door again.

"Jabed!" I called.

Jabed came running. He knows by my tone of voice when I'm real serious about something. I pointed to the door and said, "It's Blackie!" and he went straight to the door and opened it.

A gust of wind-driven rain came in along with Blackie. Jabed had to lean against the door to shut it, the wind was blowing so hard.

And Blackie—well, I felt so sorry for that poor little cat, I got down on my knees and took her up in my arms. She was soaked through and through and didn't stop shivering till I'd held her up against me for a good two minutes. Then when I let her go and stood up, she did something she'd never, ever, done before. She jumped onto a chair and from that onto the kitchen table, and made beckoning motions with that one white paw as if to say, "Come closer! I've something important to tell you!"

I felt it so strong that I reached for Jabed's hand and both of us stepped right up to the table like we were kids in school and the teacher had said, "Come here!"

"You mustn't let him go!" Blackie said then, in a voice we knew only too well. "He has to be punished!"

I looked at my husband. "Jabed!" I whispered. "It's Nina!"

Jabed just stood there returning the stare of those yellow eyes.

"We were in his car on Cemetery Road and he

wanted to—to make love to me," Blackie went on, sort of sobbing the words out in Nina Petrillo's voice. "Then he tried to force me to do what he wanted, and when I fought him he got angry and—and choked me to death. And when he discovered I was dead, he buried my body where he knew no one would ever think to look for it."

I finally found my voice and said, "Where was that?"

"We were on Cemetery Road, like I said," replied Blackie in the sobbing voice of the missing girl. "He just drove to the cemetery and went from one grave marker to another looking at the dates on them. When he found one so old it wasn't likely to be visited any more, he dug down and buried me above the coffin already in it."

I was so frightened I couldn't get a word out. But not Jabed. I'm real proud of my husband for what he did then.

Pulling up a chair, he sat down and rested his arms on the table, then leaned forward with his face up close to Blackie's and said, "What'd he dig with, Nina?"

"A license plate off his car. To break up the ground, he used a tire-changing tool."

"And which grave are you talking about?"

"It says on the headstone, 'Martha Anne Dolliver, Beloved Wife of Jonathan Dolliver, 1837–1904.' Like I said, he chose a grave so old that no one would be likely to visit it and discover he'd disturbed it."

"Now tell me," Jabed said, "how is it you can talk to us through this little cat here? You and all those others, I mean."

"What others? I don't know about any others."

"Well, there've been some, believe me. Just tell me how *you're* able to do it."

"Cats are spiritual creatures," said Nina. "Some are, anyway. Tonight this one just happened to come and bed down next to the grave Arnold put me in." The voice stopped for a few seconds, then went on with a note of determination in it, like Nina herself was actually standing there in front of us with her fists clenched. "You won't let Arnold get away with it, will you?" she said. "I'll never be able to rest right if he does."

"We'll make sure he's punished," Jabed promised.

"Thank you. Oh, thank you both!" Blackie cried, then jumped down from the table and trotted off to do her tour of the house as usual. She hadn't meowed first, I noticed—she was staying human a lot longer by this time—so she was still Nina at that point but no doubt too upset to talk any more.

"Jabed," I said then, "what are we to do?"

"Call the police of course," said my husband.

"And tell them a *cat*—"

"What else? If they want to think we've lost our minds, that's up to them. But even if they do, they'll go out there to the cemetery and look. You can bank on it." He reached for my hand. "Come on, Sarah. Let's call them."

Have I told you our telephone is on a table in the hall, at the foot of the stairs? Well, it is. We went to it and Jabed took it up and dialed the number. We don't have that fancy 911 thing in our small town; you dial the police station. The number was on a list right there before the phone.

I heard the phone at the station ringing. Then from the staircase behind me I heard the voice of Arnold

Pritchard, telling Jabed to put the phone down. "Or," Arnold snarled, "I'll drop you where you stand."

We both turned, Jabed still holding the telephone to his ear, and there was Arnold, in his pajamas, halfway down the stairs with his hunting rifle. He aimed the gun at us. "Put it down," he snarled again. "Right now! This minute!"

It seemed to take forever for Jabed to lower the phone from his ear.

"She was here, wasn't she?" Arnold screamed in a voice like—well, like he was a child again, on the verge of having hysterics. "I didn't kill her, did I? She got out of there and came here to tell you. I heard her!" His hands were shaking so hard I thought the gun would go off by itself and probably kill one of us, and my heart all but stopped beating. "Where is she?" Arnold shouted. "Where'd she go?"

He was crazy, that's what he was. Plain crazy, from hearing the voice of that girl he'd murdered and gone to such pains to bury in a place where she would never be found.

But it wasn't Jabed or me who answered him.

It was the same voice again—Nina's—from the darkness on the landing above him.

"I'm right here, Arnold," it said. And something even darker than the darkness—except for one little patch of white—launched itself from the upstairs hall and landed in a scratching, clawing heap on Arnold's head.

The rifle flew out of Arnold's hands and got to the bottom of the stairs long before Arnold himself finished falling down them. Jabed had plenty of time to snatch it up. So when Arnold finally reached the bottom and managed to scramble back onto his feet, there was Jabed pointing the weapon straight at him and saying to me, "Call the police, Sarah. Tell them we have Nina's killer right here and they should come and get him." And to Arnold he added, "You make one move, mister, and there'll be another grave in that cemetery, I promise you."

So there you are. The police came and took Jabed's no-good nephew away, and then, in spite of all that rain and wind, they went on out to the cemetery. Jabed went with them. Sure enough, someone had dug up the sod over that old grave and replaced it, and when they took it up again, using a searchlight on the police car to light up what they were doing, they found Nina Petrillo buried there, and she'd been choked to death like she said.

The man who killed her is in prison now for the rest of his life, where he belongs. As for Blackie, when we looked for her that night after Arnold got back from the cemetery, we couldn't find her. With so many people coming and going, she must have slipped out sometime when the door was opened. But she came calling again a few days later and talked to us in yet another voice from the cemetery, and she still visits us every so often.

She's getting pretty old now, though. It can't go on much longer.

We'll miss that little black cat when she dies. If we know about it when it happens, and can find her, we hope to get permission to bury her right there in the cemetery among her many friends.

# THE ALEXANDRIAN CAT

## by Steven Saylor

We were sitting in the sunshine in the atrium of Lucius Claudius's house, discussing the latest gossip from the Forum, when a terrible yowling pierced the air.

Lucius gave a start at the noise and opened his eyes wide. The caterwauling terminated in a feline shriek, followed by a scraping, scrambling noise and then the appearance of a gigantic yellow cat racing across the roof above us. The red tiles offered little traction to the creature's claws and it skittered so close to the edge that for a moment I thought it might fall right into Lucius's lap. Lucius seemed to think so as well. He scrambled up from his chair, knocking it over as he frantically retreated to the far side of the fish pond.

The big cat was quickly followed by a smaller one, which was solid black. The little creature must have had a particularly aggressive disposition to have given chase to a rival so much larger than itself, but its careless ferocity proved to be its downfall—literally, for while its opponent managed to traverse the roof without a misstep, the black cat careered so recklessly across the tiles that at a critical turning it lost its balance. After an ear-rending cacophony of feral screeching and claws scraping madly against tiles, the black cat came plummeting feet-first into the atrium.

Lucius screamed like a child, then cursed like a

man. The young slave who had been filling our wine cups came running as fast as he could.

"Accursed creature!" cried Lucius. "Get it away from me! Get it out of here!"

The slave was joined at once by others, who surrounded the beast. There was a standoff as the black cat flattened its ears and growled while the slaves held back, wary of its fangs and claws.

Regaining his dignity, Lucius caught his breath and straightened his tunic. He snapped his fingers and pointed at the overturned chair. One of the slaves righted it, whereupon Lucius stepped onto it. No doubt he thought to put as much distance between himself and the cat as possible, but instead he made a terrible error, for by raising himself so high he became the tallest object in the atrium.

Without warning, the cat gave a sudden leap. It broke through the cordon of slaves, bounded onto the seat of Lucius's chair, ran vertically up the length of his body, scrambled over his face onto the top of his head, then pounced onto the roof and disappeared. For a long moment Lucius stood gaping.

At last, assisted by his slaves (many of whom seemed about to burst out laughing), Lucius managed to step shakily from the chair. As he sat, a fresh cup of wine was put in his hand and he raised it to his lips with an unsteady hand. He drained the cup and handed it back to the slave. "Well!" he said. "Go on now, all of you. The excitement's over." As the slaves departed from the atrium, I saw that Lucius was blushing, no doubt from the embarrassment of having so thoroughly lost his composure, not to mention having been got the better of by a wild beast in his own home, and in front of his slaves. The look on his chubby, florid face was so comic that I had to bite my lips to keep from smiling.

"Cats!" he said at last. "Accursed creatures! When I was a boy, you hardly saw them at all in Rome. Now they've taken over the city! Thousands of them everywhere, wandering about at will, squabbling and mating as they please, and no one able to stop them. At least one still doesn't see them much in the countryside; farmers run them off because they frighten the other animals so badly. Weird, fierce little monsters! I think they come from Hades."

"Actually, I believe they came to Rome by way of Alexandria," I said quietly.

"Oh?"

"Yes. Sailors first brought them over from Egypt, or so I've heard. Seafarers like cats because they eat the vermin on their ships."

"What a choice—rats and mice, or one of those fearsome beasts with its claws and fangs! And you, Gordianus—all this time you've sat there as if nothing were happening! Oh, but I forget, you're used to cats. You and your Egyptian concubine have a cat which you keep as a kind of pet, don't you? As if the creature were a dog!" He made a face. "What do you call the thing?"

"Bethesda has always given her cats the name of Bast. It's what the Egyptians call their cat-god."

"What a peculiar people, to worship animals as if they were gods. No wonder we've practically taken over their government. A people who worship cats can hardly be fit to rule themselves."

I kept silent at this bit of conventional wisdom. My friend Lucius Claudius has a sweet nature and a kind heart, but he is a Roman patrician after all, and he often subscribes to the values of his class without question. I might have pointed out that the cat-worshipers he so offhandedly disdained had managed to create a culture of exquisite subtlety and monumental achievements while Romulus and Remus were still suckling a she-wolf, but the day was too hot to engage in historical debate.

"If the creature comes back, I shall have it killed," Lucius muttered under his breath, nervously eyeing the roof.

"In Egypt," I said, "such an act would be considered murder, punishable by death."

Lucius looked at me askance. "Surely you exaggerate! I realize that the Egyptians worship all sorts of birds and beasts, but it doesn't prevent them from stealing their eggs or eating their flesh. Is the slaughter of a cow considered murder?"

"Perhaps not, but the slaying of a cat most certainly is. In fact, when I was a young man in Alexandria, one of my earliest investigations involved the murder of a cat."

"Oh, Gordianus, you must be joking! You're not saying that you were actually hired to track down the killer of a cat, are you?"

"It was a bit more complicated than that."

Lucius smiled for the first time since we had been interrupted by the squabbling cats. "Come, Gordianus, don't tease me," he said, clapping his hands for the slave to bring more wine. "You must tell me the story."

I was glad to see him regain his good spirits. "Very well," I said. "I shall tell you the tale of the Alexandrian cat."

The precinct called Rhakotis is generally acknowledged to be the most ancient part of Alexandria, the

place where the city took root and about which it grew
into a great metropolis. The principal landmark of
Rhakotis is the Temple of Serapis, a magnificent marble edifice constructed on a huge scale and decorated
with fabulous conceits of alabaster, gold, and ivory.
Romans who have seen the temple begrudgingly admit
that for sheer splendor it might (mind you, *might*)
rival our own austere Temple of Jupiter—a telling
comment on Roman provincialism rather than on the
respective architectural merits of the two temples. If
I were a god, I know in which house I would choose
to live.

The temple is an oasis of light and splendor surrounded by a mazelike wilderness of winding streets.
The houses in Rhakotis, made of hardened earth, are
built high and jammed close together. The streets are
narrow and strung with ropes upon which the inhabitants hang laundry and fish and plucked fowl to dry.
The air is generally still and hot, but occasionally a
sea breeze will manage to cross the Island of Pharos
and the great harbor and the high city wall to stir the
tall palm trees which grow in the little squares and
gardens of Rhakotis.

In Rhakotis, one can almost imagine that the Greek
conquest never occurred. The city may be named for
Alexander and ruled by a Ptolemy, but the people
of the ancient district are distinctly Egyptian, darkly
complected with dark eyes and the type of features
one sees on the old statues of the Pharaohs. These
people are different from us, and so are their gods,
which are not the Greek and Roman gods of perfect
human form but strange hybrids of animals and men,
frightful to look at.

One sees many cats in Rhakotis. They wander about
as they wish, undisturbed, sunning themselves in

patches of light, chasing grasshoppers, dozing on
ledges and rooftops, staring at the inaccessible fish and
fowl hung, with the laundry, beyond their reach. But
the cats of Rhakotis do not go hungry; far from it.
People set bowls of food out on the street for them,
muttering incantations as they do so, and not even a
starving beggar would consider taking such conse-
crated food for himself—for the cats of Rhakotis, like
all cats throughout Egypt, are considered to be gods.
Men bow as they pass them in the street, and woe
unto the crass tourist from Rome or Athens who dares
to snigger at such a sight, for the Egyptians are as
vengeful as they are pious.

I found myself residing in Rhakotis for a number
of reasons. For one thing, a young Roman of little
wealth could find lodgings there to suit his means. But
Rhakotis offered far more than cheap dwellings. To
feed my mind, I could listen to the philosophers who
lectured to their students and debated one another on
the steps of the library attached to the Temple of Serapis. To feed my stomach, vendors at crowded street
corners hawked exotic delicacies unheard of in Rome.
As for the other appetites common to young men,
those were easily satisfied as well; the Alexandrians
consider themselves to be the most worldly of people,
and any Roman who disputes the point only demon-
strates his own unworldliness.

One morning I happened to be walking through one
of the district's less crowded streets when I heard a
noise behind me. It was a vague, indistinct noise, like
the sound of a roaring crowd some distance away. The
government of Egypt is notoriously unstable, and riots
are fairly common, but it seemed too early in the day
for people to be raging through the streets. Nevertheless, as I paused to listen, the noise became louder

and the echoey din resolved into the sound of angry human voices.

A moment later, a man in a blue tunic appeared from around a bend in the street, running headlong toward me, his head turned to look behind him. I hurriedly stepped out of the way, but he blindly changed his course and ran straight into me. We tumbled to the ground in a confusion of arms and legs.

"Numa's balls!" I shouted, for the fool had caused me to scrape my hands and knees on the rough paving stones.

The stranger suddenly stopped his mad scramble to get to his feet and stared at me. He was a man of middle age, well groomed and obviously well fed. There was absolute panic in his eyes, but also a glimmer of hope.

"You curse in Latin!" he said hoarsely. "You're a Roman, then, like me?"

"Yes."

"Countryman—save me!" By this time we were both on our feet again, but the stranger moved in such a spastic manner and clutched at me so desperately that I thought he might pull us to the ground again.

The noise of angry voices grew nearer. The man looked back to the way he had come. Fear danced across his face like a flame. He clutched me with both hands and kept his eyes on the bend.

"I swear, I never touched the beast!" he whispered hoarsely. "The little girl said I killed it, but it was already dead when I came upon it."

"What are you saying?"

"The cat! I didn't kill the cat! It was already dead, lying in the street. But they'll tear me limb from limb, these mad Egyptians! If I can only reach my house—"

At that moment, a number of people appeared at

the bend in the street, men and women dressed in the tattered clothing of the poorer classes. More people appeared, and more, shouting and twisting their faces into expressions of pure hatred. They came rushing toward us, some of them brandishing sticks and knives, others shaking their bare fists in the air.

"Help me!" the man shrieked, his voice breaking like a boy's. "Save me! I'll reward you!" The mob was almost upon us. I struggled to escape his grip. At last he broke away and resumed his headlong flight. As the angry mob drew nearer, for a moment it seemed that I had become the object of their quest. Indeed, a few of them headed straight for me, and I saw no possibility of escape. "Death comes as the end," goes the Egyptian poem, and I felt it drawing very near.

But a man near the front of the crowd, notable for his great long beard curled in the Babylonian fashion, saw the mistake and shouted in a booming voice, "Not that one! The man in blue is the one we want! Up there, at the end of the street! Quick, or he'll escape us again!"

The men and women who had been ready to strike me veered away at the last moment and ran on. I drew into a doorway, out of sight, and marveled at the size of the mob as it passed by. Half the residents of Rhakotis were after the Roman in blue!

Once the mob had passed, I stepped back into the street. Following the mob were a number of stragglers unable to keep up the pace. Among them I recognized a man who sold pastries from a shop on the Street of the Breadmakers. He was breathing hard but walked at a deliberate pace. In his hand he clutched a wooden rod for rolling dough. I knew him as a fat, cheerful baker whose chief joy was filling other people's stom-

achs, but on this morning he wore the grim counte-
nance of a determined avenger.

"Menapis, what is happening?" I said, falling into
step beside him.

He gave me such a withering look that I thought
he did not recognize me, but when he spoke it was
all too clear that he did. "You Romans come here
with your pompous ways and your ill-gotten wealth,
and we do our best to put up with you. You foist
yourself upon us, and we endure it. But when you
turn to desecration, you go too far! There are some
things even a Roman can't get away with!"

"Menapis, tell me what's happened."

"He killed a cat! The fool killed a cat just a stone's
throw from my shop!"

"Did you see it happen?"

"A little girl saw him do it. She screamed in terror,
naturally enough, and a crowd came running. They
thought the little girl was in danger, but it turned out
to be something far worse. The Roman fool had killed
a cat! We'd have stoned him to death right on the
spot, but he managed to slip away and start running.
The longer the chase went on, the more people came
out to join it. He'll never escape us now. Look up
ahead—the Roman rat must be trapped!"

The chase seemed to have ended, for the mob had
come to a stop in a wide square. If they had overtaken
him, the man in blue must already have been trampled
to a pulp, I thought, with a feeling of nausea. But as
I drew nearer, the crowd began to chant: "Come out!
Come out! Killer of the cat!" Beside me, Menapis
took up the chant with the others, slapping his rolling
pin against his palm and stamping his feet.

It seemed that the fugitive had taken refuge in a
prosperous-looking house. From the faces that stared

in horror from the upper-story windows before they were thrown shut, the place appeared to be full of Romans—the man's private dwelling, it seemed. That he was a man of no small means I had already presumed from the quality of his blue tunic, but the size of his house confirmed it. A rich merchant, I thought—but neither silver nor a silvery tongue was likely to save him from the wrath of the mob. They continued to chant and began to beat upon the door with clubs.

Menapis shouted, "Clubs will never break such a door! We'll have to make a battering ram." I looked at the normally genial baker beside me and a shiver ran up my spine. All of this—for a cat!

I withdrew to a quieter corner of the square, where a few of the local residents had ventured out of their houses to watch the commotion. An elderly Egyptian woman, impeccably dressed in a white linen gown, gazed at the mob disparagingly. "What a rabble!" she remarked to no one in particular. "What are they thinking of, attacking the house of a man like Marcus Lepidus?"

"Your neighbor?" I said.

"For many years, as was his father before him. An honest Roman trader, and a greater credit to Alexandria than any of this rabble will ever be. Are you a Roman, too, young man?"

"Yes."

"I thought so, from your accent. Well, I have no quarrel with Romans. Dealing with men like Marcus Lepidus and his father made my late husband a wealthy man. Whatever has Marcus done to bring such a mob to his door?"

"They accuse him of killing a cat."

She gasped. A look of horror contorted her wrinkled face. "That would be unforgivable!"

"He claims to be innocent. Tell me, who else lives in that house?"

"Marcus Lepidus lives with his two cousins. They help him run his affairs, I believe."

"And their wives?"

"The cousins are married, but their wives and children remain in Rome. Marcus is a widower. He has no children. Look there! What madness is this?"

Moving through the mob like a crocodile through lily pads was a great uprooted palm tree. At the head of those who carried it I saw the man with the Babylonian beard. As they aligned the tree perpendicular to the door of Marcus Lepidus's house, its purpose became unmistakable: it was a battering ram.

*"I didn't kill the cat!"* Marcus Lepidus had said. And, *"Help me! Save me!"* And—no less significantly, to my ears—*"I'll reward you!"* It seemed to me, as a fellow Roman and as a man of honor who had been called on for help, that my course was clear: if the man in blue was innocent of the crime, it was my duty to help him however I could. If duty alone did not suffice, the fact that my stomach was growling and my purse was nearly empty tipped the scales conclusively.

I would need to act swiftly.

The way to the Street of the Breadmakers, usually thronged with people, was almost deserted; the shoppers and the hawkers had all run off to kill the Roman, it seemed. The shop of Menapis was empty—peering within, I saw that piles of dough lay unshapen on the table and the fire in his oven had gone out. The cat had been killed, he said, only a stone's throw from his shop, and it was at about that distance,

around the corner on a little side street, that I came
upon a group of shaven-headed priests who stood in
a circle with bowed heads.

Peering between the orange robes of the priests, I
saw the corpse of the cat sprawled on the paving
stones. It had been a beautiful creature, with sleek
limbs and a coat of midnight black. That it had been
deliberately killed could not be doubted, for its throat
had been cut.

The priests knelt down and lifted the dead cat onto
a small funeral bier, which they hoisted onto their
shoulders. Chanting and lamenting, they began a slow
procession toward the Temple of Bast.

I looked around, not quite sure how to proceed. A
movement at a window above caught my eye, but
when I looked up there was nothing to see. I kept
looking until a tiny face appeared, then quickly disappeared again.

"Little girl," I called softly. "Little girl."

After a moment she reappeared. Her black hair was
pulled back from her face, which was perfectly round.
Her eyes were shaped like almonds and her lips
formed a pout. "You talk funny," she said.

"Do I?"

"Like the other man."

"What other man?"

She appeared to ponder this for a moment, but did
not answer. "Would you like to hear me scream?" she
said. Not waiting for a reply, she did so.

The high-pitched wail stabbed at my ears and
echoed weirdly in the empty street. I gritted my teeth
until she stopped. "That," I said, "is quite a scream.
Tell me, are you the little girl who screamed earlier
today?"

"Perhaps."

"When the cat was killed, I mean."

She wrinkled her brow thoughtfully. "Not exactly."

"Are you not the little girl who screamed when the cat was killed?"

She considered this. "Did the man with the funny beard send you?" she finally said.

I thought for a moment and recalled the man with the Babylonian beard, whose shout had saved me from the mob in the street—"The man in blue is the one we want!"—and whom I had seen at the head of the battering ram. "A Babylonian beard, you mean, curled with an iron?"

"Yes," she said, "all curly, like sunrays shooting out from his chin."

"He saved my life," I said. It was the truth.

"Oh, then I suppose it's all right to talk to you," she said. "Do you have a present for me, too?"

"A present?"

"Like the one he gave me." She held up a doll made of papyrus reeds and bits of rag.

"Very pretty," I said, beginning to understand. "Did he give you the doll for screaming?"

She laughed. "Isn't it silly? Would you like to hear me scream again?"

I shuddered. "Later, perhaps. You didn't really see who killed the cat, did you?"

"Silly! Nobody killed the cat, not really. The cat was just playacting, like I was. Ask the man with the funny beard." She shook her head at my credulity.

"Of course," I said. "I knew that; I just forgot. So you think I talk funny?"

*"Yes, I do,"* she said, mocking my accent rather cruelly, I thought. Alexandrian children acquire a sharp sense of sarcasm very early in life. "You do talk funny."

"Like the other man, you said."

"Yes."

"You mean the man in the blue tunic, the one they ran after for killing the cat?"

Her round face lengthened a bit. "No, I never heard him talk, except when the baker and his friends came after him, and then he screamed. But I can scream louder."

She seemed ready to demonstrate, so I nodded quickly. "Who then? Who talks like I do? Ah, yes, the man with the funny beard," I said, but I knew I must be wrong even as I spoke, for the man had looked quite Egyptian to me, and certainly not Roman.

"No, not him, silly. The other man."

"What other man?"

"The man who was here yesterday, the one with the runny nose. I heard them talking together, over there on the corner, the funny beard and the one who sounds like you. They were talking and pointing and looking serious, the one with the beard pulling on his beard and the one with the runny nose blowing his nose, but finally they thought of something funny and they both laughed. 'And to think, your cousin is such a lover of cats!' said the funny beard. I could tell they were planning a joke on somebody. I forgot all about it until this morning, when I saw the funny beard again and he asked me to scream when I saw the cat."

"I see. He gave you the doll, then he showed you the cat—"

"Yes, looking so dead it fooled everybody. Even the priests!"

"You screamed, people came running—then what happened?"

"The funny beard pointed at a man who was walking up the street and he shouted, 'The Roman did it! The man in blue! He killed the cat!' " She recited the lines with great conviction, holding up her doll as if it were an actor.

"The man with the runny nose, who talked like me," I said. "You're sure there was mention of his *cousin*?"

"Oh yes. I have a cousin, too. I play tricks on him all the time."

"What did this man with the Roman accent look like?"

She shrugged. "A man."

"Yes, but tall or short, young or old?"

She thought for a moment, then shrugged again. "Just a man, like you. Like the man in the blue tunic. All Romans look the same to me."

Then she screamed again, just to show me how well she could do it.

By the time I got back to the square a band of soldiers had arrived from the palace and were attempting, with limited success, to push back the mob. The soldiers were vastly outnumbered, and the mob would only be pushed back so far. Rocks and bricks were hurled against the building from time to time, some of them striking the already cracked shutters. It appeared that a serious attempt had been made to batter down the door, but the door had lost only a few splinters.

A factotum from the royal palace, a eunuch to judge by his high voice, appeared at the highest place in the square, on a rooftop next to the besieged house. He tried to quiet the mob, assuring them that justice would be done by King Ptolemy and his servants. It was in Ptolemy's interest, of course, to quell what might become an international incident; the murder of a wealthy Roman merchant by the people of Alexandria could cause him great political damage.

The eunuch warbled on, but the mob was unimpressed. To them, the issue was simple and clear: a Roman had ruthlessly murdered a cat, and they would not be satisfied until the Roman was dead. They took up their chant again, drowning out the eunuch: "Come out! Come out! Killer of the cat!"

I had decided to get inside the house of Marcus Lepidus. Caution told me that such a course was mad—for how could I ever get out alive once I was in?—and, at any rate, apparently impossible, for if there were a simple way to get into the house the mob would already have found it. Then it occurred to me that someone standing on the rooftop where Ptolemy's eunuch had stood could conceivably jump or be lowered onto the roof of the besieged house.

It all seemed like a great deal of effort, until I heard the plaintive echo of the stranger's voice inside my head: *"Help me! Save me!"*

The building from which the eunuch spoke had been commandeered by soldiers, as had the other buildings adjacent to the besieged house, as a precaution to keep the mob from gaining entry through an adjoining wall or setting fire to the whole block. It took some doing to convince the guards to let me in, but the fact that I was a Roman and claimed to know Marcus Lepidus eventually gained me an audience with the king's eunuch.

Royal servants come and go in Alexandria; those who fail to satisfy their masters become food for crocodiles and are quickly replaced. This royal servant was clearly feeling the pressure of serving a monarch who might snuff out his life with the mere arching of an eyebrow. He had been sent to quell an angry mob and to save the life of a Roman citizen, and at the moment his chances of succeeding looked distinctly uncertain. He could call for more troops, perhaps, and slaughter the mob, but such a bloodbath could lead to an even graver situation, given the instability of the Egyptian state. Complicating matters even more was the presence of a high priest of Bast, who dogged (if I may use that expression) the eunuch's every step, yowling and waving his orange robes and demanding that justice be done at once in the name of the murdered cat.

The eunuch was receptive to any ideas that I might offer. "You're a friend of this man the mob is after?" he asked.

"This *murderer,*" the high priest corrected.

"An acquaintance, yes," I said—and truthfully, if having exchanged a few desperate words after colliding in the street could be called an acquaintance. "In fact, I'm his agent. He's hired me to get him out of this mess." This was also true, after a fashion. "And I think I know who really killed the cat!" This was not quite true, but might become so if the eunuch would cooperate with me. "You must get me into Marcus Lepidus's house. I was thinking that your soldiers might lower me onto his roof by a rope."

The eunuch became thoughtful. "By the same route, we might rescue Marcus Lepidus himself by having him climb a rope up onto this building, where my men can better protect him."

"Rescue a cat-killer? Give him armed protection?" The priest was outraged. The eunuch bit his lip.

At last it was agreed that the king's men would supply a rope by which I could make my way onto the roof of the besieged house. "But you cannot return to this building by the same route," the eunuch insisted.

"Why not?" I had a sudden vision of the house

being set aflame with myself inside it, or of an angry mob breaking through the door and setting upon all the inhabitants with knives and clubs.

"Because the rope will be visible from the square," snapped the eunuch. "If the mob sees someone leaving the house, they'll assume it's the man they're after. Then they'll break into this building! No, I'll allow you passage to your countryman's house, but after that you'll be on your own."

I thought for a moment and then agreed. Behind the eunuch, the high priest of Bast smiled like a cat, no doubt anticipating my imminent demise and purring at the idea of yet another impious Roman departing from the shores of the living.

As I was lowered onto the merchant's roof, the household slaves realized what was happening and set up an alarm. They surrounded me at once and seemed determined to throw me into the square below, but I held up my hands to show them that I was unarmed and I cried out that I was a friend of Marcus Lepidus. My accent seemed to sway them. At last they took me down a flight of steps to meet their master.

The man in blue had withdrawn to a small chamber which I took to be his office, for it was cluttered with scrolls and scraps of papyrus. He recognized my face at once.

"But why have you come here, stranger?" he said, looking at me as if I were either a lemur sent to haunt him or a demigod to save him.

"Because you asked for my help, Marcus Lepidus. And because you offered me a reward," I said bluntly. "My name is Gordianus."

Beyond the shuttered window, which faced the square, the crowd began to chant again. A heavy object—a piece of stone or a clay bottle—struck the shutters with a crash. Marcus gave a start and bit his knuckles.

"These are my cousins, Rufus and Appius," he said, introducing two younger men who had just entered the room. Like their older cousin, they were well groomed and well dressed, and like him they appeared to be on the verge of panic.

"The guards outside are beginning to weaken," said Rufus shrilly. "What are we going to do, Marcus?"

"If they break into the house they'll slaughter us all!" said Appius, equally agitated.

"You're obviously a man of wealth, Marcus Lepidus," I said. "A trader, I understand."

"Why, yes," he said. All three cousins looked at me blankly, confused at my apparent disregard for the crisis immediately at hand. "I own a fleet of ships. We carry grain and slaves and other goods from Alexandria to Rome and elsewhere." Talking about his work calmed him noticeably, as reciting a familiar chant calms a worshiper in a temple.

"Do you own the business jointly with your cousins?" I asked.

"The business is mine," said Marcus proudly. "Inherited from my father."

"Yours alone? You have no brothers?"

"None."

"And your cousins are merely employees, not partners?"

"If you put it that way."

I looked at Rufus, the taller of the cousins. Was it fear of the mob I read on his face, or the bitterness of old resentments? His cousin Appius began to pace the room, biting his fingernails and casting what I took to be hostile glances at me.

"I understand you have no sons, Marcus Lepidus," I said.

"No. My first wife gave me only daughters; they all died of fever. My second wife was barren. I have no wife at present, but I soon will, when the girl arrives from Rome. Her parents are sending her by ship, and they promise me that she will be fertile, like her sisters. This time next year, I could be a proud father at last!" He managed a weak smile, then bit his knuckles. "But what's the use of contemplating my future when I have none? Curse all the gods of Egypt, to have put that dead cat in my path!"

"I think it was not a god who did so," I said. "Tell me, Marcus Lepidus, though Jupiter forbid such a tragedy, if you should die without a son, who would inherit your property?"

"My cousins would inherit in equal portions," said Marcus.

Rufus and Appius both looked at me gravely. Another stone struck the shutters and we all gave a start. It was impossible to read their faces for any subtle signs of guilt.

"I see. Tell me, Marcus Lepidus, who could have known, yesterday, that you would be walking up that side street in Rhakotis this morning?"

He shrugged. "I make no secret of my pleasures. There is a certain house on that street where I spend certain nights in the company of a certain catamite. Having no wife at present . . ."

"Then either of your cousins might have known that you would be coming home by that route this morning?"

"I suppose," he said, shrugging. If he was too agitated to see the point, his cousins were not. Rufus and

Appius both stared at me darkly and glanced dubiously at one another.

At that moment a gray cat came sauntering into the room, its tail flicking, its head held high, apparently oblivious to the chaos outside the house or the despair of those within. "The irony of it all!" wailed Marcus Lepidus, suddenly breaking into tears. "The bitter irony! I, of all men, would never kill a cat! The creatures adore me, and I adore them. I give them a place of honor in my home, I feed them delicacies from my own plate. Come, precious one." He stooped down and made a cradle for the cat, who obligingly pounced into his arms. The cat squirmed onto its back and purred loudly. Marcus Lepidus held the animal close to him. Caressing it seemed to soothe his own distress. Rufus appeared to share his older cousin's fondness for cats, for he smiled weakly and joined him in stroking the beast's belly.

I had reached an impasse. It seemed to me quite certain that at least one of the cousins had been in league with the bearded Egyptian in deliberately plotting the destruction of Marcus Lepidus, but which? If only the little girl had been able to give me a better description. "All Romans look the same" indeed!

"You and your cursed cats!" said Appius suddenly, wrinkling his nose and retreating to the far corner of the room. "It's the cats that do this to me. They cast some sort of hateful spell! Alexandria is full of them, making my life a misery. I never sneezed once in my life before I came here!" And with that he sneezed and sneezed and began to blow his runny nose.

What followed was not pretty, though it may have been just.

I accused Appius of plotting his cousin's death. I

told Marcus Lepidus all I had learned from the little
girl. I summoned him to the window and opened the
shutters enough to point out the bearded Egyptian,
who was now overseeing the construction of a bonfire
in the square below. Marcus had seen the man before
in the company of his cousin.

What outcome did I expect? I had meant to help a
fellow Roman far from home, to save an innocent man
from the wrath of an unreasoning mob, and to gain a
few coins for my purse in the process—all honorable
pursuits. Did I not realize that inevitably a man would
die? I was younger then, and did not always think a
thing through to its logical result.

The unleashed fury of Marcus Lepidus took me by
surprise. Perhaps it should not have, considering the
terrible shock he had suffered that day; considering
also that he was a successful businessman, and therefore to some degree ruthless; considering finally that
treachery within a family often drives men to acts of
extreme revenge.

Quailing before Marcus Lepidus, Appius confessed
his guilt. Rufus, whom he declared to be innocent of
the plot, begged for mercy on his cousin's behalf, but
his pleadings were ineffectual. Though we might be
hundreds of miles from Rome, the rule of the Roman
family held sway in that house in Alexandria, and all
power resided in the head of the household. When
Marcus Lepidus stripped off his blue tunic and ordered that his cousin Appius should be dressed in it,
the slaves of the household obeyed; Appius resisted,
but was overwhelmed. When Marcus ordered that Appius should then be thrown from the window into the
mob, it was done.

Rufus, pale and trembling, withdrew into another
room. Marcus made his face as hard as stone and

turned away. The gray cat twined itself about his feet, but the solace it offered was ignored.

The bearded Egyptian, not realizing the substitution, screamed to the others in the mob to take their vengeance on the man in blue. It was only much later, when the mob had largely dispersed and the Egyptian was able to get a closer look at the trampled, bloody corpse, that he realized the mistake. I shall never forget the look on his face, which changed from a leer of triumph to a mask of horror as he approached the body, studied its face, and then looked up at the window where I stood. He had overseen the killing of his own confederate.

Perhaps it was fitting that Appius received the fate which he had intended for his cousin. No doubt he thought that while he waited, safe and sound in the family house, the bearded Egyptian would proceed with the plot as they had planned and his older cousin would be torn to pieces on the Street of the Breadmakers. He did not foresee that Marcus Lepidus would be able to elude the crowd and flee all the way to his house, where all three cousins became trapped. Nor did he foresee the intervention of Gordianus the Finder—or for that matter, the intervention of the gray cat, which caused him to betray himself with a sneeze.

Thus ended the episode of the Alexandrian cat, whose death was terribly avenged.

Some days after telling this tale to Lucius Claudius, I chanced to visit him again at his house on the Palatine. I was surprised to see that a new mosaic had been installed on his doorstep. The colorful little tiles pictured a snarling Molossian mastiff, together with the stern caption, CAVE CANEM, "Beware the Dog."

A slave admitted me and escorted me to the garden at the center of the house. As I approached I heard a yapping noise, accompanied by deep-throated laughter. I came upon Lucius Claudius, who sat with what appeared to be a gigantic white rat on his lap.

"What on earth is that?" I exclaimed.

"This is my darling, my sweet, my adorable little Momo."

"Your doorstep shows a Molossian mastiff, which that animal most certainly is not."

"Momo is a Melitaean terrier—tiny, true, but very fierce," said Lucius defensively. As if to prove her master's point, the little lapdog began to yap again. Then she nervously began lapping at Lucius's chin, which he appeared to enjoy immensely.

"The doorstep advises visitors to beware this beast," I said sceptically.

"As indeed they should—especially unwelcomed visitors of the four-footed variety."

"You expect this dog to keep cats away?"

"I do! Never again shall my peace be violated by those accursed creatures, not with little Momo here to protect me. Is that not right, Momo? Are you not the fiercest cat-chaser who ever lived? Brave, bold little Momo—"

I rolled my eyes upward at this display of enthusiasm, and caught a glimpse of something black and sleek on the roof. It was almost certainly the cat who had terrified Lucius before.

An instant later the terrier was out of her master's lap, performing a frantic circular dance on the floor, yapping madly and baring her teeth. Up on the roof, the black cat arched its back, hissed, and disappeared.

"There, you see, Gordianus! Beware this dog, all you cats of Rome!" Lucius scooped the dog up in his arms and kissed her nose. "There, there, Momo, and disbelieving Gordianus doubted you ..."

I thought of a truism I had learned from Bethesda: there are those who love cats, and those who love dogs, and never shall the two agree. But we could at least share a cup of wine, Lucius Claudius and I, and exchange the latest gossip from the Forum.

# THE NILE CAT

## by Edward D. Hoch

Professor Bouton had never killed a man before, and so was not at all prepared for the blood which spurted from Henry Yardley's shattered head. He was still standing above the bludgeoned body, trying to think how to get the blood from his clothes, when the night security guard walked into the Egyptian Room and found him. After that, there was no point in denying it.

The detective lieutenant, a man named Fritz, was calm and professional, but with tired eyes. He sat across the table from Professor Bouton and spoke to him quietly, as if this sort of murder happened every day in the week. "You admit killing Henry Yardley?" he asked, after checking to make certain the stenographer was ready.

"Oh, yes. I admit it. If that was the poor fellow's name."

"You didn't know his name?"

"I didn't know *him*. I never saw him before in my life."

Lieutenant Fritz looked blank, but only for a moment. "His name was Henry Yardley and he was a graduate student at the University, working for his master's degree in archeology. Does that help you?"

"I told you—I never saw him or heard of him before."

Fritz picked up a pencil and began to play with it. "We're not getting anywhere, Professor Bouton. You've admitted the crime—you might as well tell us the motive. Did you two have an argument, a fight?"

"No. We never spoke to each other."

"There are only a limited number of motives for murder—hate, fear, revenge—"

"It was nothing like that."

"—gain—"

"Not really—not gain in your sense of word."

"This Yardley, was he a queer or something?"

"I have no idea. He was doing nothing, had done nothing to me in the past. As I told you, I had never seen the man, never even heard his name spoken."

The detective put down the pencil and sighed. "You mean, he just walked into the room and you killed him?"

"Exactly."

"Then you must be nuts!"

Professor Bouton was still able to smile, however slightly. "Perhaps all murderers are insane. I am no more so than the rest."

"You had a motive for killing him? And you expected to get away with it?"

"I had a motive, yes. And I did expect somehow to get away with it. Though I must admit I had no plan beyond the murder itself."

"It was premeditated?"

"Yes, within the legal meaning of the word. I thought about it for some minutes before I acted. And now that I'm arrested, nothing is changed. In fact, it may actually be better that it's happening this way."

"Better for whom? Is there a woman involved?"

Professor Bouton smiled once again. "Perhaps I should tell you the entire story, from the beginning. I think you would understand my motive then . . ."

My name—my full name—is Patrick J. Bouton. I have been associated with the University for the past twenty years, most recently as Professor of Middle Eastern Civilizations. One of my duties, and increasingly a chief one, has been to act as curator of the Egyptian Room at the University Museum. This is hardly the British Museum with its room after room of mummies and sarcophagi, but we have a nice little collection. Mainly small statues, Coptic crosses, and a really fine group of scarabs.

The prize of the collection, and the only art object in the entire museum to achieve world-wide renown, is of course the Nile Cat. It's one of several representations of Bastet, Goddess of Joy, whose shrine was at Bubastis, in lower Egypt. The statue was found back in the 1920's near the banks of the Nile, and is part of a loan collection belonging to Cadmus Verne, the investment banker.

The Nile Cat is a beautiful thing, twelve inches high and made of bronze, with large ruby eyes set deep into the head. Some art critics have called it the most important single piece of early Egyptian art ever uncovered. The owner has it insured for a quarter of a million dollars, and it's easily worth that amount.

My entire collection—the pieces acquired under my direction—has been built around the Nile Cat, which occupies the largest display case in the Egyptian Room. So you can imagine that what happened two weeks ago was quite a shock to me. Cadmus Verne had given us the loan of the statue for his lifetime, with the provision that his heirs continue the arrangement for as long as they owned the Cat. When Verne died a few months back at the age of 81, I was saddened but not particularly surprised. He had led a full and good life.

No, it was not until two weeks ago that the blow fell. His daughter, a middle-aged matron with no interest in Egyptology, came and told me the news. I'm Mrs. Constance Clark, she said. Cadmus Verne was my father. Oh, yes, it's about the statue—the Nile Cat. My husband and I have decided to withdraw it from your collection and sell it.

Sell it? I suppose my face must have revealed my dismay at her words. Sell it to whom? Where?

The French government has made an offer of $250,000 for the statue, she told me. They want it as the main exhibit in their new museum, opening next month.

Next month! Do you mean—?

I'll be selling it to them in a few weeks, she said. And that was it. There was no appeal from her decision. There could not even be a delay in the negotiations, because the new French museum also had in mind a head of Nefertiti from the National. If the Nile Cat was not available by their opening next month, the offer to Mrs. Clark would be withdrawn and they would buy the head of Nefertiti instead.

She said it and she was gone, leaving me alone with my thoughts. You must realize what those thoughts were. You must realize that I have no other interests in this world but my work. My wife has been dead for many years, and we had no children. Even my hobbies, such as they are, center around this museum and its contents. After years of building it, of making it an important part of the University, I was on the verge of losing my prize exhibit.

Well, I determined not to go down without a fight. By the terms of Verne's will, the statue had to remain with us unless it was sold. And I knew that the French offer was a once-in-a-lifetime thing. The Nile Cat might be important to me, and to a new French museum, but there were very few others who would pay that price for it. They didn't need to—the big museums have their own treasures.

One week ago, I finally got in touch with the French museum's representative in New York. I pleaded with him, begged him, but to no avail. The statue would be purchased from Mrs. Clark and flown to Paris for the opening. I came back home a broken man.

I think it was then that I decided to murder Mrs. Clark.

Yes, murder. The idea can come to the mildest of men, if the provocation is sufficient. I would kill her and save my precious statue.

But it was not that easy. For one thing, she was traveling now somewhere in the west. For another, her death would accomplish exactly nothing. The statue would still be sold, by her husband, by her family. A quarter of a million dollars is a great deal of money.

I hit upon a second plan, which in many ways was more fantastic than the first. I would buy the statue from her myself, borrowing the money against my salary of $12,000 a year. But of course the bank only laughed at that. I am only six years from compulsory retirement. Where, the bank asked, would I earn the money to repay the loan in six years? Especially with the interest.

So where did that leave me? Last night I walked out to the Egyptian Room and stood for a long time staring at the Nile Cat. I thought of stealing it, of hiding it somewhere until the French offer was withdrawn. But then it would still be gone from my museum, which was where it belonged. And could I ever return it? Mrs. Clark would have collected the insurance, and my problems would have multiplied. Besides, she would immediately guess that I had taken it, and send the police to search my house. I could never bring myself to destroy it, and I lacked the skill to find a really clever hiding place. I do not have a criminal mind.

She called me today from the west coast and said the men would come for it tomorrow morning. This was to be my last night with the beautiful Nile Cat in my museum. I appealed to her again, but of course it was useless. Nothing could be done to save the Nile Cat. Nothing.

I thought about it for a long time. I thought about Cadmus Verne and his middle-aged daughter. I thought about the French museum half a world away. But mostly I thought about the Cat, and how to keep it here.

And then I guess it came to me. Tonight. Just a little while ago. I walked into the Egyptian Room and there was only one person in sight—this fellow Yardley. I went over to the display case and unlocked it and took out the Nile Cat and smashed his skull with it . . .

"You see now why I did it?" Professor Bouton asked, looking up from his hands.

"I guess I do," the detective said, very softly.

"My beloved Nile Cat is now a murder weapon—Exhibit A in an investigation and trial. Just the investigation alone would delay its release for weeks. Now that you have me for trial, it will be months before the statue can be returned to this museum. By the time Mrs. Clark can get her hands on it, the French sale will have collapsed. The Nile Cat will rest in my museum forever."

"Yes," the detective said. He motioned to the stenographer and pressed a buzzer on his desk.

"And even though I've confessed, the laws of this state require a plea of Not Guilty in a first-degree murder case. I'll be tried in some months—perhaps I might even appeal my conviction. It could be years before the Nile Cat gets back to her. It could be years . . ."

# THE SEARCHING CATS
## by Frances and Richard Lockridge

The cat appeared soundlessly on the open window sill—the window which had been forced open. The cat was spotlessly black and for a moment, poised there, he looked around the room with unblinking yellow eyes.

The cat looked at M. L. Heimrich, captain, New York State Police, a man most often concerned with homicide, and now so concerned. The cat looked away again, dismissing the man. The cat dropped to the polished tile floor of the living room. Then he spoke, once, on a note which seemed to Heimrich to have a curious insistence. The cat seemed to wait for an answer.

When there was no answer, the cat began to move— to glide around the floor, nose close to the floor. The cat's progress was erratic; the cat circled among chairs and under tables; now and then the cat paused and Heimrich could see his nostrils quiver. But always he went on again, engrossed and, it seemed to the watching man, impelled. Heimrich had never before seen a cat behave so—search so. Search, Heimrich decided after a time, for something he would never find again.

"It's no good, fellow," Heimrich said, and the cat paused and looked up, as if he had understood the words and waited to be told more. (Which was, of course, absurd.) "Your man's dead, fellow," Heimrich said, and the cat still seemed to wait. "Murdered," Heimrich told him. The cat waited a moment longer and then went back to sniffing the green tile floor.

Heimrich, having other things to do, walked across the living room, ignored by the black cat, and out of the small, pleasant, country house. It was about four o'clock, then, in the afternoon.

At a few minutes after four, Russell Ashby circled his white farmhouse and sounded the horn of the pickup truck to tell Jane he was home. He ran the truck into the shed which served as a garage and walked back to the house—a tall man in slacks and a jacket with suede-patched elbows. He took long strides on the path to the house and, when he saw Jane standing in the doorway, began to nod his head and smile at her.

It was a kind of pantomime of triumph. But the set expression—was it of anxiety?—on his wife's young face did not alter, and then Ashby slapped his left hip pocket, where his wallet was, to make what should have been evident, clearer yet. But still her face did not brighten.

He walked up on the porch, his footsteps emphatic on the boards. She stepped out onto the porch to meet him and there was an odd rigidity in her slender body, matching the rigidity of her face—a rigidity unbecoming to so lovely a face.

"Got it," Russell Ashby said. "All I had to do was . . ." He stopped; her eyes stopped his words. "What's the matter, baby?" he said, in a very different tone.

"Russ," she said, "where have you been?"

"Been?" he said. "What's the matter, Jane? You knew—" He broke off. "Oh," he said, "afterward.

That's it. Think I'd got run over? Went to look at Jenkins's north field. See if it's worth haying. Took longer than—"

"Russ," Jane Ashby said, and her young voice shook. "Russ—Mr. Bailey's dead. They say—Russ, they say somebody killed him. Broke into the house and—killed him. Russ—somebody from the police called. Wanted—"

She did not go on. He held her close and could feel her body trembling. Over her head he looked, flatly, at nothing. And waited. After a time, stumbling on the words, she told him what everybody around East Belford had known for an hour or more. "Everybody but me," Russell Ashby said, his voice steady, uninflected.

Thwaite Bailey, the richest man around, had been found dead by his daughter, who had walked the hill path from the "big" house to her father's house at about three o'clock. She had telephoned him first and got no answer, and had been worried and walked the quarter of a mile which separated the original Bailey house from the low, contemporary house Bailey had built for week ends when he turned the old house—too big for anybody, the old house was—over to his daughter and Sidney Combe, her husband.

Margaret Combe had found her father dead in the doorway of his bedroom, his head crushed. She had found the little house, which had so much glass it glittered like a jewel in its green valley, ransacked.

"They think he was taking a nap," Jane Ashby said, sitting straight in her living room. "That somebody broke in, thinking he wouldn't be there in the middle of the week. And that whoever it was made a noise that wakened Mr. Bailey and then—killed him. Russ ..."

"Yes?" Russell Ashby said.

"Russ—Sid says Mr. Bailey had a lot of money in the house. A—a thousand dollars. That he always had. And—it isn't there, Russ. *It isn't there!*"

"No," Russ Ashby said. "It's in my pocket."

She put hands over her eyes—the biggest ever, he thought. The brownest ever.

"Hold it, baby," Russ said. "Like we planned—I said did he want to invest in an outfit that needed a push over a hump. Because of the way he and Dad felt about each other. I made a pitch, Jane. And— look." He took his billfold from his hip pocket and they both looked—looked at twenty fifty-dollar bills. "I said a check would be just as good but he said, 'Here, son. Take it.' It was—a gesture, I guess. He was always a little like that."

Thwaite Bailey had been like that, as a good many people knew. It was a quirk. Rich men—and men as generous in service as with money—are entitled to quirks.

"Russ," she said, "when were you there?"

"About two," he said.

"He'd been dead about an hour," Jane Ashby said, "when Marge found him. They say that ... Russ, did anybody see you? There, I mean? Because ..."

He looked at her strangely. "You mean," he said, "because of that other thing?"

She did not answer. That was good enough, or bad enough. "It was a long time ago," Russ Ashby said, slowly.

It had been—long before Clint Ashby had died and left his son a dairy farm which was now—in spite of everybody's advice—an Aberdeen Angus breeding farm; long before Russ went to Korea in the Marines. It had been before Russ Ashby grew up; when he was a "wild kid." With other wild kids he had broken into a closed country house. "For the hell of it." But Russell Ashby had been the one caught—and booked. Clinton Ashby had made good and the charges had been dropped. But ...

"Sid was walking his dog," Russell Ashby, the grown-up Russell Ashby, said now. He spoke slowly. "On the hill. He was going away when I saw him—his back was to me. Swinging that squire's walking stick of his. I left the truck on Shady Lane and cut across by the path ..."

Someone knocked at the front door. The knocking was not loud. There was no threat in it.

"Russ," Jane said, in a very low voice, a hurried voice. "Russ—I'm scared. *Terribly scared.* They won't believe ..."

Russell Ashby went to the door and let in two large, solid men—men not in uniform; Captain M. L. Heimrich and Sergeant Charles Forniss, of the New York State Police.

Heimrich said, "Mr. Ashby?" and then, "We'd like to ask you a couple of questions." Heimrich and Forniss did not wait for more, but went on into the living room. "Oh," Heimrich said. "Mrs. Ashby?" She was a remarkably pretty young woman, he thought; she looked frightened. Which was reasonable. She nodded her head, standing, fear in her face. "Sit down," Heimrich said, and then, "You, too, Mr. Ashby." He waited until they sat down. Then he sat on a straight chair. Forniss remained near the door, standing, looking very large.

"Mr. Thwaite Bailey was killed this afternoon," Heimrich said. "About the time you were there, Mr. Ashby."

Heimrich closed bright blue eyes. And waited. And Jane Ashby, fear rioting in her eyes, waited, too.

Waiting, she held her breath. That was evident to Heimrich—the cessation, utter if momentary, of breath movement in her body. Heimrich looked at Russell Ashby and Ashby looked only at his wife— and looked as if he listened. Heimrich saw Ashby's chest rise, slowly. It seemed a long time before Russell Ashby spoke.

"I was there," Ashby said. "He was all right when I went in—when he let me in. He was all right when I left."

"Yes," Heimrich said, "you were there. Your fingerprints are there. On the desk drawer."

"Maybe," Ashby said. "I don't know what I touched. I've said I was there. Mr. Bailey was an old friend of father's. Of mine, too. I dropped by to see him now and then. He—"

"Your prints are on record," Heimrich said. "From the other time. You know what I mean?"

Again Russell Ashby and his wife looked at each other—looked quickly, then away again. Ashby said, "I know what you mean."

"The same thing," Heimrich said. "Except—murder, this time. A window forced. But this time—a man killed."

"I was a kid then," Ashby said. "A long time ago, when I was a kid."

"Yes," Heimrich said. "Mr. Combe—Sidney Combe— says you were carrying something when you left the house. He couldn't make out what it was. He was taking a walk—walking his dog. It was about two o'clock, he says. You went out of the house and around it toward the path that leads down to Shady Lane. Walking very fast, Mr. Combe says."

"Most of the time," Russ Ashby said, "I walk fast.

Most of the time I take the path. I wasn't carrying anything. Sid's wrong about that."

"Better show him, Charley," Heimrich said, and Forniss went out the door. He came back almost at once. He carried a stick of firewood—a stick about three feet long and a little over two inches in diameter; a stick like a club. "Found it halfway down the path," Heimrich said. "To where you parked your car in the lane. And—there's blood on this, Mr. Ashby. Not a lot. Didn't bleed much, Mr. Bailey didn't. But—enough."

"I don't know anything about it," Ashby said. "You claim this was what I was carrying? You claim it's got my prints on it?"

"Now, Mr. Ashby," Heimrich said. "Rough wood. Wouldn't take prints worth anything, naturally. It was used to force the window. The way you and the other kids forced the other window. Then—to kill Mr. Bailey." Heimrich paused.

"Mr. Combe says his father-in-law had about a thousand dollars in the desk drawer. Says he kept it there as—as a kind of petty cash. Mr. Combe's term for it."

He watched. For a moment neither of the Ashbys spoke. Then—slowly, as if so simple a movement were incredibly difficult—Jane Ashby brought her hands from her eyes. Heimrich could see no expression in her eyes.

"He loaned it to us," she said, in a voice which was blank like her eyes. "Show them, Russ."

Russell Ashby looked at her for a long moment. Then he showed them. Heimrich took the crisp bills out of Ashby's billfold, riffled them, put them back, then put the billfold in his own pocket.

"We'll give you a receipt for this, Mr. Ashby," Heimrich said. "At the station house."

They left Jane Ashby then—left her sitting in a chair, with her face buried in her hands again, her slender body shaking again. "I'll be back," Russell Ashby said, and she did not seem to hear him.

That was about five o'clock. At a quarter after seven, Heimrich went into the taproom of the Maples Inn, on the main street of East Belford, and ordered a before-dinner drink. He sipped the drink and thought of murder—and of the tall young man at the police station, still denying murder. A stubborn young fool, Russell Ashby was, to deny what was so obvious.

Heimrich sighed. He thought of Ashby's dark-haired wife—was she still sitting so, with hands hiding her face, shutting out a world which had crumbled? There was no good in thinking of that.

He thought, instead, of Margaret Combe, who had gone through a bright afternoon to invite her father over for tea. If it was necessary to think of such things, think of *her* white face, *her* blank eyes. With nobody better, stronger, than Sidney Combe to stand with her.

Combe, the country squire—Ashby had called him that, bitterly, but, Heimrich thought, with reason. Tweeds and walking stick and dog on rawhide leash—and with the seven forty-three to catch five mornings a week to a job in town which wasn't much more than a clerk's job. Well, Combe wouldn't have to go back from this two-week vacation. He could spend the rest of his life walking his dog. He—

Heimrich, who had been looking at nothing, found he was looking at another cat. This cat was yellow. Another tom, from the shape of the forelegs—a big yellow cat standing in the doorway of the taproom and looking at Heimrich, and looking away again. I don't, Heimrich thought, seem to interest cats. The cat came into the taproom and began to sniff the floor. Two cats in one day, sniffing intricate patterns around a floor. Yellow cat and black cat, both searching. Yellow cat and—

"Marty," Heimrich said, through the service window of the bar, "what's he doing that for?"

The bartender looked at the cat.

"Smells something," Marty said. "Mrs. Latham's peke, most likely. Brought it in with her, while back. If he bothers you—"

"Not me," Heimrich said, and watched the cat's systematic sniffing of the floor, watched the yellow cat follow the scent where the little dog had gone. "Does he smell around after people?" Heimrich asked, and Marty shook his head. He said that cats don't care much how people smell. Only other cats, and dogs—

"You don't want dinner?" Marty said, because Heimrich stood up abruptly.

"Not now," Heimrich said, and went to his car, and drove toward the old Bailey house a few miles out of East Belford—toward the house, and a white-faced woman and a rather strutting man, who wouldn't have to catch the seven forty-three any more, now that his wife had inherited a few million dollars; toward a man who would be free, now, to walk his boxer on a leash any day he chose—and to take him along on leash when he went to call on people. Toward a man, at any rate, who had planned on that freedom, and might have got it but for a cat who followed a dog's scent around a room. A persistent cat, following a scent.

"I've come to have a look at that walking stick of yours," Heimrich told Sidney Combe, at the door of the old house—told a tweedy Sidney Combe, with his boxer sitting behind him, attentive, in the hall. Combe merely looked at Heimrich. "To see if there are blood traces on it," Heimrich said. "Hard to get blood off things, the lab boys tell me—"

Combe was a fool—but a frightened man maybe— to try to slam the door on Heimrich. Heimrich had a foot in it.

"Now, Mr. Combe," Heimrich said. "That's no good. Where would you go? Your mind was working better earlier. When you smeared a little of Mr. Bailey's blood on the club, for example. And planted it on the path. When you took advantage of the fact that Ashby went around for a loan, and you saw him. When you tried to make it all look like a robbery, because Ashby broke into a place when he was a kid. Disappointed not to find the money, Mr. Combe? Mr. Bailey had given it to Ashby. But that worked out all right, too, or looked like working—"

Combe gave up trying to close the door. He said he didn't know what Heimrich was talking about.

"Now, Mr. Combe," Heimrich said. "A black cat, among other things. Cats can't testify, naturally. But I watched the cat and—I can testify, you know."

Combe really didn't know what Heimrich was talking about, then. Heimrich told him, later, about the cat—told him after he had got the East Belford substation on the telephone and said to let Russell Ashby go and come pick Sidney Combe up. Heimrich followed the police car which had Combe in it only as far as the Maples Inn. He stopped off there to finish his dinner. He started into the taproom but stopped at the door.

Russell and Jane Ashby were sitting at a corner table, with food in front of them, and no great interest in food. They were looking at each other as if, to the other, each was new. They wouldn't want to see him, Heimrich thought. They had each other to look at—and a whole future to talk about.

A future, Heimrich thought, that a past might have ruined, but fortunately had not. Thanks, in large part, to a dead man's cat—inquisitive, as cats are notoriously. And, Heimrich thought, as policemen have need to be, however obvious the truth seems.

# WHO KILLED WEE WINKY?

## by Barbara Owens

The contestants on *One in a Million* were being introduced as Mrs. Martin settled happily in front of her little black and white set with her breakfast tea and toast. The host, Rod Rooney, already had the studio audience in a fine mood. Mrs. Martin watched hopefully as Rod prepared to ask his first question. Would he do it today?

Yes. Just as the camera moved in for a closeup of his face, Rod looked directly at her and smiled. Mrs. Martin glowed, flushing warm all over.

"Did you see that, Wink? That was just for me. Today will be a good day."

The big orange tomcat stretched beside her on the sofa flicked an ear at the sound of his name but did not open his eyes. Mrs. Martin sighed, stroking him. She liked it when her day began so pleasantly.

Mrs. Martin had lived alone for a very long time. Sometimes she could scarcely remember Leonard and what life had been like when he was alive. It was just as well. Those earlier years held nothing but ugly memories—never enough money; an endless succession of cheap, dark, too-small apartments; and the smell. Oh, that smell. Leonard had hauled beer for a living. It had taken Mrs. Martin months after he was gone to get rid of the stink of beer in her home.

She had never stopped trying to convince Leonard to better himself, and she had devoted years to protecting Carol from the poverty and shame that he provided. And what good had it done? Carol ran away at seventeen to get married. Now she lived in California and in twenty years had never once invited her mother to visit. She rarely even wrote. No appreciation at all for the sacrifices her mother had made. Sometimes Mrs. Martin idly wondered if she'd recognize Carol today.

It was all Leonard's doing. Then he had taken sick at fifty and lingered three long years. She'd had to wait on him night and day, while his medicine and operations ate away at their pitiful savings. The savings went long before Leonard did. And he'd actually had the nerve to cry at the end and beg her to say just once that she loved him. Mrs. Martin had sniffed and turned away.

So she'd been reduced to living out her years in this dismal two-room apartment. In a big ugly building that squatted like a toad in a run-down Chicago neighborhood. She rarely went out except to market, and she had nothing to do with her trashy neighbors. They were always playing nasty tricks on her, although the various building managers never believed it. Her imagination, they said. Ha!

But she had forced herself to find small contentments. She lived on the meager benefits Leonard left her. She had her TV family who had become close friends. And, of course, she had Wee Winky. Such a tiny wink he'd been when she found him crying in an alley six years ago. Now he was the center of her life. Mrs. Martin had never loved anyone or anything the way she loved Wee Winky.

Twice during her morning TV shows he went to the

back door asking to go out, but Mrs. Martin couldn't tear herself away from the set.

"In a little while, darling," she cooed to him. "We'll go out soon."

Right in the middle of a wonderful scene on *Let Us Live,* while Laura was at the hospital trying to find out if Michael had pulled through the operation, someone knocked at the front door. As usual, Mrs. Martin ignored it, but the knocking continued, accompanied by a persistent voice.

"Hey, Mrs. Martin, I know you're in there. It's Bob Singleton."

Annoyed, she rose and backed slowly to the door, keeping her eyes on poor anguished Laura until the last possible moment. The building manager's narrow face with its silly walrus moustache looked at her through the crack in the door.

"Open up," he said. "You been complaining about a leaky faucet. Well, I'm here to take a look at it."

Pursing her lips distastefully, Mrs. Martin took the chain off the door. Just as Bob Singleton started through it an orange streak shot across the room and between his bowed legs, and before either of them could move, Winky was down the hall, around the corner, and out of sight.

Bob blinked after him. "What the hell was that?"

Mrs. Martin's hands flew to her face and she let out a little scream. "Winky! Oh, now see what you've done! Go after him! My Winky—Winky, come back here!"

Bob Singleton sighed. "All right, don't get all upset. I'll get him."

He lumbered away down the hall with Mrs. Martin pattering right behind him. At the landing she leaned over and called after him, "Don't you scare him! He's not used to strangers. Winky? Come back, sweet-heart."

Bob appeared on the landing below. "Don't see him," he said.

"He has to be there!" Mrs. Martin insisted in a shrill voice. "I saw him go down the stairs!"

Bob shrugged. "Well, he can't get out of the building. I'll find him."

But an hour of searching produced no cat. Mrs. Martin, wringing her hands and calling frantically, finally demanded that they canvass the building. Bob reluctantly agreed.

Unaware that she still wore her bedroom slippers, Mrs. Martin stood at his shoulder while they went door-to-door. Some residents were out, some barely understood English, and some were not at all pleased at being disturbed. It was almost lunchtime when they reached a door on the sixth floor labeled Diaz. Bob Singleton shuffled in front of it.

"Listen, I know this lady works nights. She's probably sleeping. I'll come back to her later."

"Certainly not!" Mrs. Martin cried. "You don't understand! Winky's never been outside the apartment alone. We have to find him!"

The woman who finally answered the door was round and rumpled from sleep. When Bob finished his little explanation, she stared at him in disbelief. "A cat? You wake me up for a cat?" She seemed ready to unleash a torrent, but when she caught sight of Mrs. Martin's tearful face, her own softened. "Lady," she said, "I been asleep. I don't see your cat. I see him, I tell you, okay?" And she closed the door.

"That's the last apartment," Bob said.

"He's gone. My Winky's gone." Mrs. Martin clasped her hands prayerfully.

"Aw, he'll come back, especially when he gets hungry. Look, Mrs. Martin, I got to get back to work. Maybe that old cat's waiting for you downstairs right now."

But he wasn't, and after a few quiet sniffles, Mrs. Martin phoned the police. The officer who answered sounded surprised at first, but he was courteous, and he wrote down all the information she gave him, reading it back at her insistence.

After she hung up, Mrs. Martin filled Winky's little dish with fresh liver that Mr. Vitale chopped special for her every day and sat with it on the back walkway, calling to him, until it got too cold and dark to stay outside.

The tiny apartment seemed huge and empty. She cuddled Winky's pillow while she ate a bowl of soup and watched *Tuesday Night Theater* on TV. It was a sad story, and soon Mrs. Martin's tears mingled freely with the chicken noodle. At the end the poor wretched woman on the screen was left alone, sobbing pitifully into the fadeout, "No one cares. No one cares."

Mrs. Martin blew vigorously into a tissue. "You are so right, my dear. None of them—they don't care."

All through the long sleepless night she rocked in her rocking chair, holding Winky's pillow. She peered frequently through the frosted back door, but the liver in Winky's dish remained untouched, slowly turning dark and hard.

When the first rays of morning sun began to lighten the room, Mrs. Martin stirred in her chair and blinked red-rimmed eyes. "Well, he's dead," she announced sadly to the empty room. "My Winky's dead and no one cares. One of them caught and killed him just to spite me. I'm an old woman. What can I do?"

After breakfast she tidied up the room and called the police station. The officer told her no, he didn't have any word on a missing orange cat.

"Of course not!" Mrs. Martin snapped. "What do you care?"

Bob Singleton's sloppy wife said he was on the fourth floor fixing a jammed door and wouldn't have time today to go chasing after a cat. Feeling like a thundercloud, Mrs. Martin sat down with a cup of tea to watch *One in a Million.*

The contestants were so silly and stupid today that poor Rod forgot to give her his special smile. Mrs. Martin's mind began to wander.

But it came back to her with a snap. "—one in a million!" Rod was shouting. Lights were flashing, horns trumpeting, and the music broke into the song it played when someone won the bank. A woman screamed off-camera, and Rod was grinning close up. "She did it! She did it!" Suddenly his eyes looked directly into Mrs. Martin's and he repeated with emphasis, *"Mrs. Diaz did it!"*

Mrs. Martin sat for several long minutes wrapped in cold white silence. Could she believe her ears? Rod had never spoken directly to her before. But he was her friend. Why would he lie?

"Mrs. Diaz?" Mrs. Martin whispered finally. "Killed my Winky? Why, Rod? Tell me why!"

She squinted desperately at the screen, but the show was proceeding normally and Rod would not look at her again.

Mrs. Martin stared briefly into her teacup, her mind ascramble. Finally she rose and left her apartment, creeping down the back stairs to her storage locker in the basement.

At 4:00 A.M. on the following morning, Doris Diaz

finished her shift at the all-night market and drove the few short blocks home. It was cold, and she hurried up the back steps of her building, anxious for her soft, warm bed. The fifth-floor landing light was out, and as Doris rounded the corner in the dark, something rose up out of the shadows—a shapeless form wearing a man's heavy coat and a wide-brimmed hat pulled down over the ears.

Doris Diaz had lived on Chicago's west side all her life, and her mouth opened instinctively on a scream. But her foot slid off the edge of an icy step and she stumbled backward into the old wooden railing. A hand appeared from the shape to cover her gaping mouth, pushing the scream down her throat and adding just enough impetus to send her backward over the rail. She made a ripe, squashing sound when she hit the parking lot five stories below.

Later that morning, Mrs. Martin was washing her breakfast dishes when she heard voices in the hall outside her front door. Through her small spying crack she saw Bob Singleton with a big man in a police uniform.

Mrs. Martin widened the crack. "Are you here about my cat?"

The officer turned to look at her. "Ma'am?"

He was very young. He had a big open face covered with freckles and his smile was pleasant. He looked very much like her beloved brother Dennis.

She opened the door still wider. "My cat, Winky. Have you found him? I think he's dead."

Before the officer could speak, Bob Singleton interrupted. "There's been a little accident here, Mrs. Martin."

She narrowed the crack. "What kind of accident?"

"You remember Mrs. Diaz on the sixth floor?"

Mrs. Martin nodded dumbly.

"Looks like she took a fall from one of the top floors," the nice young man spoke up. "Sorry to tell you, she's dead. I don't suppose you heard anything?"

"Oh my," Mrs. Martin said. "This awful old building isn't safe to live in. Do you think she'd been drinking? They all do."

The officer looked startled. "Well, I'm sorry we bothered you. Don't let it upset you." The two men turned to go.

"Wait!" Mrs. Martin said. "What is your name?"

"Officer Burdick, ma'am," he said, turning back.

"What about my cat?"

He looked thoughtful. "You've lost a cat, Mrs. Martin?"

"I thought you'd know. I made a report. His name is Wee Winky, a lovely orange tom. I'm so worried. He's never been out alone and he's all I have left in this world."

She managed an effective quaver in her voice, but her heart ached at having to pretend. She knew Wink was dead, and she knew who'd killed him, but the officer must never know that.

Officer Burdick smiled kindly. "Well, that's too bad. I'll sure keep an eye out for him." Again, he turned to go.

"Would you like to come in for a cup of tea?"

As soon as she said it, she was astounded at herself. No one but a succession of building managers had put a foot through her door in years. But this young man was very appealing.

"I'd like to, ma'am," he said. "But I'm on duty. I'm sorry." And he sounded like he was. "Good morning to you."

"You can't mistake Wee Winky," she called after

him. "He has a white moustache right under his nose."
Officer Burdick waved.

Mrs. Martin closed her door. "Well," she said.
"Well, well, well." She settled on the sofa with Wink's
pillow, smoothing it sadly while her old set warmed
up.

Rod Rooney avoided looking directly at her during
his show today, but several times she caught him looking at her from the corner of his eye. Mrs. Martin
nodded to show him that she had gotten his message
and taken care of things.

As soon as *Let Us Live* began, it was obvious that
Laura had received bad news. Her eyes shone with
tears, and as the camera pulled away from her face,
Mrs. Martin saw that she was sitting in the hospital
waiting room with Michael's mother sobbing and
clinging to her hand. Mrs. Martin's own eyes misted.
"Oh no," she whispered. "Not Michael."

The camera panned to the hallway and the figure
of a doctor walking slowly toward them. When Laura
saw him, she sprang to her feet.

"There!" she cried, pointing to him. "He's responsible!" Her stricken face filled the screen. "He's the
one!" Her streaming eyes looked directly into Mrs.
Martin's. "The butcher! The butcher!!" The screen
blanked out to a commercial.

Mrs. Martin felt faint. She rose on tottering legs and
turned off the set. Confusion filled her aching head.

"Mr. Vitale?" she murmured incredulously. "But I
thought—Rod said—Why would Mr. Vitale—"

Was that why Rod had avoided looking at her this
morning? Had he made a mistake? Mrs. Martin's eyes
widened. Or, worse yet, was he playing a trick on her?

"Mr. Vitale!" she said aloud. Then, "Oh dear. Poor
Mrs. Diaz."

She was up early the following morning after another sleepless night. The day was gray and dreary; frost rimmed the kitchen window. Mrs. Martin dressed warmly in coat, hat, and gloves.

Mr. Vitale's butcher shop was only a short walk, but her nose was quite cold by the time she reached it. The shop was not open yet, but Mrs. Martin could see him at the slicer. She rapped smartly on the glass.

"Not open yet!" he shouted without looking up. Mrs. Martin tapped again. "Come back pretty soon!"

Mrs. Martin pressed her face against the glass. Mr. Vitale looked at her, cast his eyes to heaven, and came to open the door a slit.

"Mrs. Martin, I'm not open yet, you see that?"

Mrs. Martin smiled sweetly. "I'm so sorry, Mr. Vitale. I'm hungry for a nice little lamb chop for my supper. I had to be out anyway. I didn't think you'd mind if I slipped in."

"Not ready yet," he grumbled, still blocking the door. "You come back."

Mrs. Martin placed her hand against the door as if to steady herself, pushing it against him. "Oh, it's so cold this morning. I feel quite weak."

Mr. Vitale sighed gustily. "Come in, Mrs. Martin, come in."

She followed close at his heels as he crossed the small shop. She had looked closely, but she'd seen no hint of guilt at what he'd done. He was an evil man. All the years of chopping liver special for Winky and now her poor darling could be hanging in his frozen storage room. She had to close her eyes at the thought.

"Today's lamb is still in the back," Mr. Vitale said. "I give you some from yesterday, special price."

"Oh no." Mrs. Martin shook her head. "Day-old

lamb just won't do. I'll have the fresh, if you don't mind."

He minded. He pressed his lips together and rolled his eyes. "I'm a busy man today, Mrs. Martin, all alone. My son takes his wife to the doctor. Lamb from yesterday be fine if you cook it right." He repeated heavily, "Special price."

Mrs. Martin's chin began to quiver. "I've been your customer for years, Mr. Vitale. Have I ever asked for a favor before?"

With a final tragic look he turned and stalked into the meat locker at the rear of the shop. Mrs. Martin, right behind him, slammed the door, wrestling home the special burglar bolt that his son had insisted upon installing recently. Ignoring the sound of the panic buzzer and Mr. Vitale's pounding on the door, she tore a length of butcher paper from its roll and lettered it carefully in grease pencil: CLOSED. SICK TODAY. She taped it to the front door as she went out, taking care to be certain that the door locked behind her.

As she walked home she looked and called into every alley and alcove, just in case. Oh, Wink, I'm only a poor helpless old woman. What can I do?

Early the next morning someone knocked at the door.

"Sorry to bother you again, Mrs. Martin," Officer Burdick said through the crack she opened. "And I'm sorry, but it's not about your cat."

He looked surprised when she opened the door wide. "Good morning. Won't you come in for a cup of tea?"

The young policeman looked cold and tired. "I can't, ma'am. I'm here on police business."

"I see," Mrs. Martin murmured. "Still that Mrs. Diaz?"

"No, ma'am. I'm afraid we've had a murder. We're questioning everyone in the area."

Mrs. Martin gasped. "Murder! In the building? Why, they're all killing each other out there, aren't they?"

"No, ma'am. It's a Mr. Vitale. He owned the meat market down the street. Have you seen any suspicious characters in the neighborhood lately?"

Mrs. Martin managed to look shocked. "Why, I've known Mr. Vitale for years. Suspicious, you say? They all look suspicious to me. Was it a robbery?"

"Now, don't you worry," Officer Burdick reassured her. "We think it might have been a grudge killing. Someone locked Mr. Vitale in his freezer."

"Oh my. No one is safe anymore. It's very frightening, I can tell you, for an old woman alone like me."

The officer closed his notebook. "You just stay inside and keep your doors locked. You'll be all right."

"Are you sure you wouldn't like a cup of tea? It's so cold outside." She was getting much better at quavering. "I'm so lonely now without my Winky."

Officer Burdick's smile was gentle. "I'm sure you are. I'm watching out for him, like I said. I'll bet he turns up."

Mrs. Martin felt a surprising surge of real emotion. "You're a very nice young man. You remind me of my dear dead brother Dennis."

The freckled face blushed. "You know, I was just thinking you remind me of my grandma. You take care now." And he clumped off down the hall.

Mrs. Martin closed her door with satisfaction. "Well," she said with relish, "finally that is that."

*Let Us Live* featured Helen and Barney today instead of Laura. Their troubles continued with their wayward daughter, Liz. Afterwards, Mrs. Martin took a small bundle of washables to the basement laundry room. It was warm and deserted at this hour, so she stationed herself in a quiet corner to daydream about happier days with Winky. In a few minutes she heard steps outside in the hallway. Bob Singleton and another man. They went past the laundry-room door without seeing her and into the storage-locker room. She could hear their voices quite clearly.

"—wife said you was around the other day with that loony old woman looking for her cat. That what they pay you for nowadays?"

Bob's answer was muffled, the other man said something, then they both laughed loudly.

"How'd you guess?" Bob said. Then, in falsetto, "Okay, officer, I confess. I overdosed him on fleas. I know I'll get the chair."

More laughter, then the other man carried a box back past the door. Mrs. Martin didn't know him, just another one of the swarthy ones who had gradually taken over the building.

She sat very still, having trouble finding air to breathe. Of course. Bob Singleton. He had picked Winky up when he first followed him down the stairs—hidden him somewhere until they had finished searching the building. Mrs. Martin closed her tired eyes. Winky would have been afraid. He probably cried for her. Then Bob had killed him just to spite her. Rod and Laura must have been in on it, too. She shook her sad head. Mrs. Diaz and Mr. Vitale had died by mistake. It had been Bob Singleton all along, and he had pretended to help her, pretended to care.

She slipped stealthily into the storage room. Bob

was kneeling with his back to her, working on one of the compartment locks.

"Mr. Singleton?" she said right at his ear.

He started violently, dropping the lock and cracking his head against the door. "Mrs. Martin! You scared the hell out of me!"

"I'm so sorry. I was just wondering if you'd heard anything about my Winky."

He didn't even have the grace to blush or look away. Instead, he rubbed his head gingerly. "Nope. Don't give up, though. I still think he'll show up."

"Well," she said, lowering her eyes demurely, "I've been meaning to thank you for helping me look for him. Would you like to come up for a cup of tea?"

She'd never noticed before what a mean little face he had. "Well, thanks," he said, "but I'm pretty busy. I ain't much of a tea drinker anyway."

"I can make coffee then," she offered earnestly. Again she lowered her eyes. "But maybe you'd rather not. You probably think I'm just a silly old woman." She produced a tear and wiped it away.

"Uh," Bob said. Mrs. Martin waited patiently. "Tell you what. Maybe I could stop by in the morning for a few minutes. Would ten o'clock be okay?"

"Oh yes, ten will be fine. Thank you." Mrs. Martin smiled to herself all the way upstairs.

Back in her kitchen, she climbed on a chair to search the high back shelf of her cupboard until she located the container of rat poison. It was almost full.

By 9:30 the next morning there were fresh home-made cookies and a pot of steaming coffee laid out on her little dining table. The empty poison container had been dropped discreetly down a neighbor's garbage chute. Mrs. Martin waited, sipping a cup of tea and humming a happy little tune.

When a knock came at her door she jumped, hands flying to her throat. Her heart gave a couple of sharp ugly slaps. Then two deep breaths and she was able to go to the door and open it, a smile forming prettily on her lips.

"Hi!" Officer Burdick said with a grin that stretched his freckles to their limit. "You'll never guess what I found."

Mrs. Martin faltered, her eyes moving from his big cheerful face down to the crook of his arm where he held—dirty, bedraggled, but unmistakably—"Winky!" Mrs. Martin cried. "Oh, it's—you've—little Winky!"

She reached out blindly. Burdick placed the cat gently into her arms and watched her fold it to her breast.

"Found him in an alley just a few blocks from here, white moustache and all. I brought him right over. He sure looks sorry, doesn't he?"

Tears fell helplessly. "Oh, I thought he was—how can I ever thank you—oh, my Winky's home and you—"

Burdick thought she looked like she was going to fall. He placed a strong hand on her elbow. "Sure looks like he could use something to eat."

"Oh yes, of course. I—a little warm milk—oh, Winky, I missed you, it's just been terrible—"

Officer Carl Burdick stood tall in the center of the tiny room, watching her fly around warming milk and crooning to the cat. Bless her old soul, she'd forgotten he was there.

A plate of cookies and a pot of hot coffee sat invitingly on a small table across the room. He eyed the spread thoughtfully. She'd been after him to come in and he'd kept turning her down. What the hell, a few minutes wouldn't make any difference. Poor thing was lonely. Made him feel good just watching her and the cat. He stepped up to the table, poured himself a cup of coffee, and selected two large cookies.

Yessir, it was worth it. After all the dirt he was forced to deal with on the streets out there, moments like this made it all worthwhile.

# PROFESSOR KRELLER'S SECRET

## by Ingram Meyer

They were walking single file along the uneven rocky path. Large cottonwood trees grew on both sides, the branches spreading umbrella-like above their heads. The lake would be just a hundred yards or so to their left. Pixy, carrying a high, aluminum-framed backpack, walked in front. He was completely hidden; only his legs showed from behind. The backpack was bright red, and his corduroys dark green.

"A giant walking tomato," thought Grandma. "What a funny little man." And not for the first time did she wonder why on earth she had ever gone into partnership with that small, ridiculous detective. She pulled her large beat-up vinyl suitcase on casters by a leather grasp. It wasn't an easy feat, either, on this awful hikers' trail. Her arm was getting sore.

"You all right, Gran?" called Pixy from behind his backpack.

"Yeah, great. This miserable suitcase is like a big fat dog, jumping and dipping behind me. How much farther is that blasted house?"

"Must be coming up soon. Mooshi said it was a mile from the highway.—There! There it is now."

And there it was. Both detectives stopped, mouths open.

"THIS is Mooshi Winthrop's hideaway?" Grandma cried. "THIS is where she writes all those wonderful love stories? It's a terrible place!"

Pixy had to admit that it was one of the worst houses he had ever seen. It was an ugly old place, originally a brown clapboard house but now mended all over with odd pieces of plywood and shingles. The roof was overgrown with thick, brownish moss, and the chimney was crumbly. There was an outhouse to the right. It wouldn't be haunted, would it? Oh man, he hoped not! If there was one thing that he, Pixy, was afraid of, it was the supernatural. He looked up at the four small windows, two on either side of the entrance, and thought that on the whole it wasn't the kind of place that ghosts would choose to occupy. Shabby and unattractive it was, but not especially creepy.

Grandma sat down on her suitcase.

"That thing will snap open," warned Pixy, but she didn't bother to answer. Instead she asked, "Did you know that rich and famous Mooshi Winthrop, author of over two hundred romantic novels, lived in a cheap ramshackle like this? You were the one who went to her hotel to negotiate the contract."

"Well, yes and no." Pixy was leaning against a craggy dead tree trunk, easing the weight of his backpack.

"What kind of an answer is that, Pixy!" She got up from her suitcase—it had creaked dangerously, for she was a large person—and took off her heavy tweed jacket.

Pixy almost laughed aloud. Good heavens, what a sight she was. Smart navy skirt and lace-trimmed white blouse, a beautiful cameo pin at her throat, silver hair coiled all around her head and held by a large glittering mother-of-pearl clip.—And then there were the legs! Thick crinkly cotton stockings, shabby faded sneakers with knotted laces and holes in the toes. That was Grandma all right. Not his granny, not anybody's granny, but for some reason or other called so by half their home town because of her several ex-husbands and accordingly other ex-this-and-thats. Ten years ago she had finally decided to become something other than a housewife for a change. She had looked all over for an important and glamorous job to do, then decided that her next door neighbor Pixy was really the only person she knew who led a fairly exciting life. She had bought a partnership in his business, and Grandma had become a private detective.

"What does 'yes and no' mean, Pixy?" she asked again, sharply.

"Well, Gran, it's like this. Mooshi told me her hideaway was quaint and rustic—"

Grandma sniffed. "Quaint and rustic, my foot! This is an awful place to send a person detecting. Outhouse in the yard, for goodness sake! I haven't seen such a thing since I married my first husband."

"Mooshi writes about olden times," said Pixy. "This setting probably inspires her stories about—"

"—knights in shining armor? Handsome, charming young gentlemen asking for the hand of beautiful aristocratic maidens?" laughed Grandma. "Well, one never knows. Writers are said to be strange people. Let's unlock the door and see what the house looks like on the inside."

"I promised Mooshi we'd stay here for a few days. Do you think we'll be able to find out what's behind all those strange happenings in her neighbor Professor Kreller's cabin? It would be located a little farther along this trail, but the trees seem way too dense to get a view of it from here."

"Well, we sure as hell can't see anything from this place. And to tell you the truth, Pixy, I for one don't fancy creeping through these woods and spying on someone else's house. But, as always, we're damned short on money. Sleuthing is a poor man's occupation." Grandma sighed deeply.

"Mooshi is loaded. Regardless of her funny taste in living quarters and all, that lady is *rich*. We solve this mystery, and the rent will get paid once again." Pixy stuck the large cast iron key into the lock, whistling. And Grandma pulled up her suitcase, and she too was in good spirits once again.

On the inside the house was quite clean and cosy, albeit tacky. There were only two big rooms. On the left was a bedroom, with a kingsize bed, a stool, a large mirrored dresser, and a cedar trunk. And on the right was the combination kitchen and living room, with a huge black woodburning stove, a modern refrigerator with a cat on top, a round maple table with four chairs, a brown saggy sofa, and three big overstuffed armchairs, none of them matching. Then there was a rather lovely corner china cabinet, which also had a cat on top.

"Oh, how cute!" cried Grandma. "Look at the darling beautiful grey Persian cats. Here, kitty, kitty!" She left her suitcase by the door and dashed over to the one on the fridge. She reached up and tried to grab it. But the cat stood up, leaned on its hindlegs, flattened its ears—and hissed.

"Gee, if you want to be like that, then I'll talk to your friend!" Grandma was insulted. She was a cat lover, and she seldom met a feline who didn't fall instantly in love with her. She stood on her toes and tried to get the other cat, but this one went almost berserk. It flew over to the sofa, jumped on the table, and landed with a thud behind the big stove. It growled and spat and wagged its bushy tail furiously. Grandma was in shock.

"Maybe they've got rabies," said Pixy. He stood pressed against the bedroom door, shaking. Cats weren't his favorite animals under any circumstances.

"They don't look sick to me. They're just unfriendly. How Mooshi Winthrop can keep such badly behaved pets is beyond me."

She grabbed a broom from a hook beside the door and swatted at them. Pixy held the front door wide open, but the cats wouldn't budge. They had flattened themselves under the stove, and four yellowish-green eyes squinted nastily at Grandma and Pixy.

"Oh well," said Grandma. "They aren't very nice, are they? But if we leave the door open, they'll probably go outside eventually. Let's unpack our stuff and get settled. I get the bedroom, and you get the couch."

Oh sure, he, Pixy, would get the saggy sofa!

Grandma had percolated a pot of coffee, and they were sitting in wooden armchairs in front of the house. Pixy had put on bluejeans and a grey T-shirt with a large green alligator on it. Grandma had also changed. She now wore a pale yellow caftan, with big orange and brown flowers.

"This *is* nice!" she sighed contentedly. "I can almost see how one can write romantic novels in this setting."

"I don't know about romantic, Gran. Seems more a setting for a nice murder story. It's deserted here. House is crooked, trees are high."

Grandma had to laugh. She stirred a little more

sugar into her coffee, tried it, put in half a spoonful more. Then she said, "How about a Dracula thing? There are apt to be oodles of bats around."

"Bats! Here?"

"Well, of course. Where else do you think they'd live? Bats live in attics and under eaves, especially in old houses. They also love hollow tree trunks—like those over there by the outhouse. Just wait until twilight. You'll see them swarming all over the place."

"Stop it, Gran! You give me the creeps. You were just kidding, huh? We're not going outside at night, are we?" Pixy had, all of a sudden, visions of hundreds of shadowy, soundless bats descending on everything. Horrible!

"We won't have to work at night, will we?" he asked again. "We can't see anything in the dark anyhow."

Grandma just looked at him. How that little chicken had ever solved all those so-called unsolvable crimes he had to his credit was beyond her. But then again, those had been bright-light downtown things. You put her partner into isolated lonely places, especially older houses, and Pixy became a coward. Grandma knew darn well that he believed in ghosts. It was almost laughable, but it was a nuisance nevertheless.

"I only hope we won't get in trouble for snooping around Mooshi's neighbor," she said.

"She was awfully upset when I talked to her. I mean," said Pixy, "who wouldn't be upset when people start disappearing into thin air just like that. And with the police shrugging the whole thing off as nonsense."

"Can't blame them, though. Nobody ever officially reported any of those people missing in the first place." Grandma drank the last of her coffee. "Want some more?"

He shook his head. "Two cups are my limit."

She went on. "Maybe there's a sea monster in the lake, and it gobbles them all up."

For a minute Pixy thought Grandma was serious, then decided she was teasing him once more. He sighed. This just wasn't his sort of case. But of course with business being so slow these days, they had to accept any kind of detective work. And, as his partner had pointed out, they could more or less look on this job as a paid vacation. If Mooshi Winthrop wanted to throw away her money for such a silly thing, who were they to argue? Writing fiction day in and day out probably made her imagination run wild in every other respect as well. Disappearing guests at the Kreller cabin, for goodness sake!

"You think that maybe they drowned in the lake?" he asked. "Maybe their bodies got caught on something on the bottom."

"I don't think anything. Mooshi lost a few of her marbles, living here in the woods all by herself. Just look at her crazy cats. Even they aren't normal. You told me Mooshi admitted that Kreller had laughed off the whole thing anyhow. Said that nobody was missing at all, and for her to keep her nose out of his business. And to tell you the truth, Pixy, I'm inclined to agree with him. She really must have snooped around his cabin a lot, for how else could she know that his guests didn't leave by boat? It's a big lake."

"There is that. But she insists that only Professor Kreller himself left by the trail last week. And the two old ladies, his guests, weren't anywhere around here. Mooshi looked everywhere for them. The cabin was locked and the boat moored securely. And that wasn't the only time something strange has happened over there. Last November Professor Kreller came along this trail, past Mooshi's house, with two middle-aged men dressed in hunting gear. They were a noisy bunch, too. At nights she heard them laugh and carry on raucously. And—okay, she spied on them—they were drinking whisky and playing cards almost the whole time. And then at the end Professor Kreller was the only one who left. Mooshi went over to his cabin, but it was all boarded up for the winter. His boat was on blocks up on land. She was especially annoyed because he had left his cats behind to fend for themselves while he was gone. They were shy and Mooshi just left them alone." Pixy got up from the hard chair, stretching himself.

Grandma picked up the empty coffee cups. "Why don't we take a little stroll over to Kreller's place now," she said. "He's supposed to have a guest there again this week. We can just walk right up to the cabin and say hi. We'll tell them we're here on holiday."

The professor's cabin was a beautiful A-frame building, with a balcony on top and a large porch in front. It was painted sky blue with white trim.

"No outhouse here," said Pixy. "What a smart weekend cottage!"

"Yes, it *is* lovely. That little separate thing over there must be for an electric pump." Grandma went over to it—it was a miniature of the main house—and tried the door but it was locked. They then went to the front door and knocked, but there was no answer.

"Must be fishing. Let's go down to the lake," said Grandma.

The lake was fifty yards or so behind the house. The grounds in between had been cleared and beautifully landscaped, with a luscious green lawn and flowers and shrubs bordering it. The embankment by the lake was turned into a rockery; steps made of large granite chips led down to a wooden landing. There a small white and blue boat was moored, its outboard motor tipped upwards.

"Don't seem to be around here, either. Probably went for a walk in the woods," said Grandma.

They were going back around the house when Pixy whispered, "There is someone inside the house. I just saw a curtain move."

The detectives stopped. Sure enough, the curtain did twitch. Grandma hollered, "Hello there!" The curtain fell into place, but no one opened the front door.

"What an unfriendly neighbor," said Pixy. "No wonder Mooshi says the professor is weird."

They had just turned their backs to the house again when a terrific noise came from inside. There was crashing and banging. There was hissing and screeching, intermingled with long-drawn-out meowing.

"Damned cats!" exclaimed Pixy. "They seem to be especially crazy in these parts of the woods."

Later Pixy chopped wood for the stove while Grandma peeled potatoes, cut up carrots and broccoli, and prepared T-bone steaks. Mooshi's freezer and refrigerator were filled with goodies, and the two hungry detectives weren't going to save on food during their stay. Grandma loved her food—her figure showed it—and it wouldn't hurt to put a few pounds on her skinny little partner. She decided to make a vanilla pudding and bake a chocolate cake for dessert. Maybe a small pie for a bedtime snack would be a good idea as well.

She had seen a package of frozen blueberries in the freezer.

She also put a bowl of canned milk and some cut-up pieces of smoked ham out for the cats. Then she pushed the bowls under the sofa where they were hiding now.

It was a hot evening. They were sitting in the twilight, in the wooden garden chairs again. Grandma used a plastic fly swatter and Pixy a small leafy tree branch to hit at the pesky mosquitoes and gnats. Pixy looked suspiciously at the black birds flying above. Or were they bats? He didn't feel too good but he was not going to admit his discomfort to his partner.

Over at the Kreller cabin, they seemed to be having a lot of fun. The loud laughter of two men, one voice deep, the other scratchy, drifted periodically over to the Winthrop house.

The detectives had finished their blueberry pie and sweet tea when Grandma said, "You know, Pixy, I feel like a little walk. Let's go over and have a look at the other place again."

"Now?! In the dark, with the ba—, er, things flying—"

"Sure. We'll just follow the trail again. It's not very far. Come on." Grandma was already at the corner of the house. Pixy followed reluctantly. Bats wouldn't come down to his level, he hoped. He put his hand into his pockets and he stooped.

Through gaps in the foliage they had a fairly clear view of Professor Kreller's front porch. A large, elderly man with a mane of white hair and a bushy mustache was just pouring red wine from a gallon jug into two big goblets. He was apparently telling a very funny story, for the other man, a tallish Oriental-looking person, was laughing so hard that he had to wipe tears from his eyes. From inside the house came jazzy music.

Pixy started to snap his fingers in tune, but Grandma shushed him.

"Let's go up and introduce ourselves," whispered Pixy. "They seem to have lots of wine."

"We do not drink!" Grandma shot back at him. Honestly, if she didn't watch over him almost every minute of his life, her young partner would go to the dogs. Boozing it up, for heaven's sake. She had weaned him of that the day she became his partner.

Pixy shrugged his shoulders, and the two detectives went back to their own place.

They were cooking breakfast, Grandma making the waffles and Pixy scrambling eggs, when they heard someone go past the house. Grandma opened the door.

"Good morning! You must be Miss Winthrop's neighbor, Professor Kreller."

"Morning to you, too." The professor stopped, shook back his long white hair, and came over. "Looks like we're in for another hot day."

"It does that. Won't you come in for a cup of freshly percolated coffee? Miss Winthrop kindly lent us her house for a little vacation." Grandma wiped her hands on her apron. Pixy came and stood beside her.

"No, no," the professor said. "But thank you ever so much anyway. I'm in quite a hurry to get to the university."

"Perhaps your guest would like to come over for a visit," said Pixy. "He might get lonely all by himself."

"Guest? What guest?" Professor Kreller looked astonished. "I've been working most of the week, all by myself, on the book I'm writing. Well, nice to have met you. Give my regards to Miss Winthrop." And with that he disappeared among the cottonwood trees.

Grandma and Pixy looked at each other, then rushed inside the house. They took the food off the stove and hurried down the trail towards Kreller's cabin. Grandma was remarkably quick for such a big person, and her partner could hardly keep up with her.

Both front door and back door were locked. They tried to look through the windows, but all the curtains were drawn. It was uncommonly quiet everywhere. Grandma tried the doorknob of the pumphouse. It turned, and the door opened inwards. An earsplitting shriek filled the air, and a furious Siamese cat came flying out. It jumped right over Pixy and sped around the cabin.

"My goodness," exclaimed Grandma. "Professor Kreller locked one of his poor cats in here by mistake."

"Are you sure it was by mistake!" cried Pixy. "Gran, it was an Oriental cat!"

"So?"

"The guest. The guest who wasn't—but whom *we* know was."

"Pixy! You are not seriously suggesting—no, even you wouldn't!" But she did take a look inside the pumphouse. There was nothing in it but a galvanized tank with a couple of valves and switches. "Come, let's get back to Mooshi's house and get on with another couple of days' vacation. We haven't even eaten our breakfast yet."

"What *about* the guest, Gran? We know there was one here last night. We both saw him with our own eyes. I mean, we are being paid for finding out about these disappearing guests," said Pixy uneasily. "Where could that man be?"

"Left by boat most likely. Come on, don't worry, Pixy. Mooshi Winthrop is a fool. And of course the professor had a guest."

"He denies it, though.'

"Oh, well. You heard him say he's writing a book. So the logical explanation for his denying having anybody here is that he has hired a ghost writer. Many a good book has been written by hired professional writers. Famous people, like movie stars and politicians, use them all the time."

"But, Gran, he's a university professor."

"Sure. Probably professor of something funny. Perhaps he has some very interesting things to say but no talent for writing them down."

The partners spent most of the afternoon down by the lake. Pixy went swimming, and Grandma sat on a big flat rock and dangled her bare feet in the cool water. Then they went back to the house, where she fried a whole chicken and cooked the rice, and he prepared the salad. They ate outside, balancing their plates on their knees. This was the good life! Later Grandma washed and Pixy dried the dishes, and the kitchen corner was neat again in no time. The cats had gotten a plate with scraps.

The detectives had just decided to take yet another little walk, this time into the woods opposite the lake, when they heard branches snapping and the sound of rolling pebbles from the direction of the trail. After a moment Mooshi Winthrop came puffing and stumbling out from among the trees.

"Oh, thank goodness you're still around!" she cried, then sank exhausted into the nearest garden chair. Her pepper and salt hair was tousled, and her blouse had crept out of her skirt. She was perspiring.

"My, am I ever glad to find you alive and well!"

Grandma had rushed into the house and come out again with a tall glass of orange juice.

"You get cooled off first, Mooshi. Then tell us why you are so surprised that we're still here." Grandma took the only other chair, and Pixy perched on a nearby tree stump. "Pixy did tell you we'd stay for several days." Oh boy, she hoped the owner of this house wouldn't immediately look into either her fridge or her freezer. Grandma had sort of a bad conscience about all the food she and her partner had already consumed.

Mooshi drank half the juice in one gulp. "Yes, it was so silly of me to worry about you two. But with those people going missing and all, and then the professor's strange death this noon—"

"Death? Professor Kreller is *dead*?" cried Pixy.

"But we just talked to him this morning!" Grandma was just as shocked. "He came by here on his way to the university."

"Yes, and on his way there he dropped dead. Seems that one minute he was walking along the sidewalk in front of the university library, the next he was dead in the bushes. Was supposed to have some nasty scratches on his arms, but otherwise they think he just died of old age." Mooshi drank the last of her juice. "I got the whole story from my nephew who was one of Professor Kreller's students.—Biology, you know."

Grandma and Pixy told Mooshi then about their strange encounter with the professor. Pixy tried to elaborate on Kreller's cats, but the women just looked funny at him. That is, Mooshi shrugged it off until

Grandma said, "Oh, by the way, I fed your two cats. Guess they aren't used to strangers, though."

"Cats?" asked Mooshi.

"Yes, your beautiful long-haired grey ones. They seem to love sitting on top of your china cabinet. They don't go outside much, do they?"

"But I have no cats!" cried Mooshi. She rushed into the house and looked wildly around. Grandma and Pixy followed, and they too were shocked, for now there were other cats here as well. In fact, cats seemed to be everywhere. Green and yellow eyes were peeking from under the sofa, from atop the refrigerator and the china cabinet, from behind the armchairs.

"I can count five now," said Grandma. "At supper time there were only two here. Whose could they be? The professor's?"

"There's the Siamese one from Kreller's pumphouse." Pixy moved toward it, but it hissed.

Mooshi was in tears. How was she going to get them out of her place? She wasn't fond of cats, and now here were all these full-grown ones in her dear little house. She sniffled.

"And what is going to happen to the professor's book now?" asked Pixy. "I wonder what it's about. Cats, maybe? It's probably still in his cabin. Perhaps it even has something to do with disappearing people." And seeing Grandma's disapproving looks, he added quickly, "Maybe it has nothing at all to do with those things—should we take another look at the cabin?"

They had walked up to the Kreller place. The front door stood wide open now, but otherwise all seemed empty and quiet. It was rapidly getting dark, and the place didn't look all that inviting any more.

"It seems as dead as its owner. The cats must have

felt it, too. You think they opened the door themselves?" asked Pixy as he switched on the lights.

They looked uneasily around. It was a man's room, but very cosy. There was a large desk, a fireplace, dark brown vinyl upholstered armchairs, and low bookshelves all along the walls.

Pixy went over to the desk. An inch-high stack of typed papers, probably *the* manuscript, lay beside a covered typewriter. There was a pile of reference and technical books, a dictionary, and several thin cardboard folders on it. One of the folders had slipped down to the floor, and Pixy picked it up. It had scratches on it, as if one of the cats had tried to sharpen its claws there. Inside the folder were several newspaper clippings, some with pictures. Mooshi came over and looked at a couple of them, then exclaimed, "Oh my, oh my—I recognize those people in the photos! Please, let's go over to my house and take these clippings with us. I can't stand this place another minute!"

Back at the Winthrop house Pixy riffled through the newspaper clippings, with Grandma and Mooshi looking over his shoulder. Nobody said a word. The five cats sat side by side on top of the china cabinet, their eyes big and round and much friendlier. Their loud purring filled the room.

First they inspected the pictures of two middle-aged, bearded men. The headline read: "MacDonald Brothers Acquitted in Hotel Murders for Lack of Evidence."

"They look exactly like the two hunters Professor Kreller brought to his cabin last November," whispered Mooshi.

Pixy pulled out the next clipping. It was a very clear photo of two sweet-looking elderly ladies, with neat white curls around their faces and lace around their throats. The caption said: "Retired Teachers Acquitted in Murder of Millionaire Cousin."

"Those by any chance the two little old ladies who were Kreller's guests a couple of weeks ago?" asked Grandma.

Mooshi could only nod her head. Everything was horrid. She glanced at the cats. Oh dear, would they stay here now? Could she, Mooshi Winthrop, actually get used to those creatures—five of them yet! She shuddered. How could one write romantic novels under those circumstances? Maybe she should try her hand at something different? Maybe ghost stories?

They came to the last clipping, the one of a tall, slim, Oriental-looking young man.

"'Suspect in Holdup Killing Released for Lack of Evidence,'" Pixy read aloud. "That was Professor Kreller's last guest, huh?"

Mooshi shivered. And from the top of the china cabinet the Siamese cat let out a shrill, drawn-out cry.

They were walking single file back along the uneven rocky path, Pixy in front with his backpack and Grandma following with her rolling suitcase.

"Got the check in your purse, Gran?" called Pixy.

"Oh yes. And a nice one it is, too," she answered. "Funny she should have paid us, seeing we didn't really solve the mystery of the missing people. *You* didn't believe the thing about the cats by any chance, did you, Pixy? About the professor being a one-man law enforcer, luring the murder suspects to his remote cabin and turning them into—"

"Who, me?!" It was a good thing Grandma couldn't see her partner's face behind his high backpack, as Pixy blushed.

For Pixy believed indeed that Professor Kreller had been some sort of magician.

# THE BLACK CAT
## by Lee Somerville

She was an old cat, coal black, lean and ugly. Her right ear had been chewed and her old hide showed scars, but she had a regal look when she sat under the rosebushes in the plaza and surveyed us with yellow-green eyes.

If the witch cat had a name, we never knew it. Miss Tessie fed it, as she fed other strays. She even let the old cat sleep in her store in rainy weather. But mostly the cat slept under the rosebushes in our plaza in Caton City, Texas. We have a pretty little plaza, or square, here in the center of town. It has a fountain and a statue of a tired Confederate soldier facing north, ready to defend us from Northern invaders, and a bit of grass and lots of rosebushes.

Nobody dared to pet the old cat. People gave the cat scraps of bread and meat from hamburgers and hot dogs. She accepted this placidly, as a queen accepts homage from peons. Now and then a stray dog came through our small dusty town, saw the cat, and made a lunge at it. The cat would retreat to the base of the fountain, turn, lash with a razor-sharp claw that sliced the poor dog's nose. The dog would run howling while townspeople laughed. Our dogs, having learned the hard way, left that cat alone.

When I was fourteen, my mother's jailbird distant

relative, Cousin Rush, came to live with us. My little brother Pete and I had to give up our room to this scruffy relative, but that wasn't the only reason I disliked him. I despised his dumpy figure and his smelly cigars and his scaly bald head and his way of looking at me with beady small eyes and nodding and winking.

Mama told me to show Cousin Rush the town, and I had to do it. This was the day before Halloween, and half the town was in the theater across the street from the plaza, rehearsing for the Heritage Festival we have every Halloween night. Miss Tessie was in the front of the theater, selling plastic masks of Cajun Caton and Davy Crockett. We have this play about Cajun Caton and a Delaware Indian, Chief Cut Hand, saving the town from Comanches on a Halloween night in the early 1800s. It ends with Cajun Caton, town hero, leaving his eight children and one wife later on and going off with Davy Crockett and getting killed in the Alamo during the Texas Revolution against Mexico in 1836.

Cousin Rush bought a mask from Miss Tessie. He smiled and flirted and talked of the Importance of History. His face smiled, but his eyes remained cold and scornful, and I could tell he thought this heritage business was hillbilly country foolishness. He'd already told me Caton City was a hick town filled with stupid people. It didn't compare with real towns.

As we started walking across the plaza, the black cat jumped from the rosebushes and ran in front of us.

To keep walking in a straight direction would have meant bad luck. I sidestepped, made a little circle, and prevented bad luck. I'm not superstitious, not really, but no use taking chances.

Cousin Rush laughed at me. Then, to show his scorn

of superstition and black cats, he did a fat-legged little hop and skip and kicked that cat in the stomach.

The old cat doubled up on Cousin Rush's sharp-toed shoe. She clawed at his sock, then bounced into a rosebush. She landed on her feet, stood there, weaving, hurt. Cousin Rush kicked again, and she dodged. She ran into the street, stopped, looked at Cousin Rush with yellow-green eyes. As he popped his hands together, making a threatening noise, she stood her ground for a moment, then ran into Miss Tessie's store.

"You didn't have to do that," I said.

Cousin Rush stood there, the October sun beating down on his bald head and his cigar sticking out of his fat face. "You country bumpkins don't have to act ignorant, but you do. The only way to deal with a black cat running across your path is to kick the manure out of the cat. It's a callous world, Brian, and the only way to deal with it is to skin your buddy before he skins you."

"We don't act that way here," I disagreed.

"You are fools," he stated. He blew cigar smoke and looked at people milling around in front of the theater, talking and being friendly. "Now, tell me about this Heritage Festival you'll have tomorrow night. As I understand it, half the town is in the play, including the sheriff and his deputy. The other half— and that includes a lot of people that make this a sort of homecoming—will buy tickets and make cash contributions to the historical society. I understand this crazy old maid, this Miss Tessie, has collected a neat bit of cash."

"She's raising money for a historical marker to honor her ancestor, Cajun Caton."

"Yes. That's the idiot the town is named for."

"He was not an idiot. Caton and Davy Crockett were both killed in the Alamo, and they were Texas heroes."

Cousin Rush blew more smoke. "And there are at least a hundred people in this town descended from Caton. I understand that during the finale of this play, which Miss Tessie wrote, it has become a custom for every man in the audience to put on a mask to honor Cajun Caton or Davy Crockett? Hmmm."

I didn't like the sudden suspicion I had. I'd heard Mama and Dad talking in whispers, telling that Rush had served time in a Texas penitentiary for small-time robbery. I didn't like the cold, greedy look on my cousin's face.

I could have reported my suspicion to Sheriff Mitchell or to Deputy Haskins except for one thing—my mother was an Adams. Every Adams is intensely loyal to other Adamses, and don't you forget it. Cousin Rush was Rushid E. Sarosy, and his daddy had been a shoe salesman in Dallas, but his mama was Verney Adams to start with. Verney was a hot little blonde who was born with a female urge and grew up around it. She left Caton County fifty-six years ago for the big city, but she was still an Adams.

I had a suspicion, from the calculating look on his face, that Cousin Rush would burglarize some place tomorrow night when everybody was in the theater, or he'd rob the box office at the theater, wearing a mask like everybody else would wear.

I couldn't talk to Mama about my suspicions. If I was wrong and Cousin Rush didn't do anything bad, she'd say I was disloyal to the name of Adams.

As we left the Plaza, the old black cat that Cousin Rush had kicked came out of Miss Tessie's store and looked at us as if she were casting a spell. I shivered.

I still wonder if what happened that night was just coincidence.

My little brother Pete had been unsuccessfully baiting that animal trap for a week. The trap was in the back yard. Here in Caton City, which is in northeast Texas, just south of Oklahoma and not far from Arkansas between the Red River and the Sulphur River, things were different. Coyotes and raccoons and possums and other animals came into town at night to raid garbage cans. Pete had been baiting that animal trap, actually a cage, for a week with cornbread, beans, cabbage, and such, hoping to catch a raccoon and make a pet of it. On this night, with a big moon beaming down, he had jerry-rigged a Rube Goldberg device that would turn on a light if the trap door was triggered.

Cousin Rush had our room now, so we slept in beds on our big screened-in back porch. About midnight the signal light came on to show the trap door had slammed down. Pete got out of bed in his underwear and ran barefoot to the trap, waving a flashlight.

He came back in a hurry. "Brian, we got trouble!"

I sat up, sniffed. "I smell it." The smell of skunk was not all that strong, showing the animal was fairly content, but it was definitely skunk.

"You got to shoot it."

"Hell, no! If you shoot that skunk, it'll make a smell that will wake up the town," I cautioned. "It has plenty of food and water and room to move around in that cage-trap. After it eats, it will probably go to sleep, won't it?"

Pete thought this over. "I guess so, unless it's disturbed."

"Okay. I'll make sure the yard gates are closed, so

no dogs or other animals can disturb that skunk. We'll figure what to do after it gets daylight tomorrow. Let sleeping skunks sleep, that's my motto."

After Pete had gone back to bed, I lay awake, thinking. I could take a long fishing pole, hold the cage as far from me as possible, and move gently. I'd have to get that skunk out of our back yard somehow. . . .

I finally went to sleep and dreamed that Cousin Rush robbed Miss Tessie of all the Heritage Festival money. He got by with it because he was wearing a mask and all the men in the crowd he joined afterward wore masks. Nobody knew which masked man had the money. I woke up. Then I went to sleep again and this time I dreamed Cousin Rush didn't get away with it after all. He came out of the theater with the money still in his hands, and the old black cat cast a spell on him and made him throw the money in the air.

And I dreamed the old cat was really a witch in disguise.

When I woke up, it was Halloween Day and I still didn't know what to do about Cousin Rush. Maybe I was suspicious of him because I didn't like him.

But later in the day, as I listened to him talk with Miss Tessie, I became more alarmed. Oh, it was just general talk, discussion of the fact that Cajun Caton wasn't really a cajun. He was from Henry County, Tennessee, and he had picked up that nickname in Louisiana in what Miss Tessie described as an "indiscreet house."

I watched as Cousin Rush got his Oldsmobile filled with gas and the tires and oil checked. Looked like he was planning for a trip. He couldn't go to Houston, because police would arrest him if he went back there. He'd have trouble with his fourth wife in Dallas, and was wanted on charges there. But the way he was fussing around his car, it looked as if he would go somewhere in a hurry.

Long before the Heritage Play started that night, he parked his car on the north side of the plaza near the biggest rosebush. Then he went into the theater early, carrying a cape and a mask as some other men were doing.

I stood looking across the plaza, worried. The black cat came from the rosebushes, sat on the base of the fountain, and stared back at me. Darkness came, and a full moon rose. Stars shone.

Looking at that cat, I knew what I had to do. Maybe it wouldn't work, but maybe it would. I had to try.

After the play was well under way, with everyone except me in the theater, I got a long fishing pole and some cord. Cautiously, holding my breath at times, I carried that animal cage-trap the three blocks to the plaza. The skunk, his belly full of cornbread and cabbage and beans, slept most of the time.

I learned later that during the last two minutes of the play a man wearing a mask and a cape went inside the box office where Miss Tessie was counting money. He didn't speak a word, but he pushed a small pistol in Miss Tessie's face and motioned for her to sit down. He tied her to the chair. She opened her mouth to scream, and he jammed a handkerchief in it. Nobody would have heard if she had screamed because the audience and the cast were singing the finale.

The man put his pistol inside his cape, took handfuls of the paper money she'd been sorting. He stuffed money in his pockets and inside the cape pockets, and left with some money in his hands.

He walked out of the theater as the townspeople, wearing capes and masks, also walked out.

I knew which one was Cousin Rush. I could tell by the prissy walk and the dumpy figure.

A couple of kids ran ahead of him across the plaza, but I pulled the cord I had rigged to the trap door. With that door open, and with all the noise, the skunk would come out. He would not be disturbed or afraid, because skunks are not usually afraid. Even a grizzly bear would tippy-toe around a skunk.

The two kids apparently saw him, hollered, "Uh-oh," detoured slightly, and kept running. Cousin Rush paid them no attention.

Then Miss Tessie's old black cat ran out of the rose-bushes, ran right in front of Cousin Rush, ran back into the bushes.

Cousin Rush slowed in his fast walk to the Olds-mobile. It was a beautiful night, bright as day with white moonlight and black shadows. Just as Cousin Rush got near his car, a small black animal came out of the rosebushes again, right in front of him.

If he had climbed in his car without noticing, he would have gotten away with robbery. Being Cousin Rush and being naturally mean, and probably thinking this was Miss Tessie's old black cat, he kicked the skunk.

Then he bent over, ready to kick again. He got that spray full in his face. He staggered back, threw both arms in the air, hands spread wide. Money fluttered high, caught the wind, and blew all over the plaza. Cousin Rush fought for breath, ran into the monu-ment, bounced off, stumbled against the fountain, coughed, gasped, vomited, waved his hands again.

He tore off his mask and cape, and money came from the pockets inside the cape and swirled in the air. People stood watching, wondering.

Somebody found Miss Tessie bound and gagged and

cut her loose. She ran into the street, screaming she'd been robbed.

With all those dollar bills and five-dollar bills and ten-dollar bills floating in the air around Cousin Rush, he became the Prime Suspect. Nobody went near him for a while, though. The smell was nauseating.

Finally Sheriff Mitchell spoke firm words to Deputy Haskins. Haskins looked reluctant, but Mitchell gave the orders. Don't take him to our clean jail, he said. Take him to the old county stables and lock him up for the night.

The skunk got away in all the excitement. Nobody would have touched him anyway. I knew I would pick up the cage-trap when everybody left, or I'd be incriminated. I didn't want Mama to know I'd had anything to do with trapping Cousin Rush.

Citizens picked up the money that was blowing around and put it in a well-ventilated place for the night. Then people left for the American Legion Barbecue and Dance. Some of those who had gotten close to skunk smell while picking up the money might have to stay outside the Legion Hall, but they'd eat barbecue and drink Blanton Creek bourbon and they'd survive.

As the crowd left the plaza, and as Deputy Haskins started Cousin Rush walking twenty feet ahead of him to the stables, I saw Miss Tessie's old black cat sitting on the base of the fountain. Her eyes glinted in the Halloween moonlight, and I'll swear that cat was laughing.

# PHUT PHAT CONCENTRATES

## by Lilian Jackson Braun

Phut Phat knew, at an early age, that humans were an inferior breed. They were unable to see in the dark. They ate and drank unthinkable concoctions. And they had only five senses—the two who lived with Phut Phat could not even transmit their thoughts without resorting to words.

For more than a year, ever since he had arrived at the townhouse, Phut Phat had been attempting to introduce his system of communication, but his two pupils had made scant progress. At dinnertime he would sit in a corner, concentrating, and suddenly they would say, "Time to feed the cat," as if it were their own idea.

Their ability to grasp Phut Phat's messages extended only to the bare necessities of daily living, however. Beyond that, nothing ever got through to them, and it seemed unlikely that they would ever increase their powers.

Nevertheless, life in the townhouse was comfortable enough. It followed a fairly dependable routine, and to Phut Phat routine was the greatest of all goals. He deplored such deviations as tardy meals, loud noises, unexplained persons on the premises, or liver during the week. He always had liver on Sunday.

It was a fashionable part of the city in which Phut Phat lived. His home was a three-story brick house furnished with thick rugs and down-cushioned chairs and tall pieces of furniture from which he could look down on questionable visitors. He could rise to the top of a highboy in a single leap, and when he chose to scamper from first-floor kitchen to second-floor living room to third-floor bedroom, his ascent up the carpeted staircase was very close to flight, for Phut Phat was a Siamese. His fawn-colored coat was finer than ermine. His eight seal-brown points (there had been nine before that trip to the hospital) were as sleek as panne velvet and his slanted eyes brimmed with a mysterious blue.

Those who lived with Phut Phat in the townhouse were a pair, identified in his consciousness as One and Two. It was One who supplied the creature comforts—beef on weekdays, liver on Sunday, and a warm cuddle now and then. She also fed his vanity with lavish compliments and adorned his throat with jeweled collars taken from her own wrists.

Two, on the other hand, was valued chiefly for games and entertainment. He said very little, but he jingled keys at the end of a shiny chain and swung them back and forth for Phut Phat's amusement. And every morning in the dressing room he swished a necktie in tantalizing arcs while Phut Phat leaped and grabbed with pearly claws.

These daily romps, naps on downy cushions, outings in the coop on the fire escape, and two meals a day constituted the pattern of Phut Phat's life.

Then one Sunday he sensed a disturbing lapse in the household routine. The Sunday papers, usually scattered all over the library floor for him to shred with his claws, were stacked neatly on the desk. Furniture was rearranged. The house was filled with flowers, which he was not allowed to chew. All day long, One was nervous and Two was too busy to play. A stranger in a white coat arrived and clattered glassware, and when Phut Phat went to investigate an aroma of shrimp and smoked oysters in the kitchen the maid shooed him away.

Phut Phat seemed to be in everyone's way. Finally he was deposited in his wire coop on the fire escape, where he watched sparrows in the garden below until his stomach felt empty. Then he howled to come indoors.

He found One at her dressing table, fussing with her hair and unmindful of his hunger. Hopping lightly to the table, he sat erect among the sparkling bottles, stiffened his tail, and fastened his blue eyes on One's forehead. In that attitude he concentrated—and concentrated—and concentrated. It was never easy to communicate with One. Her mind hopped about like a sparrow, never relaxed, and Phut Phat had to strain every nerve to convey his meaning.

Suddenly One darted a look in his direction. A thought had occurred to her.

"Oh, John," she called to Two, who was brushing his hair in the dressing room, "would you ask Millie to feed Phuffy? I forgot his dinner until this very minute. It's after five o'clock and I haven't fixed my hair yet. You'd better put your coat on—people will start coming soon. And please tell Howard to light the candles. You might stack some records on the stereo, too.—No, wait a minute. If Millie is still working on the canapes, would you feed Phuffy yourself? Just give him a slice of cold roast."

At this, Phut Phat stared at One with an intensity that made his thought waves almost visible.

"Oh, John, I forgot," she corrected. "It's Sunday, and he should have liver. Cut it in long strips or he'll toss it up. And before you do that, will you zip the back of my dress and put my emerald bracelet on Phuffy? Or maybe I'll wear the emerald myself and he can have the topaz. John! Do you realize it's five-fifteen? I wish you'd put your coat on."

"And I wish you'd simmer down," said Two. "No one ever comes on time. Why do you insist on giving big parties, Helen, if it makes you so nervous?"

"Nervous? I'm not nervous. Besides, it was *your* idea to invite my friends and your clients at the same time. You said we should kill a whole blasted flock of birds with one stone. Now, *please,* John, are you going to feed Phuffy? He's staring at me and making my head ache."

Phut Phat scarcely had time to swallow his meal, wash his face, and arrange himself on the living-room mantel before people started to arrive. His irritation at having the routine disrupted had been lessened somewhat by the prospect of being admired by the guests. His name meant "beautiful" in Siamese, and he was well aware of his pulchritude.

Lounging between a pair of Georgian candlesticks, with one foreleg extended and the other exquisitely bent under at the ankle, with his head erect and gaze withdrawn, with his tail drooping nonchalantly over the edge of the marble mantel, he awaited compliments.

It was a large party, and Phut Phat observed that very few of the guests knew how to pay their respects to a cat. Some talked nonsense in a falsetto voice. Others made startling movements in his direction or, worse still, tried to pick him up.

There was one knowledgeable guest, however, who approached the mantel with a proper attitude of deference and reserve. Phut Phat squeezed his eyes in appreciation. The admirer was a man, who leaned heavily on a shiny stick. Standing at a respectful distance, he slowly held out his hand with one finger extended, and Phut Phat twitched his whiskers in polite acknowledgement.

"You are a living sculpture," said the man.

"That's Phut Phat," said One, who had pushed through the crowded room toward the fireplace. "He's the head of our household."

"He is obviously a champion," said the man with the shiny cane, addressing his hostess in the same dignified manner that had charmed Phut Phat.

"Yes, he could probably win a few ribbons if we wanted to enter him in shows, but he's strictly a pet. He never goes out, except in his coop on the fire escape."

"A coop? That's a splendid idea," said the man. "I should like to have one for my own cat. She's a tortoise-shell long-hair. May I inspect this coop before I leave?"

"Of course. It's just outside the library window."

"You have a most attractive house."

"Thank you. We've been accused of decorating it to complement Phut Phat's coloring, which is somewhat true. You'll notice we have no breakable bric-a-brac. When a Siamese flies through the air, he recognizes no obstacles."

"Indeed, I have noticed you collect Georgian silver," the man said in his courtly way. "You have some fine examples."

"Apparently you know silver. Your cane is a rare piece."

"Yes, it is an attempt to extract a little pleasure from a sorry necessity." He hobbled a step or two.

"Would you like to see my silver collection down-stairs in the dining room?" asked One. "It's all early silver—about the time of Wren."

At this point, Phut Phat, aware that the conversation no longer centered on him, jumped down from the mantel and stalked out of the room with several irritable flicks of the tail. He found an olive and pushed it down the heat register. Several feet stepped on him. In desperation, he went upstairs to the guest room, where he discovered a mound of sable and mink and went to sleep.

After this upset in the household routine, Phut Phat needed several days to catch up on his rest—so the ensuing week was a sleep blur. But soon it was Sunday again, with liver for breakfast, Sunday papers scattered over the floor, and everyone sitting around being pleasantly routine.

"Phuffy! Don't roll on those newspapers," said One. "John, can't you see the ink rubs off on his fur? Give him the *Wall Street Journal*—it's cleaner."

"Maybe he'd like to go outside in his coop and get some sun."

"That reminds me, dear. Who was that charming man with the silver cane at our party? I didn't catch his name."

"I don't know," said Two. "I thought he was someone you invited."

"Well, he wasn't. He must have come with one of the other guests. At any rate, he was interested in getting a coop like ours for his own cat. He has a long-haired torty. And did I tell you the Hendersons

have two Burmese kittens? They want us to go over
and see them next Sunday and have a drink."

Another week passed, during which Phut Phat discovered a new perch. He found he could jump to the
top of an antique armoire—a towering piece of furniture in the hall outside the library. Otherwise, it was
a routine week, followed by a routine weekend, and
Phut Phat was content.

One and Two were going out on Sunday evening to
see the Burmese kittens, so Phut Phat was served an
early dinner and soon afterward he fell asleep on the
library sofa.

When the telephone rang and waked him, it was
dark and he was alone. He raised his head and chattered at the instrument until it stopped its noise. Then
he went back to sleep, chin on paw.

The second time the telephone started ringing, Phut
Phat stood up and scolded it, arching his body in a
vertical stretch and making a question mark with his
tail. To express his annoyance, he hopped on the desk
and sharpened his claws on Webster's Unabridged.
Then he spent quite some time chewing on a leather
bookmark. After that he felt thirsty. He sauntered
toward the powder room for a drink.

No lights were burning and no moonlight came
through the windows, yet he moved through the dark
rooms with assurance, side-stepping table legs and
stopping to examine infinitesimal particles on the hall
carpet. Nothing escaped him.

Phut Phat was lapping water, and the tip of his tail
was waving rapturously from side to side, when something caused him to raise his head and listen. His tail
froze. Sparrows in the backyard? Rain on the fire es-

cape? There was silence again. He lowered his head and resumed his drinking.

A second time he was alerted. Something was happening that was not routine. His tail bushed like a squirrel's, and with his whiskers full of alarm he stepped noiselessly into the hall, peering toward the library.

Someone was on the fire escape. Something was gnawing at the library window.

Petrified, he watched—until the window opened and a dark figure slipped into the room. With one lightning glide, Phut Phat sprang to the top of the tall armoire.

There on his high perch, able to look down on the scene, he felt safe. But was it enough to feel safe? His ancestors had been watchcats in Oriental temples centuries before. They had hidden in the shadows and crouched on high walls, ready to spring on any intruder and tear his face to ribbons—just as Phut Phat shredded the Sunday paper. A primitive instinct rose in his breast, but quickly it was quelled by civilized inhibitions.

The figure in the window advanced stealthily toward the hall, and Phut Phat experienced a sense of the familiar. It was the man with the shiny stick. This time, though, his presence smelled sinister. A small blue light now glowed from the head of the cane, and instead of leaning on it the man pointed it ahead to guide his way out of the library and toward the staircase. As the intruder passed the armoire, Phut Phat's fur rose to form a sharp ridge down his spine. Instinct said, Spring at him! But vague fears held him back.

With feline stealth, the man moved downstairs, unaware of two glowing diamonds that watched him in the blackness, and Phut Phat soon heard noises in the dining room. He sensed evil. Safe on top of the armoire, he trembled.

When the man reappeared, he was carrying a bulky load, which he took to the library window. Then he crept to the third floor, and there were muffled sounds in the bedroom. Phut Phat licked his nose in apprehension.

Now the man reappeared, following a pool of blue light. As he approached the armoire, Phut Phat shifted his feet, bracing himself against something invisible. He felt a powerful compulsion to attack, and yet a fearful dismay.

Get him! commanded a savage impulse within him.

Stay! warned the fright throbbing in his head.

Get him! Now—now—*now!*

Phut Phat sprang at the man's head, ripping with razor claws wherever they sank into flesh.

The hideous scream that came from the intruder was like an electric shock. It sent Phut Phat sailing through space—up the stairs—into the bedroom— under the bed.

For a long time he quaked uncontrollably, his mouth parched and his ears inside-out with horror at what had happened. There was something strange and wrong about it, although its meaning eluded him. Waiting for Time to heal his confusion, he huddled there in darkness and privacy. Blood soiled his claws. He sniffed with distaste and finally was compelled to lick them clean. He did it slowly and with repugnance. Then he tucked his paws under his warm body and waited.

When One and Two came home, he sensed their arrival even before the taxicab door slammed. He should have bounded to meet them, but the experience had left him in a daze, quivering internally, weak and unsure.

He heard the rattle of the front door lock, feet climbing the stairs and the click of the light switch in the room where he waited in bewilderment under the bed.

One instantly gave a gasp, then a shriek. "John! Someone's been in this room. We've been robbed!"

Two's voice was incredulous. "What! How do you know?"

"My jewel case. Look! It's open—and empty!"

Two threw open a closet door. "Your furs are still here, Helen. What about money? Did you have any money in the house?"

"I never leave money around. But the silver! What about the silver? John, go down and see. I'm afraid to look. No! Wait a minute!" One's voice rose in panic. "Where's Phut Phat? What's happened to Phut Phat?"

"I don't know," said Two with alarm. "I haven't seen him since we came in."

They searched the house, calling his name—unaware, with their limited senses, that Phut Phat was right there under the bed, brooding over the upheaval in his small world, and now and then licking his claws.

When at last, crawling on their hands and knees, they spied two eyes glowing red under the bed, they drew him out gently. One hugged him with a rocking embrace and rubbed her face, wet and salty, on his fur, while Two stood by, stroking him with a heavy hand. Comforted and reassured, Phut Phat stopped trembling. He tried to purr, but the shock had constricted his larynx.

One continued to hold Phut Phat in her arms—and he had no will to jump down—even after two strange men were admitted to the house. They asked questions and examined all the rooms. "Everything is insured," One told them, "but the silver is irreplaceable. It's old and very rare. Is there any chance of getting it back, Lieutenant?" She fingered Phut Phat's ears nervously.

"At this point it's hard to say," the detective said. "But you may be able to help us. Have you noticed any strange incidents lately? Any unusual telephone calls?"

"Yes," said One. "Several times recently the phone has rung, and when we answered it there was no one on the line."

"That's the usual method. They wait until they know you're not at home."

One gazed into Phut Phat's eyes. "Did the phone ring tonight while we were out, Phuffy?" she asked, shaking him lovingly. "If only Phut Phat could tell us what happened! He must have had a terrifying experience. Thank heaven he wasn't harmed."

Phut Phat raised his paw to lick between his toes, still defined with human blood.

"If only Phuffy could tell us who was here."

Phut Phat paused with toes spread and pink tongue extended. He stared at One's forehead.

"Have you folks noticed any strangers in the neighborhood?" the lieutenant was asking. "Anyone who would arouse suspicion?"

Phut Phat's body tensed and his blue eyes, brimming with knowledge, bored into that spot above One's eyebrows.

"No, I can't think of anyone," she said. "Can you, John?"

Two shook his head.

"Poor Phuffy," said One. "See how he stares at me? He must be hungry. Does Phuffy want a little snack?"

Phut Phat squirmed.

"About these bloodstains on the window sill," said the detective. "Would the cat attack an intruder viciously enough to draw blood?"

"Heavens, no!" said One. "He's just a pampered little house pet. We found him hiding under the bed, scared stiff."

"And you're sure you can't remember any unusual incident lately? Has anyone come to the house who might have seen the silver or jewelry? Repairman? Window washer?"

"I wish I could be more helpful," said One, "but, honestly, I can't think of a single suspect."

Phut Phat gave up!

Wriggling free, he jumped down from One's lap and walked toward the door with head depressed and hind legs stiff with disgust. He knew who it was. He knew! The man with the shiny stick. But it was useless to try to communicate. The human mind was closed so tight that nothing important would ever penetrate. And One was so busy with her own chatter that her mind—

The jingle of keys caught Phut Phat's attention. He turned and saw Two swinging his key chain back and forth, back and forth, and saying nothing. Two always did more thinking than talking. Perhaps Phut Phat had been trying to communicate with the wrong mind. Perhaps Two was really number one in the household and One was number two.

Phut Phat froze in his position of concentration, sitting tall and compact with tail stiff. The key chain swung back and forth, and Phut Phat fastened his blue eyes on three wrinkles just underneath Two's hairline.

He concentrated. The key chain swung back and forth, back and forth. Phut Phat kept concentrating.

"Wait a minute," said Two, coming out of his puzzled silence. "I just thought of something. Helen, remember that party we gave a couple of weeks ago? There was one guest we couldn't account for. A man with a silver cane."

"Why, yes! The man was so curious about the coop on the fire escape. Why didn't I think of him? Lieutenant, he was terribly interested in our Georgian silver."

Two said, "Does that suggest anything to you, Lieutenant?"

"Yes, it does." The detective exchanged nods with his partner.

"This man," One volunteered, "had a very cultivated voice and a charming manner."

"We know him," the detective said grimly. "We know his method. What you tell us fits perfectly. But we didn't know he was operating in this neighborhood again."

One said, "What mystifies me is the blood on the window sill."

Phut Phat arched his body in a long, luxurious stretch and walked from the room, looking for a soft, dark, quiet place. Now he would sleep. He felt relaxed and satisfied. He had made vital contact with a human mind, and perhaps—after all—there was hope. Someday they might learn the system, learn to open their minds and receive. They had a long way to go before they realized their potential—but there was hope.

# A FELINE FELONY

## by Lael J. Littke

Jerome Kotter looked like a cat. However, this did not bring him any undue attention from his schoolmates since almost all of them had an unusual quality or two. Beverly Baumgartner had a laugh like a horse. Bart Hansen was as rotund as an elephant. Carla Seaver's long neck resembled that of a giraffe. And Randy Ramsbottom always smelled remarkably like a dog on a rainy day.

The only person who worried about Jerome's unusual appearance was his father, who quietly set about arming his son to face a world in which he was a bit different. He taught Jerome gentle manners, assuring him that no matter how different he looked he would always get along fine if he acted right. He taught him to recite all the verses of "The Star-Spangled Banner" by heart. He encouraged him to read the Bible. And he taught him to sing the songs from the best-known Gilbert and Sullivan operettas. He felt Jerome was well equipped to face the world.

When Jerome got to high school he became the greatest track star that Quigley High had ever produced, although he had to be careful because the coaches from rival schools cried foul when Jerome resorted to running on all fours.

Altogether, Jerome's school years would have been quite happy—if it hadn't been for Benny Rhoades.

Whereas Jerome was tall, polite, studious, and well groomed with silken fur and sparkling whiskers, Benny was wizened, unkempt, rude, and sly. His face was pinched and pointed and his hair stuck up in uneven wisps. He hated anyone who excelled him in anything. Almost everybody excelled him in everything, and since Jerome surpassed him in the one thing he did do fairly well—running—he hated Jerome most of all. When Jerome took away his title of champion runner of Quigley High, Benny vowed he would get even if it took him the rest of his life.

One of Benny's favorite harassments was to tread on Jerome's tail in study hall, causing him to yowl and thereby incurring the wrath of the monitor. Benny tweaked Jerome's whiskers and poured honey in his fur. He did everything he could think of to make Jerome's life miserable.

When it came to Benny Rhoades, Jerome found it hard to follow the admonitions of his father—that he should love his enemies and do good even to those who used him spitefully. He looked forward to the day when he would finish school and get away, for he had to admit in his heart that he loathed the odious Benny. It rankled him to think that Benny was the only person who could make him lose his composure and caterwaul in public, thus making people notice that despite his suave manner and intellectual conversation he was a bit different. To keep his temper he took to declaiming "The Star-Spangled Banner" or passages from the Bible. Once he got all the way through the "begats" in Genesis before he took hold of himself and regained his composure.

Just before Jerome was graduated from college,

Benny stole all the fish from Old Man Walker's little fish cart and deposited them in Jerome's car, after which he made an anonymous phone call to the police. The police, who had always regarded Jerome as the embodiment of what they would like all young men to be, preferred to believe his claim of innocence; but then again, looking as he did, it was natural for them to believe that he might have swiped a mess of fish.

People began to whisper about Jerome when he passed on the street. They pointed out that although his manners were perfect, he did have those long swordlike claws, and they certainly wouldn't want to be caught alone with him in any alley on a dark night. And wasn't there a rather feline craftiness in his slanted eyes?

Jerome left town after graduation enveloped in an aura of suspicion and an aroma of rotting fish which he never could dispel completely from his car.

Jerome decided to pursue a career as a writer of advertising copy in New York, reasoning that what with all the strange creatures roaming about in that city no one was apt to notice anything a bit different about him. He was hired at the first place he applied, Bobble, Babble, and Armbruster, Inc., on Madison Avenue. Mr. Armbruster had been out celebrating his fourteenth wedding anniversary the night before and had imbibed himself into near oblivion trying to forget what devastation those fourteen years had wrought. When Jerome walked into his office he naturally figured him to be related to the ten-foot polka-dot cobra that had pursued him the night before, and thought he would fade with the hangover. After ducking behind his desk for a little hair-of-the dog, he hired Jerome. By the time Mr. Armbruster had fully recovered from his celebration, Jerome had proved himself capable at his job and affable with the other employees, so he was allowed to stay. Mr. Armbruster naturally put him on the cat-food account.

Before long Jerome fell in love with his secretary, Marie, a shapely blonde, who thought Jerome's sleek fur and golden eyes sexy. He wanted to ask her for a date, but first, in all fairness, he thought he should find out how she felt about him.

"Marie," he said one day as he finished the day's dictation, "do you like me as a boss?"

"Oh, yes," breathed Marie. "Gee, Mr. Kotter, you're the swellest boss I ever had. You're so different."

Jerome's heart sank. "Different? In what way, Marie?"

"Well," said Marie, "Mr. Leach, my old boss, used to pinch me sometimes. And he used to sneak up behind me and kiss me." She peered coyly at Jerome from under her lashes. "You're a perfect gentleman, Mr. Kotter. You're real different."

Jerome was enchanted and wasted no further time asking her out to dinner.

For several weeks everything was wonderful. Then, unexpectedly, Benny Rhoades turned up. Jerome looked up from his desk one day to see his nemesis standing in the doorway.

"Man," said Benny, "if it ain't Jerome Kotter." He grinned.

"Benny Rhoades," exclaimed Jerome. "What are you doing here?"

"Man, you're the most," said Benny softly. "I work in the mail room, man. You're gonna see a lot of me, Jerome."

Jerome's tail twitched.

"Why did you come here?" he asked. "Why don't you leave me alone?"

Offended innocence replaced the calculating look on Benny's pasty face.

"Why, man, I ain't done a thing. A man's got to work. And I work here." He lounged against the doorjamb. "I hear you're a real swingin' cat around here. I wonder how long that's gonna last."

"Get out," said Jerome.

"Sure, Mr. Kotter, sir. Sure. Think I'll drop by your secretary's desk. Quite a dish, that Marie."

"You stay away from her." Jerome could feel the fur around his neck rising. His whiskers bristled.

Benny smiled and glided away like an insidious snake.

From that time on Benny did what he could to torment Jerome. He held up his mail until important clients called the bosses to complain about lack of action on their accounts. He slammed Jerome's tail in doors, usually when some VIP was visiting the office. Worst of all, he vexed Marie by hanging around her desk asking for dates and sometimes sneaking up to nibble at her neck. Marie hated him almost as much as Jerome did.

Jerome didn't know quite what he could do about it without jeopardizing his job, of which he had become very fond. The other people at the agency liked him, although they regarded him as a trifle eccentric since he always insisted on sampling the cat food he wrote about. But then, everyone to his own tastes, they said.

Things came to a head one evening when Jerome invited Marie to his apartment for a fish dinner before going out to a show. They were just sitting down to eat when the doorbell rang.

It was Benny.

"Cozy," he murmured, surveying the scene. He slammed the door shut behind him.

"A real swingin' cat," he said, sidling into the room. He produced a small pistol from his pocket.

"Are you out of your mind, Benny?" said Jerome. "What do you think you're doing?"

"I lost my job," smiled Benny.

"What's that got to do with me?"

"Marie complained that I bothered her. They fired me." Benny's small eyes glittered. "I'll repay her for the favor, then I'll take care of you, Jerome. I'll fix it so they'll think you shot her for resisting your charms, and then shot yourself. Everybody knows a big cat like you could go beserk anytime."

"You're a rat," said Marie. "You're a miserable, blackhearted little rat."

Jerome stepped protectively in front of her.

"Sticks and stones may break my bones but names will never hurt me," chanted Benny gleefully.

Jerome was looking at Benny thoughtfully. "A rat," he said. "That's what he is. A rat. Funny it never occurred to me before." His tail twitched nervously.

Benny didn't like the look on Jerome's face. "Stay away from me, man. I'll shoot."

Before Benny could aim, Jerome leaped across the room with the swift, fluid motion of a tiger. He knocked Benny to the floor and easily took the gun from him.

"A rat," repeated Jerome softly.

Benny looked at Jerome's face so close to his own. "What are you going to do?" he squeaked, his own face pinched and white and his beady eyes terror-stricken. "What are you going to do?"

Jerome ate him.

* * *

It took a long time to get the police sergeant to take the matter seriously. Marie had urged Jerome to forget the whole thing, but Jerome felt he must confess.

"You say you ate this guy Benny?" the sergeant asked for the twentieth time.

"I ate him," said Jerome.

"He was a rat," said Marie.

The sergeant shook his head. "We get all kinds," he muttered. "Go home. Sleep it off." He sighed. "Self-defense, you say?"

"Benny was going to shoot both of us," said Marie.

"Where's the body?" asked the sergeant.

Jerome shook his head. "There is no body. I ate him."

"He was a rat," said Marie.

"There's no body," said the sergeant. "We sent a coupla men up to your apartment and there's no body and no sign of anybody getting killed. We even called this Benny's family long distance to find out if they knew where he is, but his old man said as far as they are concerned he died at birth. So go home."

"I ate him," insisted Jerome.

"So you performed a public service. I got six kids to support, buddy. I don't want to spend the next two years on a headshrinker's couch for trying to make the Chief believe I got a six-foot cat here who ate a guy. Now go home, you two, before I get mad."

Jerome remained standing in front of the desk.

"Look," said the sergeant. "You ate a guy."

"A rat," corrected Marie.

"A rat," said the sergeant. "So how do you feel?"

"Terrible," said Jerome. "I have a most remarkable case of indigestion."

"You ate a rat," said the sergeant. "Now you've got a bellyache. That's your punishment. Remember when you ate green apples as a kid?" He sighed. "Now go home."

As they turned to leave, Jerome heard the sergeant muttering to himself about not having had a vacation in four years.

Despite his indigestion, Jerome felt marvelous. "Let the punishment fit the crime," he said with satisfaction. He took Marie's arm in a courtly fashion and sang softly as they walked along. "My object all sublime, I shall achieve in time, to let the punishment fit the crime, the punishment fit the crime. . . ."

"Gee, Mr. Kotter," said Marie, gazing up at him in admiration. "You're so different from anyone else I ever went with."

"Different?" asked Jerome. "How, Marie?"

"Gee," said Marie, "I never went out before with anybody who quoted poetry."

# THE CAT IN THE BAG

## by Charles Peterson

I am sitting on a park bench minding my own business, which at the moment consists of the study of some passing statistics like 5'6", 120 pounds, 34-26-34, when this little bimbo in the grey fedora and pencil mustache sits down next to me, hems and haws a bit, then says, "Are you by any chance Kit the Cat Burglar?"

I perform a sitting high jump of eighteen and a quarter inches—a new intramural record.

True, on the date of this park bench episode, I am still in the burgling business. Nowadays, of course, I am plain Augie Augenblick, having paid my debt to society—at least as much of it as they could tag me with—but even at the time whereof I speak I am not anxious to have my business advertised in the public parks. So I murmur, "Excuse me!" and prepare to leave a large void in the immediate area.

Grey Fedora hauls me back by the jacket sleeve. "Because if you are," he goes on, "I have a five-grand proposition for you."

The words "five grand" induce a certain immobility, and though I am prompt with many disclaimers, in case he is concealing a tape recorder and police badge about his person, I express curiosity to hear what this proposition may be, supposing (ho! ho!) that I am this Kit what's-his-name.

"I want you to steal a cat," says Grey Fedora.

"You have a very perverted idea of what cat burglars do," I say, frowning. "Excuse me again."

Again he hauls me back, and this time he presses a business card into my hand. It is so heavily embossed as to be readable in Braille, and says

### RENFREW T. SNYDE, JR.
Senior Account Executive
Snyde, Fingle and Chatsworthy, Advertising.

"You have no doubt heard of Scat Cat Food. The Feast for Finicky Felines?" he begins, with a hopeful expression.

I look blank. "No, but I've heard of Sweetums Cat Cuisine."

Mr. Snyde sighs and twitches his mustache. "That's the problem. Everybody knows about Sweetums; nobody knows about Scat. It's those dratted television commercials starring Sweetums."

"The cat with the $25,000 diamond-studded collar?"

"Hah!" Mr. Snyde's mustache quivers mirthlessly. "People who believe in cats that wear $25,000 diamond collars generally believe in tooth fairies, too. But Sweetums *is* the problem. We've learned that Muckley and Swerge, the agency for Sweetums Cat Cuisine, is about to begin production of a new series of commercials."

A light begins to dawn. "And you want me to steal Sweetums beforehand." "Precisely!" says Mr. Snyde.

Once Mr. Snyde and I have formalized the arrangements, I begin my preparations. Ordinarily, I prefer an ad lib approach to purloinment, but this being a commissioned assignment I feel impelled to plan rather carefully, and among the first steps is that of checking out the establishment where Sweetums lives when not on camera or opening shopping centers. It is an oldish house standing by itself in the middle of a couple of acres—doubtless an elementary business precaution for an outfit whose stock in trade come with yaps, yips, barks, howls, growls and yowls that could raise eyebrows in the typical suburb. There is a chain-link fence, behind which are dog runs and kennels, but the place appears not much more difficult to get into than, say, your average used car lot. I manage to catch several of Sweetums' TV spots, and can see why Mr. Snyde's client has problems. Most cats can give you a disdainful look that makes you feel you have gravy spots on your necktie, but Sweetums is positively uncanny. When she stares at you over that diamond collar and suggests that your cat deserves Sweetums Cat Cuisine, you get this strange urge to trot out and buy the stuff even if you must then buy a cat to feed it to.

But the commercials give me an idea of what to look for, and a feature story in a recent TV magazine even tells me where—Sweetums' own room toward the back of the house, with a balcony that might have been designed with a burglar's ease and convenience in mind.

With a few other details taken care of, it is a dark and moonless night suitable for stratagems, spoils and cat-nappings when I approach the McGurk Animal Farm, that being Sweetums' formal address. I am anticipating, and prepared for, a certain amount of what-the-helling to erupt when the dogs scent an intruder. But all is quiet. As I tiptoe by, I find that the Dobermans are in dreamland, the Schnauzers are snoring, the beagles are blissfully blank and the German Shepherds counting sheep.

I pause to mull this over. If I didn't know better, I would think that someone kindly disposed to burglars had slipped each of them a mickey, just as I had planned to do. It is odd, to say the least, and I wonder briefly if perhaps I should scrub the mission. But, finding nothing else to cause alarm, I pull the black knit hood over my head, clamber over the chain-link fence and scamper up a handy trellis to the balcony with no more uproar than a marshmallow falling into tapioca pudding. Another few moments and I have the window open (a bit of noise there, but unavoidable) and am entering the house.

At the same time, I hear the sound of a window being softly closed somewhere else.

*Curiouser and curiouser,* I think, freezing.

I haven't thawed appreciably when the sound of soft footsteps approaching congeals the bloodstream once more. Then a door opens and a figure slips through, so close that I can reach out and touch him.

Except that he happens to touch me first, at which there are symptoms of sudden paralysis in both of us, and the yelp that emerges from the other is so high-pitched that I realize he is really a she.

"Good grief!" she says, making a quick recovery. "You nearly scared me to death! I didn't expect you so soon," she continues, in a low whisper. "I was just checking to see that everything was all set."

"Um!" I say, feeling that some comment is called for but unwilling to contribute anything that might be misinterpreted. There is a stab of light from a tiny flash. "No lights!" I gasp.

"Sorry!" says the girl. "I never met a burglar before. I'm Jennifer Potter, junior account executive for Muckley and Swerge. And you're—?"

"No names, no K.P." I respond, thinking that this situation is growing goofier by the minute. She evidently thinks so, too, for she giggles. "Right! I keep forgetting. You have a very nice voice for a burglar."

"I'm a very nice burglar."

"I'm glad. Sweetums doesn't take to everybody, you know, and I was kind of worried that—well—" briskly—"let's get on with it, shall we? You're here to kidnap Sweetums, so let's go."

"H-How did you know?"

"It was my idea to begin with," says Jennifer Potter, proudly, "of course, I just figured we'd hide Sweetums away for a few days, but Mr. Muckley thought we should stage a real kidnapping. That way, we could legitimately call in the police and get some great publicity—just as, by an odd coincidence, we're about to announce the new broccoli-flavored Sweetums Cat Cuisine. Then, according to the plan, Sweetums will be rescued at risk of life and limb and *voila!*—TV coverage, newspaper stories, features in all the magazines, America's most beloved feline restored to the bosom of her adoring public ... here you are," says Miss Potter, guiding my hand to some kind of cushioned wicker basket. "Go ahead—kidnap away!"

"One small problem."

"Oh?"

"There's no cat to kidnap."

"You're kidding!"

The penlight snaps on again and a finger of light probes the basket, which I now see is painted gold with a red velvet cushion and the name "Sweetums" picked out in rhinestones on the back.

"She must be here!" insists Miss Potter who, now

that I have enough light to see her by, turns out to be worth considerably more wattage. She has soft brown hair that tumbles fetchingly over her eyes, and a tilted little nose over a rather wide, humorous mouth—only right now it is not looking humorous at all. Her flash sweeps the room, which is pretty sparsely furnished at best, but even more sparsely furnished with cats.

"I thought I heard a window closing as I came in," I offer. "That one, probably."

We look and find that the catch has been snapped from the outside, where there is another balcony—the twin of the one I climbed in on. And the light reveals a muddy footprint on the floor.

"That's not mine," I point out.

Jennifer Potter stiffens. "Good grief! Somebody beat us to Sweetums! Mr. Muckley's going to kill me!"

She may have company, I learn when I report to Mr. Snyde the following a.m. He is sitting on the park bench, reading the morning paper, and standing nearby—at first I take it for an outcropping of rock— is a very large person whose face looks as though it had been thrown together by a Mother Nature anxious to break for lunch. Mr. Snyde chuckles and I am sure he is reading the front page feature on the disappearance of Sweetums.

"Well, I see you were successful," he says.

"Not so's you could notice it," I reply.

He glances up sharply. "What's that supposed to mean?"

"I don't have the cat. Somebody got there first." I explain about the Muckley and Swerge kidnap plot and how J. Potter evidently confused me with the hired heister.

Mr. Snyde gives me a long look, and I sense a sudden cold front passing by. "Cut the clowning," he says. "Where's the cat?"

"Cross my heart and hope to die——" I begin, before thinking this is perhaps an unfortunate choice of words, as Mr. Snyde crooks a finger and says, "Humbert!"

The nearby monolith stirs and lumbers forward. "Yus, Mr. S.?"

"Humbert," says Mr. Snyde, "I want you to take a good look at this gentleman."

Humbert turns a beady little eye on me. The effect is akin to that of an elephant examining a peanut of suspicious antecedents.

"It is now nine-thirty," notes Mr. Snyde. "In the event that he fails to bring us a cat named Sweetums by six this evening, I want you to turn him inside out and play tunes on his ribs like a xylophone."

"Yus, Mr. S."

"Following which, you may push his nose so far around his head that he'll have to smell the flowers through the back of his neck."

"Yus, Mr. S."

"Following which, you may chastise him severely."

"Yus, Mr. S.," Humbert replies, registering a lively approval of the scenario.

"As for you," Mr. Snyde says, turning to me, "I don't know what your game is, but if you're thinking of holding me up for more dough, forget it. Humbert and I will expect you here at six. With cat. Understood?"

"Yus, Mr. S.," I say.

I have not, up to this point, taken much time to analyze the situation, but it is amazing how the prospect of being taken apart like a Tinker Toy by Humbert tends to concentrate the mind. For the first time, I give some thought to the following points:

A. Somebody, using a modus operandi very much like that of Kit the Cat Burglar, has made off with Sweetums.

B. It wasn't Kit the Cat Burglar.

C. Therefore, who? Or is it whom?

There are only three possible candidates I can think of; "Nervous" Sam Purvis, who is presently on sabbatical up at the state pen; "Easy Eddie" Magruder, who hasn't been heard from since he inadvertently robbed the wife of the local mob boss and is rumored to be part of the sub-base of the interstate highway; and Frank "Fingers" Fenster.

It has to be Frank, but he is not all that evident, either, and it takes hours of running down leads before I find myself, late that afternoon, about to rap on the door of a third floor room on the east side. Odd noises and muffled curses emanate from behind the door, to cease abruptly as I knock. A wary voice says, "Whozat?"

"This is Mr. Muckley," I reply, in the commanding tone I imagine an advertising agency account executive might employ.

"Waitaminnit!" There are more noises, followed by the unmistakable sound of a cat being stuffed into a bag, before the the door opens.

"Hey, you ain't Muckley!" says Fingers, recoiling and preparing to slam the door.

"True, but I thought you might not let me in if I said I was the Avon lady. May I?" Since I have taken the precaution of sticking a .32 in his midriff, he invites me in. I wave him to a chair as I close the door, and he sits down, looking humble.

He also looks as though he has recently gone feet first through some sort of shredding machinery, or perhaps an agricultural combine. His hair is awry, one sleeve is ripped, his face is dotted with bits of adhesive tape and there are more bits speckling his hands.

"I understand you have a cat here," I begin.

"Hah!" says Fingers, bitterly. "What I have here is a cross between a buzz-saw and an octopus!" He nods toward a burlap bag that is writhing in a corner and expressing feline outrage. "And how come you know so much?" A gleam of comprehension appears in his eye. "Say! Was that you comin' in as I was goin' out last night? Hey, you must be Kit the Cat burglar!"

I acknowledge this and Fingers looks at me with mingled awe and admiration. "Say, that was a slick job of slippin' that catch! I didn't hear a thing until you was almost in the room!"

"Well, I hardly heard you leaving, either."

Fingers shrugs modestly. "Aw, I do my best, but—"

"You did fine. Leaving that footprint, though—that wasn't too neat."

"That Muckley guy—it was his idea," says Fingers, defensively. "Said he needed some evidence for the fuzz. Say, could I have your autograph before you go?"

The amenities satisfied, Fingers relaxes and resumes binding up his wounded digits and I am about to return to the subject of Sweetums when I am startled to hear a voice crying, "Get me out! Get me out!" Then I realize this must be Sweetums' version of "Meow!" And although I am not quite sure why I'm doing it, I start untying the bag. Fingers reacts with terror as he notices what I'm doing.

"Don't let her out!" he pleads. "She'll wreck the joint!"

But it is too late. A blur emerges at high speed from the bag, orbits the room several times, causing Fingers to leap behind a chair, then finally comes to rest as an orange-colored cat clad in a diamond collar. The face that launches thousands of bags of Sweetums Cat Cuisine wears the kind of expression you might surprise on Queen Victoria, had she just slipped on a banana peel, and it sweeps over Fingers like a laser beam. He winces, picks up his chair and assumes a lion-tamer's stance as Sweetums takes a step toward him, hissing. Then, surprisingly, she dismisses him with a sniff, her fur subsides, and she walks over and starts rubbing against my leg. I pick her up and darned if she doesn't start purring as if I am a long lost buddy who just turned up to repay a loan. Fingers is goggle-eyed, and remarks that he never woulda believed it.

"Jennifer Potter said she doesn't take to every-body," I explain.

"She with the ad agency? I only met Muckley—and I wish he had mentioned that before I took on this job. I didn't plan on getting skinned alive for a lousy five bills!"

"Is that all you're getting? Fingers, old pal, I think we have the makings of a mutual assistance pact here!"

He is somewhat dubious at first, but when I tell him I have a customer for Sweetums who is willing to lay out $5000—which I propose to split with him—his eyes light up like Fourth of July sparklers and he is even willing to gift-wrap Sweetums for me, provided he can do it from ten feet away with tongs. The upshot of the negotiations is that I am speeding on my way to rendezvous with Mr. Snyde and Humbert with min-utes to spare before the six o'clock deadline. Looking as though canaries wouldn't melt in her mouth, a docile Sweetums is seated beside me, grooming herself and occasionally looking at me with those unsettling green eyes. I have the odd impression that she is suppressing a grin, as though she were getting a big charge out of this variation in the routine. I admonish her to be on her best behavior as we approach Mr. Snyde.

"Ah!" he breathed, as we come into view. "I knew I could count on you. Didn't I say so, Humbert? 'Kit the Cat Burglar is a man of his word,' I said! You may put the brass knuckles away for now, Humbert."

"Yus, Mr. S.," says Humbert, masking his disappointment.

"And now," says Mr. Snyde, unclasping the diamond collar from Sweetums' neck, "I'll just remove this little item. . . ."

"I thought you told me that was a fake," I say. "What do you want that for?"

"Because, my poor chump," says Mr. Snyde, "it's *not* a fake—as you might have found, had you done your homework as I did. The whole point of this exercise was to get you to steal it for us, since neither Humbert nor I are really qualified."

"For a fee of five thousand dollars," I remind him.

Mr. Snyde looks astonished. "Five thousand dollars? Did I say anything that sounded like five thousand dollars, Humbert?"

"No, Mr. S."

"I thought not. Humbert never forgets."

"And I haven't forgotten the name of your advertising agency, either."

"Oh, that!" Mr. Snyde fans out a bunch of business cards, all with different names and companies on them. "You'd be surprised how easy it is to set yourself up in business. All you need is a supply of paste-board and a friendly printer."

"So it's all a scam? You weren't planning to stash the cat away someplace to spike some TV commercials?"

"Oh, we'll stash the cat someplace, all right," says Mr. Snyde. "The lagoon in this park seems a convenient spot. Do you have a sack and a rock handy, Humbert?"

"Yus, Mr. S."

Humbert looms menacingly as I utter an exclamation of protest, and Mr. Snyde says. "You weren't thinking of making a fuss, I trust?"

Baffled, I can only watch as Humbert grabs Sweetums by the scruff of the neck despite her yowl of indignation, and prepares to insert her into the sack he produces from a back pocket. Then all at once a look of agony and alarm spreads over his face. His nose twitches. His eyes begin to water. His face turns the color of a Hawaiian sunset. He struggles with a series of strangled gasps, then goes, "ATCHOOOO!" in a blast that shakes leaves from the trees, sends the park pigeons into hysterics and registers on Richter scales for miles around.

"ATCHOO!" he erupts again. And again. As Sweetums seizes the opportunity to clout him a good one across the chops, he adds, "OW!" and continues in this vein, dropping the sack, dropping Sweetums— who vanishes in the underbrush—and, in an especially violent paroxysm, stepping on Mr. Snyde's foot, thereby adding the latter's yelps of anguish to what is fast developing into a localized debacle. "Cats bake be sdeeze!" Humber explains apologetically, between explosions.

"Come on, you oaf!" snarls Mr. Snyde, hopping on

one foot. He throws me a poisonous look. "Forget the cat! Let's get out of here!"

Humbert's sneezes grow fainter as the two of them leg it across the park, Mr. Snyde limping to keep up, and presently Sweetums reappears from under a bush with a regal air, as though she has just been off reviewing the troops. I pick her up and she cries, "My hero!" At least, that's what it sounds like, though on further reflection I realize it is only another "Meow!"

I am not anxious to return to Fingers and confess that the deal has fallen through, as I foresee a bit of difficulty in convincing him that I really didn't collect the five grand, and that consequently he and I have a fifty-fifty split of zero. With some trepidation I give his door the code knock we'd agreed on earlier, and the feeling grows when, upon entering, I find three additional persons seated around Fingers' table, all giving me looks that could bore holes in a bank vault. One of them is Jennifer Potter, and I assume even before Finger's introductions that the others are Messrs. Muckley and Swerge. They are wearing dark three-piece suits, Muckley being stocky, swarthy and forceful-looking while Swerge is tall and thin, with big eye-glasses giving him the appearance of an agitated stork.

There is a lot of "Aha!"-ing as I heave into view, and the initial relief at finding Sweetums unharmed is succeeded by a storm of vituperation. I gather that Fingers and I are going to be strung up by the thumbs as soon as they find a rope and a stout lamp-post, and Muckley is expanding on this topic, explaining how delighted he will be, personally, to turn us over to the authorities, when Fingers looks alarmed.

"Hey, waitaminnit!" he protests. "You hired me!"

"And you tried to double-cross us!"

"I'll tell everybody it was all a publicity stunt!"

"Who's going to believe you?"

"What kind of a deal is this?" demands Fingers, rhetorically.

"Rawr!" says Sweetums, but no one pays any attention to her except Jennifer, in whose lap she is sitting, and me. The cat gives me a long look, slowly winks one eye, and cocks her head toward the cupboard in the pullman kitchen. I follow her glance—toward her food and water dishes.

"Sorry you feel that way," I remark. "We'd hoped to settle things peacefully, but I guess we'll have to mention it."

"Mention what?" says Swerge, blinking behind his spectacles.

"Oh, nothing. Just a kind of amusing sidelight, that's all."

"What's amusing" asks Muckley, suspiciously.

"The fact that all the while we had Sweetums, she refused to eat anything but Scat, The Feast for Finicky Felines." They follow my gaze to the bag of cat food in the kitchen and the room falls suddenly silent.

"I beg your pardon?" says Muckley.

"I beg your pardon?" says Swerge.

"I beg your pardon?" says Jennifer, making it a clean sweep.

"Scat, The Feast for Finicky Felines," I repeat. "You've heard of it, I suppose? Sweetums seemed to think it was caviar—couldn't get enough. I'm sure her fans would be interested in knowing."

Muckley and Swerge exchange looks. "Er—do you have to mention it?"

"I'm afraid so."

"It—er—could embarrass our client."

"Think how embarrassed Fingers and I will be, serving terms in the slammer."

A hint of perspiration beads Swerge's brow. "Perhaps we've been a bit hasty. after all, it's not as though Mr. Kit here actually profited from this—this. . . ."

"It seems to me," says J. Potter, firmly, "that we owe these two a vote of thanks for recovering America's favorite cat from a band of ruthless criminals, who are doubtless still being pursued by the police, the F.B.I. and Interpol, with arrests expected momentarily."

Muckley and Swerge consider this. "Well," they respond, "when you look at it *that* way. . ."

And that is how Fingers and I wind up splitting the reward for Sweetums' return—under different names, of course—and I am sufficiently pleased with the outcome to overlook Mr. Snyde's slurs on my planning abilities. Because, after all, I *had* checked out that ad agency of his and found there was no such outfit— which sort of made me wonder what he was really after, if not to sabotage some competitive TV spots. It could only have been the diamond collar, so one of my preparatory moves involved having a duplicate made by a friend who specializes in such things. That was the one Snyde got. And then, just in case it might cause a stir if Sweetums came back minus her famous collar, I had my friend make me another. That was the one Muckley and Swerge got.

As to who got the real diamond collar, well, I'm afraid that's a secret between Sweetums and me, and Sweetums isn't talking. Although I'm not at all sure she couldn't, if she felt like it.

# THE WITCH'S CAT

## by Manly Wade Wellman

Old Jael Bettiss, who lived in the hollow among the cypresses, was not a real witch.

It makes no difference that folk thought she was, and walked fearfully wide of her shadow. Nothing can be proved by the fact that she was as disgustingly ugly without as she was wicked within. It is quite irrelevant that evil was her study and profession and pleasure. She was no witch; she only pretended to be.

Jael Bettiss knew that all laws providing for the punishment of witches had been repealed, or at the least forgotten. As to being feared and hated, that was meat and drink to Jael Bettiss, living secretly alone in the hollow.

The house and the hollow belonged to a kindly old villager, who had been elected marshal and was too busy to look after his property. Because he was easy-going and perhaps a little daunted, he let Jael Bettiss live there rent free. The house was no longer snug; the back of its roof was broken in, the eaves drooped slackly. At some time or other the place had been painted brown, before that with ivory black. Now both coats of color peeled away in huge flakes, making the clapboards seem scrofulous. The windows had been broken in every small, grubby pane, and mended with coarse brown paper, so that they were like cast and blurred eyes. Behind was the muddy, bramble-choked backyard, and behind that yawned the old quarry, now abandoned and full of black water. As for the inside— but few ever saw it.

Jael Bettiss did not like people to come into her house. She always met callers on the old cracked doorstep, draped in a cloak of shadowy black, with gray hair straggling, her nose as hooked and sharp as the beak of a buzzard, her eyes filmy and sore-looking, her wrinkle-bordered mouth always grinning and showing her yellow, chisel-shaped teeth.

The nearby village was an old-fashioned place, with stone flags instead of concrete for pavements, and the villagers were the simplest of men and women. From them Jael Bettiss made a fair living, by selling love philters, or herbs to cure sickness, or charms to ward off bad luck. When she wanted extra money, she would wrap her old black cloak about her and, tramping along a country road, would stop at a cowpen and ask the farmer what he would do if his cows went dry. The farmer, worried, usually came at dawn next day to her hollow and bought a good-luck charm. Occasionally the cows would go dry anyway, by accident of nature, and their owner would pay more and more, until their milk returned to them.

Now and then, when Jael Bettiss came to the door, there came with her the gaunt black cat, Gib.

Gib was not truly black, any more than Jael Bettiss was truly a witch. He had been born with white markings at muzzle, chest, and forepaws, so that he looked to be in full evening dress. Left alone, he would have grown fat and fluffy. But Jael Bettiss, who wanted a fearsome pet, kept all his white spots smeared with thick soot, and underfed him to make him look rakish and lean.

On the night of the full moon, she would drive poor
Gib from her door. He would wander to the village
in search of food, and would wail mournfully in the
yards. Awakened householders would angrily throw
boots or pans or sticks of kindling. Often Gib was
hit, and his cries were sharpened by pain. When that
happened, Jael Bettiss took care to be seen next morning with a bandage on head or wrist. Some of the
simplest villagers thought that Gib was really the old
woman, magically transformed. Her reputation grew,
as did Gib's unpopularity. But Gib did not deserve
mistrust—like all cats, he was a practical philosopher,
who wanted to be comfortable and quiet and dignified.
At bottom, he was amiable. Like all cats, too, he loved
his home above all else; and the house in the hollow,
be it ever so humble and often cruel, was home. It
was unthinkable to him that he might live elsewhere.

In the village he had two friends—black-eyed John
Frey, the storekeeper's son, who brought the mail to
and from the county seat, and Ivy Hill, pretty blonde
daughter of the town marshal, the same town marshal
who owned the hollow and let Jael Bettiss live in the
old house. John Frey and Ivy Hill were so much in
love with each other that they loved everything else,
even black-stained, hungry Gib. He was grateful; if he
had been able, he would have loved them in return.
But his little heart had room for one devotion only,
and that was given to the house in the hollow.

One day, Jael Bettiss slouched darkly into old Mr.
Frey's store, and up to the counter that served as a
post office. Leering, she gave John Frey a letter. It
was directed to a certain little-known publisher, asking
for a certain little-known book. Several days later, she

appeared again, received a parcel, and bore it to her home.

In her gloomy, secret parlor, she unwrapped her purchase. It was a small, drab volume, with no title on cover or back. Sitting at the rickety table, she began to read. All evening and most of the night she read, forgetting to give Gib his supper, though he sat hungrily at her feet.

At length, an hour before dawn, she finished. Laughing loudly and briefly, she turned her beak-nose toward the kerosene lamp on the table. From the book she read aloud two words. The lamp went out, though she had not blown at it. Jael Bettiss spoke one commanding word more, and the lamp flamed alight again.

"At last!" she cried out in shrill exultation, and grinned down at Gib. Her lips drew back from her yellow chisels of teeth. "At last!" she crowed again. "Why don't you speak to me, you little brute? . . . Why don't you, indeed?"

She asked that final question as though she had been suddenly inspired. Quickly she glanced through the back part of the book, howled with laughter over something she found there, then sprang up and scuttled like a big, filthy crab into the dark, windowless cell that was her kitchen. There she mingled salt and malt in the palm of her skinny right hand. After that, she rummaged out a bundle of dried herbs, chewed them fine, and spat them into the mixture. Stirring again with her forefinger, she returned to the parlor. Scanning the book to refresh her memory, she muttered a nasty little rhyme. Finally she dashed the mess suddenly upon Gib.

He retreated, shaking himself, outraged and startled. In a corner he sat down, and bent his head to lick the smeared fragments of the mixture away. But they revolted his tongue and palate, and he paused in the midst of this chore, so important to cats; and meanwhile Jael Bettiss yelled, "Speak!"

Gib crouched and blinked, feeling sick. His tongue came out and steadied his lips. Finally he said: "I want something to eat."

His voice was small and high, like a little child's, but entirely understandable. Jael Bettiss was so delighted that she laughed and clapped her bony knees with her hands, in self-applause.

"It worked!" she cried. "No more humbug about me, you understand? I'm a real witch at last, and not a fraud!"

Gib found himself able to understand all this, more clearly than he had ever understood human affairs before. "I want something to eat," he said again, more definitely than before. "I didn't have any supper, and it's nearly—"

"Oh, stow your gab!" snapped his mistress. "It's this book, crammed with knowledge and strength, that made me able to do it. I'll never be without it again, and it'll teach me all the things I've only guessed at and mumbled about. I'm a real witch now, I say. And if you don't think I'll make those ignorant sheep of villagers realize it—"

Once more she went off into gales of wild, cracked mirth, and threw a dish at Gib. He darted away into a corner just in time, and the missile crashed into blue-and-white china fragments against the wall. But Jael Bettiss read aloud from her book an impressive gibberish, and the dish re-formed itself on the floor; the bits crept together and joined and the cracks disappeared, as trickling drops of water form into a pool. And finally, when the witch's twiglike forefinger beckoned, the dish floated upward like a leaf in a breeze and set itself gently back on the table. Gib watched warily.

"That's small to what I shall do hereafter," swore Jael Bettiss.

When next the mail was distributed at the general store, a dazzling stranger appeared.

She wore a cloak, an old-fashioned black coat, but its drapery did not conceal the tall perfection of her form. As for her face, it would have stirred interest and admiration in larger and more sophisticated gatherings than the knot of letter-seeking villagers. Its beauty was scornful but inviting, classic but warm, with something in it of Grecian sculpture and oriental allure. If the nose was cruel, it was straight; if the lips were sullen, they were full; if the forehead was a suspicion low, it was white and smooth. Thick, thunder-black hair swept up from that forehead, and backward to a knot at the neck. The eyes glowed with strange, hot lights, and wherever they turned they pierced and captivated.

People moved away to let her have a clear, sweeping pathway forward to the counter. Until this stranger had entered, Ivy Hill was the loveliest person present; now she looked only modest and fresh and blonde in her starched gingham, and worried to boot. As a matter of fact, Ivy Hill's insides felt cold and topsy-turvy, because she saw how fascinated was the sudden attention of John Frey.

"Is there," asked the newcomer in a deep, creamy voice, "any mail for me?"

"Wh-what name, ma'am?" asked John Frey, his brown young cheeks turning full crimson.

"Bettiss. Jael Bettiss."

He began to fumble through the sheaf of envelopes, with hands that shook. "Are you," he asked, "any relation to the old lady of that name, the one who lives in the hollow?"

"Yes, of a sort." She smiled a slow, conquering smile. "She's my—aunt. Yes. Perhaps you see the family resemblance?" Wider and wider grew the smile with which she assaulted John Frey. "If there isn't any mail," she went on, "I would like a stamp. A one-cent stamp."

Turning to his little metal box on the shelf behind, John Frey tore a single green stamp from the sheet. His hand shook still more as he gave it to the customer and received in exchange a copper cent.

There was really nothing exceptional about the appearance of that copper cent. It looked brown and a little worn, with Lincoln's head on it, and a date— 1917. But John Frey felt a sudden glow in the hand that took it, a glow that shot along his arm and into his heart. He gazed at the coin as if he had never seen its like before. And he put it slowly into his pocket, a different pocket from the one in which he usually kept change, and placed another coin in the till to pay for the stamp. Poor Ivy Hill's blue eyes grew round and downright miserable. Plainly he meant to keep that copper piece as a souvenir. But John Frey gazed only at the stranger, raptly, as though he were suddenly stunned or hypnotized.

The dark, sullen beauty drew her cloak more tightly around her and moved regally out of the store and away toward the edge of town.

As she turned up the brush-hidden trail to the hollow, a change came. Not that her step was less young and free, her figure less queenly, her eyes dimmer, or her beauty short of perfect. All these were as they had been; but her expression became set and grim, her body tense, and her head high and truculent. It was as though, beneath that young loveliness, lurked an old and evil heart, which was precisely what did lurk there, it does not boot to conceal. But none saw except Gib, the black cat with soot-covered white spots, who sat on the doorstep of the ugly cottage. Jael Bettiss thrust him aside with her foot and entered.

In the kitchen she filled a tin basin from a wooden bucket, and threw into the water a pinch of coarse green powder with an unpleasant smell. As she stirred it in with her hands, they seemed to grow skinny and harsh. Then she threw great palmfuls of the liquid into her face and over her head, and other changes came. . . .

The woman who returned to the front door, where Gib watched with a cat's apprehensive interest, was hideous old Jael Bettiss, whom all the village knew and avoided.

"He's trapped," she shrilled triumphantly. "That penny, the one I soaked for three hours in a love philter, trapped him the moment he touched it!" She stumped to the table, and patted the book as though it were a living, lovable thing.

"You taught me," she crooned to it. "You're winning me the love of John Frey!" She paused, and her voice grew harsh again. "Why not? I'm old and ugly and queer, but I can love, and John Frey is the handsomest man in the village!"

The next day she went to the store again, in her new and dazzling person as a dark, beautiful girl. Gib, left alone in the hollow, turned over in his mind the things that he had heard. The new gift of human speech had brought with it, of necessity, a human quality of reasoning; but his viewpoint and his logic were as strongly feline as ever.

Jael Bettiss's dark love that lured John Frey promised no good to Gib. There would be plenty of trouble, he was inclined to think, and trouble was something that all sensible cats avoided. He was wise now, but he was weak. What could he do against danger? And his desires, as they had been since kittenhood, were food and warmth and a cozy sleeping place, and a little respectful affection. Just now he was getting none of the four.

He thought also of Ivy Hill. She liked Gib, and often had shown it. If she won John Frey despite the witch's plan, the two would build a house all full of creature comforts—cushions, open fires, probably fish and chopped liver. Gib's tongue caressed his soot-stained lips at the savory thought. It would be good to have a home with Ivy Hill and John Frey, if once he was quit of Jael Bettiss. . . .

But he put the thought from him. The witch had never held his love and loyalty. That went to the house in the hollow, his home since the month that he was born. Even magic had not taught him how to be rid of that cat-instinctive obsession for his own proper dwelling place. The sinister, strife-sodden hovel would always call and claim him, would draw him back from the warmest fire, the softest bed, the most savory food in the world. Only John Howard Payne could have appreciated Gib's yearnings to the full, and he died long ago, in exile from the home he loved.

When Jael Bettiss returned, she was in a fine trembling rage. Her real self shone through the glamor of her disguise, like murky fire through a thin porcelain screen.

Gib was on the doorstep again and tried to dodge away as she came up, but her enchantments, or something else, had made Jael Bettiss too quick even for a cat. She darted out a hand and caught him by the scruff of the neck.

"Listen to me," she said, in a voice as deadly as the trickle of poisoned water. "You understand human words. You can talk, and you can hear what I say. You can do what I say, too." She shook him, by way of emphasis. "Can't you do what I say?"

"Yes," said Gib weakly, convulsed with fear.

"All right, I have a job for you. And mind you do it well, or else—" She broke off and shook him again, letting him imagine what would happen if he disobeyed.

"Yes," said Gib again, panting for breath in her tight grip. "What's it about?"

"It's about that little fool, Ivy Hill. She's not quite out of his heart. Go to the village tonight," ordered Jael Bettiss, "and to the house of the marshal. Steal something that belongs to Ivy Hill."

"Steal something?"

"Don't echo me, as if you were a silly parrot." She let go of him, and hurried back to the book that was her constant study. "Bring me something that Ivy Hill owns and touches—and be back here with it before dawn."

Gib carried out her orders. Shortly after sundown he crept through the deepened dusk to the home of Marshal Hill. Doubly black with the soot habitually smeared upon him by Jael Bettiss, he would have been almost invisible, even had anyone been on guard against his coming. But nobody watched; the genial old man sat on the front steps, talking to his daughter.

"Say," the father teased, "isn't young Johnny Frey coming over here tonight, as usual?"

"I don't know, daddy," said Ivy Hill wretchedly.

"What's that, daughter?" The marshal sounded surprised. "Is there anything gone wrong between you two young 'uns?"

"Perhaps not, but—oh, daddy, there's a new girl come to town—"

And Ivy Hill burst into tears, groping dolefully on the step beside her for her little wadded handkerchief. But she could not find it.

For Gib, stealing near, had caught it up in his mouth and was scampering away toward the edge of town, and beyond to the house in the hollow.

Meanwhile, Jael Bettiss worked hard at a certain project of wax modeling. Any witch, or student of witchcraft, would have known at once why she did this.

After several tries, she achieved something quite interesting and even clever—a little female figure, that actually resembled Ivy Hill.

Jael Bettiss used the wax of three candles to give it enough substance and proportion. To make it more realistic, she got some fresh, pale-gold hemp, and of this made hair, like the wig of a blonde doll, for the wax head. Drops of blue ink served for eyes, and a blob of berry juice for the red mouth. All the while she worked, Jael Bettiss was muttering and mumbling words and phrases she had gleaned from the rearward pages of her book.

When Gib brought in the handkerchief, Jael Bettiss snatched it from his mouth, with a grunt by way of thanks. With rusty scissors and coarse white thread, she fashioned for the wax figure a little dress. It happened that the handkerchief was of gingham, and so the garment made all the more striking the puppet's resemblance to Ivy Hill.

"You're a fine one!" tittered the witch, propping

her finished figure against the lamp. "You'd better be scared!"

For it happened that she had worked into the waxen face an expression of terror. The blue ink of the eyes made wide round blotches, a stare of agonized fear; and the berry-juice mouth seemed to tremble, to plead shakily for mercy.

Again Jael Bettiss refreshed her memory of goetic spells by poring over the back of the book, and after that she dug from the bottom of an old pasteboard box a handful of rusty pins. She chuckled over them, so that one would think triumph already hers. Laying the puppet on its back, so that the lamplight fell full upon it, she began to recite a spell.

"I have made my wish before," she said in measured tones. "I will make it now. And there was never a day that I did not see my wish fulfilled." Simple, vague—but how many have died because those words were spoken in a certain way over images of them?

The witch thrust a pin into the breast of the little wax figure and drove it all the way in, with a murderous pressure of her thumb. Another pin she pushed into the head, another into an arm, another into a leg; and so on, until the gingham-clad puppet was fairly studded with transfixing pins.

"Now," she said, "we shall see what we shall see."

Morning dawned, as clear and golden as though wickedness had never been born into the world. The mysterious new paragon of beauty—not a young man of the village but mooned over her, even though she was the reputed niece and namesake of that unsavory old vagabond, Jael Bettiss—walked into the general store to make purchases. One delicate pink ear turned to the gossip of the housewives.

Wasn't it awful, they were agreeing, how poor little

Ivy Hill was suddenly sick almost to death; she didn't seem to know her father or her friends. Not even Doctor Melcher could find out what was the matter with her. Strange that John Frey was not interested in her troubles; but John Frey sat behind the counter, slumped on his stool like a mud idol, and his eyes lighted up only when they spied lovely young Jael Bettiss with her market basket.

When she had heard enough, the witch left the store and went straight to the town marshal's house. There she spoke gravely and sorrowfully about how she feared for the sick girl, and was allowed to visit Ivy Hill in her bedroom. To the father and the doctor, it seemed that the patient grew stronger and felt less pain while Jael Bettiss remained to wish her a quick recovery; but, not long after this new acquaintance departed, Ivy Hill grew worse. She fainted, and recovered only to vomit.

And she vomited—pins, rusty pins. Something like that happened in old Salem Village, and earlier still in Scotland, before the grisly cult of North Berwick was literally burned out. But Doctor Melcher, a more modern scholar, had never seen or heard of anything remotely resembling Ivy Hill's disorder.

So it went, for three full days. Gib, too, heard the doleful gossip as he slunk around the village to hunt for food and to avoid Jael Bettiss, who did not like him near when she did magic. Ivy Hill was dying, and he mourned her, as for the boons of fish and fire and cushions and petting that might have been his. He knew, too, that he was responsible for her doom and his loss—that handkerchief that he had stolen had helped Jael Bettiss to direct her spells.

But philosophy came again to his aid. If Ivy Hill died, she died. Anyway, he had never been given the chance to live as her pensioner and pet. He was not even sure that he would have taken the chance— thinking of it, he felt strong, accustomed clamps upon his heart. The house in the hollow was his home forever. Elsewhere he'd be an exile.

Nothing would ever root it out of his feline soul.

On the evening of the third day, witch and cat faced each other across the tabletop in the old house in the hollow.

"They've talked loud enough to make his dull ears hear," grumbled the fearful old woman—with none but Gib to see her, she had washed away the disguising enchantment that, though so full of lure, seemed to be a burden upon her. "John Frey has agreed to take Ivy Hill out in his automobile. The doctor thinks that the fresh air, and John Frey's company, will make her feel better—but it won't. It's too late. She'll never return from that drive."

She took up the pin-pierced wax image of her rival, rose, and started toward the kitchen.

"What are you going to do?" Gib forced himself to ask.

"Do?" repeated Jael Bettiss, smiling murderously. "I'm going to put an end to that baby-faced chit, but why are you so curious? Get out, with your prying!"

And, snarling curses and striking with her clawlike hands, she made him spring down from his chair and run out of the house. The door slammed, and he crouched in some brambles and watched. No sound, and at the half-blinded windows no movement; but, after a time, smoke began to coil upward from the chimney. Its first puffs were dark and greasy-looking. Then it turned dull gray, then white, then blue as indigo. Finally it vanished altogether.

When Jael Bettiss opened the door and came out, she was once more in the semblance of a beautiful dark girl. Yet Gib recognized a greater terror about her than ever before.

"You be gone from here when I get back," she said to him.

"Gone?" stammered Gib, his little heart turning cold. "What do you mean?"

She stooped above him, like a threatening bird of prey.

"You be gone," she repeated. "If I ever see you again, I'll kill you—or I'll make my new husband kill you."

He still could not believe her. He shrank back, and his eyes turned mournfully to the old house that was the only thing he loved.

"You're the only witness to the things I've done," Jael Bettiss continued. "Nobody would believe their ears if a cat started telling tales, but anyway, I don't want any trace of you around. If you leave, they'll forget that I used to be a witch. So run!"

She turned away. Her mutterings were now only her thoughts aloud:

If my magic works—and it always works—that car will find itself idling around through the hill road to the other side of the quarry. John Frey will stop there. And so will Ivy Hill—forever.

Drawing her cloak around her, she stalked purposefully toward the old quarry behind the house.

Left by himself, Gib lowered his lids and let his yellow eyes grow dim and deep with thought. His shrewd beast's mind pawed and probed at this final wonder and danger that faced him and John Frey and Ivy Hill.

He must run away if he would live. The witch's

house in the hollow, which had never welcomed him, now threatened him. No more basking on the doorstep, no more ambushing woodmice among the brambles, no more dozing by the kitchen fire. Nothing for Gib henceforth but strange, forbidding wilderness, and scavenger's food, and no shelter, not on the coldest night. The village? But his only two friends, John Frey and Ivy Hill, were being taken from him by the magic of Jael Bettiss and her book. . . .

That book had done this. That book must undo it. There was no time to lose.

The door was not quite latched, and he nosed it open, despite the groans of its hinges. Hurrying in, he sprang up on the table.

It was gloomy in that tree-invested house, even for Gib's sharp eyes. Therefore, in a trembling fear almost too big for his little body, he spoke a word that Jael Bettiss had spoken, on her first night of power. As had happened then, so it happened now; the dark lamp glowed alight.

Gib pawed at the closed book, and contrived to lift its cover. Pressing it open with one front foot, with the other he painstakingly turned leaves, more leaves, and more yet. Finally he came to the page he wanted.

Not that he could read; and, in any case, the characters were strange in their shapes and combinations. Yet, if one looked long enough and levelly enough— even though one were a cat, and afraid—they made sense, conveyed intelligence.

And so into the mind of Gib, beating down his fears, there stole a phrase:

*Beware of mirrors* . . .

So that was why Jael Bettiss never kept a mirror— not even now, when she could assume such dazzling beauty.

*Beware of mirrors,* the book said to Gib, *for they declare the truth, and truth is fatal to sorcery. Beware also, of crosses, which defeat all spells.*

That was definite inspiration. He moved back from the book, and let it snap shut. Then, pushing with head and paws, he coaxed it to the edge of the table and let it fall. Jumping down after it, he caught a corner of the book in his teeth and dragged it to the door, more like a retriever than a cat. When he got it into the yard, into a place where the earth was soft, he dug furiously until he had made a hole big enough to contain the volume. Then, thrusting it in, he covered it up.

Nor was that all his effort, so far as the book was concerned. He trotted a little way off to where lay some dry, tough twigs under the cypress trees. To the little grave he bore first one, then another of these, and laid them across each other, in the form of an **X**. He pressed them well into the earth, so that they would be hard to disturb. Perhaps he would keep an eye on that spot henceforth, after he had done the rest of the things in his mind, to see that the cross remained. And, though he acted thus only by chance reasoning, all the demonologists, even the Reverend Montague Summers, would have nodded approval. Is this not the way to foil the black wisdom of the *Grand Albert*? Did not Prospero thus inter his grimoires, in the fifth act of *The Tempest*?

Now back to the house once more and into the kitchen. It was even darker than the parlor, but Gib could make out a basin on a stool by the moldy wall, and smelled an ugly pungency: Jael Bettiss had left her mixture of powdered water after last washing away her burden of false beauty.

Gib's feline nature rebelled at a wetting; his experience of witchcraft bade him be wary, but he rose on his hind legs and with his forepaws dragged at the basin's edge. It tipped and toppled. The noisome fluid drenched him. Wheeling, he ran back into the parlor, but paused on the doorstep. He spoke two more words that he remembered from Jael Bettiss. The lamp went out again.

And now he dashed around the house and through the brambles and to the quarry beyond.

It lay amid uninhabited wooded hills, a wide excavation from which had once been quarried all the stones for the village houses and pavements. Now it was full of water, from many thaws and torrents. Almost at its lip was parked John Frey's touring car, with the top down, and beside it he lolled, slack-faced and dreamy. At his side, cloak-draped and enigmatically queenly, was Jael Bettiss, her back to the quarry, never more terrible or handsome. John Frey's eyes were fixed dreamily upon her, and her eyes were fixed commandingly on the figure in the front seat of the car—a slumped, defeated figure, hard to recognize as poor sick Ivy Hill.

"Can you think of no way to end all this pain, Miss Ivy?" the witch was asking. Though she did not stir, or glance behind her, it was as though she had gestured toward the great quarry pit, full to unknown depths with black, still water. The sun, at the very point of setting, made angry red lights on the surface of that stagnant pond.

"Go away," sobbed Ivy Hill, afraid without knowing why. "Please, please!"

"I'm only trying to help," said Jael Bettiss. "Isn't that so, John?"

"That's so, Ivy," agreed John, like a little boy who

is prompted to an unfamiliar recitation. "She's only trying to help."

Gib, moving silently as fate, crept to the back of the car. None of the three human beings, so intent upon each other, saw him.

"Get out of the car," persisted Jael Bettiss. "Get out, and look into the water. You will forget your pain."

"Yes, yes," chimed in John Frey mechanically. "You will forget your pain."

Gib scrambled stealthily to the running board, then over the side of the car and into the rear seat. He found what he had hoped to find. Ivy Hill's purse—and open.

He pushed his nose into it. Tucked into a little side pocket was a hard, flat rectangle, about the size and shape of a visiting card. All normal girls carry mirrors in their purses; all mirrors show the truth. Gib clamped the edge with his mouth, and struggled to drag the thing free.

"Miss Ivy," Jael Bettiss was commanding, "get out of this car, and come and look into the water of the quarry."

No doubt what would happen if once Ivy Hill should gaze into that shiny black abyss; but she bowed her head, in agreement or defeat, and began slowly to push aside the catch of the door.

Now or never, thought Gib. He made a little noise in his throat, and sprang up on the side of the car next to Jael Bettiss. His black-stained face and yellow eyes were not a foot from her.

She alone saw him; Ivy Hill was too sick, John Frey too dull. "What are you doing here?" she snarled, like a bigger and fiercer cat than he; but he moved closer still, holding up the oblong in his teeth. Its back was uppermost, covered with imitation leather, and hid the real nature of it. Jael Bettiss was mystified, for once in her relationship with Gib. She took the thing from him, turned it over, and saw a reflection.

She screamed.

The other two looked up, horrified through their stupor. The scream that Jael Bettiss uttered was not deep and rich and young; it was the wild, cracked cry of a terrified old woman.

"I don't look like that," she choked out, and drew back from the car. "Not old—ugly—"

Gib sprang at her face. With all four claw-bristling feet he seized and clung to her. Again Jael Bettiss screamed, flung up her hands, and tore him away from his hold; but his soggy fur had smeared the powdered water upon her face and head.

Though he fell to earth, Gib twisted in midair and landed upright. He had one glimpse of his enemy. Jael Bettiss, no mistake—but a Jael Bettiss with hooked beak, rheumy eyes, hideous wry mouth and yellow chisel teeth—Jael Bettiss exposed for what she was, stripped of her lying mask of beauty!

And she drew back a whole staggering step. Rocks were just behind her. Gib saw, and flung himself. Like a flash he clawed his way up her cloak, and with both forepaws ripped at the ugliness he had betrayed. He struck for his home that was forbidden him—Marco Bozzaris never strove harder for Greece, or Stonewall Jackson for Virginia.

Jael Bettiss screamed yet again, a scream loud and full of horror. Her feet had slipped on the edge of the abyss. She flung out her arms, the cloak flapped from them like frantic wings. She fell, and Gib fell with her, still tearing and fighting.

The waters of the quarry closed over them both.

*    *    *

Gib thought that it was a long way back to the surface and a longer way to shore. But he got there, and scrambled out with the help of projecting rocks. He shook his drenched body, climbed back into the car and sat upon the rear seat. At least Jael Bettiss would no longer drive him from the home he loved. He'd find food some way, and take it back there each day to eat. . . .

With tongue and paws he began to rearrange his sodden fur.

John Frey, clear-eyed and wide awake, was leaning in and talking to Ivy Hill. As for her, she sat up straight, as though she had never known a moment of sickness.

"But just what did happen?" she was asking.

John Frey shook his head, though all the stupidity was gone from his face and manner. "I don't quite remember. I seem to have wakened from a dream. But are you all right, darling?"

"Yes, I'm all right." She gazed toward the quarry, and the black water that had already subsided above what it had swallowed. Her eyes were puzzled, but not frightened. "I was dreaming, too," she said. "Let's not bother about it."

She lifted her gaze, and cried out with joy. "There's that old house that daddy owns. Isn't it interesting?"

John Frey looked, too. "Yes. The old witch has gone away—I seem to have heard she did."

Ivy Hill was smiling with excitement. "Then I have an inspiration. Let's get daddy to give it to us. And we'll paint it over and fix it up, and then—" She broke off, with a cry of delight. "I declare, there's a cat in the car with me!"

It was the first she had known of Gib's presence.

John Frey stared at Gib. He seemed to have wakened only the moment before. "Yes, and isn't he a thin one? But he'll be pretty when he gets through cleaning himself. I think I see a white shirt front."

Ivy Hill put out a hand and scratched Gib behind the ear. "He's bringing us good luck, I think. John, let's take him to live with us when we have the house fixed up and move in."

"Why not?" asked her lover. He was gazing at Gib. "He looks as if he was getting ready to speak."

But Gib was not getting ready to speak. The power of speech was gone from him, along with Jael Bettiss and her enchantments. But he understood, in a measure, what was being said about him and the house in the hollow. There would be new life there, joyful and friendly this time. And he would be a part of it, forever, and of his loved home.

He could only purr to show his relief and gratitude.

# CHOCOLATE

## by Leslie Meier

Peering anxiously around her apartment door, Minnie
Mittelstadt checked the hallway to see if he was there.
Since that last dreadful episode, she had decided to
take no chances. If he was there, she would simply
duck back into her apartment, lock and bolt the door,
secure the safety chain, and wait until he was gone.

She had never been so frightened, and she was certain she was lucky to have escaped with her life. Living
in the big city held plenty of terrors for a single, middle-aged woman, but Minnie had lived in the Bronx
all her life and she wasn't about to leave her pleasant
cooperative apartment in the attractive neighborhood
known as Riverdale.

Minnie simply took reasonable precautions to guarantee her safety, as she was doing today. She read all
the advice the newspapers thoughtfully provided for
single women, and carefully followed their suggestions
to thwart muggers and purse snatchers. She stayed
alert, she remained aware of who was around her, she
carried her purse close to her body, and she only carried the cash she absolutely needed. Charge cards, or
large amounts of money, she tucked securely into a
dress or skirt pocket.

Minnie didn't worry too much about being mugged;
the small amount of money she usually carried could

easily be replaced. The threat of violence, especially rape, was something else, however. Dear Mama had brought her up believing that a woman must save herself for marriage. She realized she had been saving herself for quite a while, as she was now retired from her job at a downtown department store, but she was determined to preserve that which was most precious to her.

Minnie never got in an elevator with a stranger, she never spoke to strange men on the street, and she always checked her peephole before opening the door. If she didn't recognize the delivery man or the telephone man, she asked him to hold up his identification, and then she called the company and checked before allowing him to enter her apartment. Minnie didn't believe in taking unnecessary risks. In fact, she never even went out after dark.

That's why it was so frustrating to have this situation taking place right in her own apartment house. However could the members of the cooperative association have voted to allow that dreadful man to move in, and with a dog no less?

Minnie enjoyed the fact that the cooperative allowed pets, as she was the proud owner of a beautiful Siamese cat. King Tut was every bit as regal as his name implied, and he ruled the household with a velvet brown paw. Like all Siamese cats, Tut was stunningly attractive, sporting eight lovely chocolate-brown points; one nose, two ears, one tail, and four paws. His tail curved in a question mark, his sapphire-blue eyes were crossed, and he loved to talk. "Meeyowww," he would yowl when Minnie returned from a shopping trip. "Where have you been and what have you brought me? I was so lonely without you," he would complain, or so it seemed to Minnie.

Breathtakingly agile and graceful, Tut could jump
to the top of the refrigerator in one perfect leap. He
loved to sleep up there, soothed by the slight vibration
of the motor. He also enjoyed sitting on the cushion
Minnie had placed on the window sill, where he could
watch people passing in the street. But most of all, he
liked to nap in Minnie's lap while she watched TV.
He always began by curling up in a neat ball, sleeping
like a baby while she gently stroked his silky cham-
pagne-beige tummy. Then Tut's purr would rumble
with pleasure, and Minnie would think what a lovely
little boy he was.

That creature living across the hall, owned by that
monster of a man, was something else entirely. Minnie
didn't really see why the association allowed dogs.
They were messy and unruly, they scratched the wood-
work when they jumped frantically begging for walk-
ies, and they were noisy. Yipping, barking, and
whining, that awful animal across the hall kept up a
constant racket that disturbed poor Tut. And, thought
Minnie with a sniff, even the best-trained dog seemed
inevitably to have an accident in the hallway sooner
or later.

Unpleasant as they might be, Minnie was prepared
to tolerate dogs in the building if their owners were
responsible. But that was not the case in 3A across
the hall, as the incident last week so clearly indicated.

Minnie had been minding her own business, waiting
for the elevator, with one or two bits of clothing over
her arm that she was taking to the dry cleaner. Suddenly, the door of 3A had been thrown open, and the
hideous beast ran out, his nails clicking furiously
against the tile floor. Growling and snarling, he
jumped up and began pulling at the clothes she was
holding on her arm. She tried to snatch them away,

but the dog bared his teeth at her and began savaging the garments. Frightened, terrified in fact, Minnie dropped her favorite skirt and cowered in the corner as the ferocious animal ripped and shredded it to bits.

"What's going on here?" shouted a deep, masculine voice, and Minnie shrank even farther into the corner as the occupant of 3A charged down the hall. O'Connor was his name, and Minnie couldn't help noticing he had a bristly red mustache and very large teeth, just like his apricot miniature poodle.

"I'm so sorry," said O'Connor, hooking a leash onto the naughty dog's collar. "Please allow me to replace your clothes," he told a horrified Minnie. "This will never happen again, I promise you."

"It had better not," replied Minnie indignantly, as she scuttled down the hall to the safety of her apartment.

Since that awful day, Minnie had been living as if she were under siege. Residents of Beirut and Belfast probably took fewer precautions to guarantee their safety than Minnie did. And it was all because of him, and that dog.

When she came to think about it, as she frequently did, Minnie realized that dogs have a lot of the same unpleasant characteristics as those other threatening animals, men. Like men, dogs are noisy, unruly, and unpredictable. They often have gross and disgusting habits; dogs sniff at everything and lift their legs, men tend to spit in the street. They are both impulsive and overeager, unable to delay gratification. Their animal appetites must be satisfied immediately.

When she remembered her childhood, Minnie recalled the companionable relationship she had enjoyed with dear Mama. Mama had been an excellent housekeeper, and their apartment had always been neat as a pin, and spotlessly clean as well. Mama also practiced home economy, and took pride in carefully managing the household money. She and Minnie often had a salad, or an omelet, for dinner. Such a meal was simple to prepare, easy to clean up, and inexpensive, too.

All that would change, however, when Papa was home. He was a merchant seaman, and away for months at a time. but when he returned, the placid way of life she and her mother enjoyed was turned topsy-turvy. His boots would be thrown down carelessly in the hall, his pea jacket tossed over a chair, and the scent of cigar smoke would fill the air. No matter how they tried, she and Mama couldn't keep the house properly tidy when Papa was home.

There were no more tasty cheese and egg meals, either. Men had to have meat, as her mother explained. The stench of cooking fat would linger in the kitchen, and Minnie would have to wash the greasy, blood-smeared plates and platters. The heavy meals would turn her stomach, but Papa loved his meat and potatoes. He also liked a bit of whiskey now and again, and would smack his lips in pleasure as he sipped the amber liquid. Often when Papa drank whiskey of an evening, Minnie would later hear strange bumps and moans coming from the room he shared with dear Mama. Minnie suspected it was a bit of a relief to Mama when Papa's ship sank off the coast of Greenland in an icy winter storm, taking all hands down with it. Poor Papa, Mama would often sigh, stepping back to admire a cushion she had just fluffed or a picture she had straightened.

It was a few days later that Minnie found the answer to her problem. She had just settled down on the couch with a cup of tea, anticipating a peaceful hour with *Better Living* magazine. Tut leaped gracefully up beside her, lowering his rear legs but holding his head and chest upright and occasionally twitching his tail. He watched attentively as she turned the pages, almost as if he could read.

Leafing through the magazine, Minnie was amused to see the cat examine each page intently. She was startled when he suddenly yowled and put his paw on a page, and she was amazed to see the title of the story. "CHOCOLATE," it said in large letters, and just below were the words, "The deadly treat for dogs."

As she read, Minnie was astonished to learn that eating even a small amount of chocolate can cause a severe reaction in a small dog. The most dangerous, the article informed her, was baking chocolate. As little as one half ounce of baking chocolate could be life-threatening to a small dog, such as a miniature poodle, thanks to the theobromine it contained.

In addition, she was interested to read, dogs are not very discriminating eaters and will apparently wolf down large amounts of chocolate. Even more interestingly, the symptoms might not appear for several hours, she learned.

"Aren't you the clever boy," Minnie told Tut. Tut remained quiet, but narrowed his eyes, and lifted his chin so Minnie could stroke it. As she ran her fingers back and forth under his chin, Minnie would have sworn Tut smiled.

Giving O'Connor's dog the fatal dose turned out to be easier than Minnie imagined. Meeting them in the hall one day, she listened patiently while O'Connor again offered his apologies and tried to pay her for the skirt.

"It's absolutely all right," Minnie assured him. "Just to show there are no hard feelings, let me give the dog a treat. It's chocolate, is that all right?"

"Sure, he loves everything as long as he's not supposed to have it."

That gave Minnie a bit of a start, but O'Connor didn't seem to mean anything by his comment, so she bravely offered the dog a square of baking chocolate. He seemed to enjoy it, and wagged his tail in thanks. Next time she saw O'Connor in the hallway, the dog wasn't with him.

"Where's your doggie?" she asked.

"He's dead. Darnedest thing. Just had a seizure and that was it. Too bad."

"What a shame," commiserated Minnie.

"Actually, he was getting on, and I wasn't all that fond of him. He was my wife's dog and when we got divorced and she went to California, she left him with me. I always felt a little silly walking him," confessed O'Connor.

"Really?" Minnie smiled politely.

"Yeah. So I got another dog, a real man's dog."

"Oh?"

"Wanna meet him? Hold on just a sec and I'll get him."

Minnie pushed the button for the elevator and prepared to wait. Hearing O'Connor's door open, she turned. A huge brown-and-black hound hurtled down the hall towards her, pulling O'Connor behind him. Even though the dog was leashed, the man could just barely control it.

"This is Brutus," panted O'Connor. "He's a Rottweiler. A real man's dog."

"He's certainly very large—I mean handsome," stammered a horrified Minnie, as the elevator doors slid open. "I just remembered, I forgot something in my apartment. Goodbye."

Employing great self-control, Minnie walked back down the hall. Her hands were shaking so that she had quite a struggle with the locks, but she finally gained the safety of her apartment. Once inside, she ran directly to the coffee table, and began scrabbling through the magazines, finally locating the article. Running her trembling finger down the chart so thoughtfully provided by the author, she found the listing for very large dogs, dogs weighing over seventy-five pounds.

"Oh, Tut," she wailed. "How will I ever get that dog to eat ten jumbo candy bars?"

# HELIX THE CAT

## by Theodore Sturgeon

Did you see this in the papers?

BURGLAR IS CAT
Patrolman and Watchman
Shoot "Safe-cracker"

It was a strange tale that George Murphy, night
watchman for a brokerage firm, and Patrolman Pat
Riley had to tell this morning.

Their report states that the policeman was called
from his beat by Murphy, who excitedly told him that
someone was opening the safe in the inner office.
Riley followed him into the building, and they tip-toed
upstairs to the offices.

"Hear him?" Murphy asked the policeman. The officer swears that he heard the click of the tumblers on
the old safe. As they gained the doorway there was a
scrambling sound, and a voice called out of the darkness, "Stand where you are or I plug you!"

The policeman drew his gun and fired six shots in
the direction of the voice. There was a loud feline
yowl and more scrambling, and then the watchman
found the light switch. All they saw was a big black
cat thrashing around—two of Riley's bullets had
caught him. Of the safe-cracker there was no sign.
How he escaped will probably always remain a mystery. There was no way out of the office save the door
from which Riley fired.

The report is under investigation at police
headquarters.

I can clear up that mystery.

It started well over a year ago, when I was developing my new flexible glass. It would have made me rich, but—well, I'd rather be poor and happy.

That glass was really something. I'd hit on it when I was fooling with a certain mineral salt—never mind the name of it. I wouldn't want anyone to start fooling with it and get himself into the same kind of jam that I did. But the idea was that if a certain complex sulphide of silicon is combined with this salt at a certain temperature, and the product carefully annealed, you get that glass. Inexpensive, acid-proof, and highly flexible. Nice. But one of its properties—wait till I tell you about that.

The day it all started, I had just finished my first bottle. It was standing on the annealer—a rig of my own design; a turntable, shielded, over a ring of Bunsen burners—cooling slowly while I was turning a stopper from the same material on my lathe. I had to step the lathe up to twenty-two thousand before I could cut the stuff, and Helix was fascinated by the whine of it. He always liked to watch me work, anyway. He was my cat, and more. He was my friend. I had no secrets from Helix.

Ah, he was a cat. A big black tom, with a white throat and white mittens, and a tail twice as long as that of an ordinary cat. He carried it in a graceful spiral—three complete turns—and hence his name. He could sit on one end of that tail and take two turns around his head with the other. Ah, he was a cat.

I took the stopper off the lathe and lifted the top of the annealer to drop it into the mouth of the bottle. And as I did so—*whht!*

Ever hear a bullet ricochet past your ear? It was like that. I heard it, and then the stopper, which I held poised over the rotating bottle, was whipped out of my hand and jammed fast on the bottle mouth. And all the flames went out—*blown* out! I stood there staring at Helix, and noticed one thing more:

*He hadn't moved!*

Now you know and I know that a cat—any cat— can't resist that short, whistling noise. Try it, if you have a cat. When Helix should have been on all fours, big yellow eyes wide, trying to find out where the sound came from, he was sitting sphinxlike, with his eyes closed, his whiskers twitching slightly, and his front paws turned under his forelegs. It didn't make sense. Helix's senses were unbelievably acute—I knew. I'd tested them. Then—

Either I had heard that noise with some sense that Helix didn't possess, or I hadn't heard it at all. If I hadn't, then I was crazy. No one likes to think he is crazy. So you can't blame me for trying to convince myself that it was a sixth sense.

Helix roused me by sneezing. I took his cue and turned off the gas.

"Helix, old fellow," I said when I could think straight, "what do you make of this? Hey?"

Helix made an inquiring sound and came over to rub his head on my sleeve. "Got you stopped too, has it?" I scratched him behind the ear, and the end of his tail curled ecstatically around my wrist. "Let's see. I hear a funny noise. You don't. Something snatches the stopper out of my hand, and a wind comes from where it's impossible for any wind to be, and blows out the burners. Does that make sense?" Helix yawned. "I don't think so either. Tell me, Helix, what shall we do about this? Hey?"

Helix made no suggestion. I imagine he was quite ready to forget about it. Now, I wish I had.

I shrugged my shoulders and went back to work. First I slipped a canvas glove on and lifted the bottle off the turntable. Helix slid under my arm and made as if to smell the curved, flexible surface. I made a wild grab to keep him from burning his nose, ran my bare hand up against the bottle, and then had to make another grab to keep it off the floor. I missed with the second grab—the bottle struck dully, bounced, and—landed right back on the bench? Not only on it, but in the exact spot from which I had knocked it!

And—get this, now—when I looked at my hand to see how big my hypothetical seared spot might be, it wasn't there! That bottle was *cold*—and it should have been hot for hours yet! My new glass was a very poor conductor. I almost laughed. I should have realized that Helix had more sense than to put his pink nose against the bottle if it were hot.

Helix and I got out of there. We went into my room, closed the door on that screwy bottle, and flopped down on the bed. It was too much for us. We would have wept aloud purely for self-expression, if we hadn't forgotten how, years ago, Helix and I.

After my nerves had quieted a bit, I peeped into the laboratory. The bottle was still there—but it was *jumping*! It was hopping gently, in one place.

"Come on in here, you dope. I want to talk to you."

*Who said that?* I looked suspiciously at Helix, who, in all innocence, returned my puzzled gaze. Well, I hadn't said it. Helix hadn't. I began to be suspicious as hell of that bottle.

"Well?"

The tone was drawling and not a little pugnacious. I looked at Helix. Helix was washing daintily. But—Helix was the best watchdog of a cat that ever existed. If there had been anyone else—if he had *heard* anyone else—in the lab, he'd have let me know. Then he hadn't heard. And I had. "Helix," I breathed—and he looked right up at me, so there was nothing wrong with his hearing—"we're both crazy."

"No, you're not," said the voice. "Sit down before you fall down. I'm in your bottle, and I'm in to stay. You'll kill me if you take me out—but just between you and me I don't think you can get me out. Anyway please don't try ... what's the matter with you? Stop popping your eyes, man!"

"Oh," I said hysterically, "there's nothing the matter with me. No, no, no. I'm nuts, that's all. Stark, totally, and completely nuts, balmy, mentally unbalanced, and otherwise the victim of psychic loss of equilibrium. Me, I'm a raving lunatic. I hear voices. What does that make me, Joan of Arc? Hey, Helix. Look at me. I'm Joan of Arc. You must be Beucephalus, or Pegasus, or the great god Pasht. First I have an empty bottle, and next thing I know it's full of djinn. Hey, Helix, have a lil drink of djinn ..." I sat down on the floor and Helix sat beside me. I think he was sorry for me. I know I was—very.

"Very funny," said the bottle—or rather, the voice that claimed it was from the bottle. "If you'll only give me a chance to explain, now—"

"Look," I said, "maybe there is a voice. I don't trust anything any more—except you, Helix. I know. If you can hear him, then I'm sane. If not, I'm crazy. Hey, Voice!"

"Well?"

"Look, do me a favor. Holler 'Helix' a couple of times. If the cat hears you, I'm sane."

"All right," the voice said wearily. "Helix! Here, Helix!"

Helix sat there and looked at me. Not by the flicker

of a whisker did he show that he had heard. I drew a deep breath and said softly, "Helix! Here, Helix!"

Helix jumped up on my chest, put one paw on each shoulder, and tickled my nose with his curving tail. I got up carefully, holding Helix. "Pal," I said, "I guess this is the end of you and me. I'm nuts, pal. Better go phone the police."

Helix purred. He could see I was sad about something, but what it was didn't seem to bother him any. He was looking at me as if my being a madman didn't make him like me any the less. But I think he found it interesting. He had a sort of quizzical look in his glowing eyes. As if he'd rather I stuck around. Well, if he wouldn't phone the law, I wouldn't. I wasn't responsible for myself any more.

"Now, *will* you shut up?" said the bottle. "I don't want to give you any trouble. You may not realize it, but you saved my life. Don't be scared. Look. I'm a soul, see? I was a man called Gregory—Wallace Gregory. I was killed in an automobile accident two hours ago—"

"You were killed two hours ago. And I just saved your life. You know, Gregory, that's just dandy. On my head you will find a jeweled turban. I am now the Maharajah of Mysore. Goo. Da. And flub. I—"

"You are perfectly sane. That is, you are right now. Get hold of yourself and you'll be all right," said the bottle. "Yes, I was killed. My body was killed. I'm a soul. The automobile couldn't kill that. But They could."

"They?"

"Yeah. The Ones Who were chasing me when I got into your bottle."

"Who are They?"

"We have no name for Them. They eat souls. There

are swarms of them. Anytime They find a soul running around loose, They track it down."

"You mean—any time anyone dies, his soul wanders around, running away from Them? And that sooner or later, They catch it?"

"Oh, no. Only some souls. You see, when a man realizes he is going to die, something happens to his soul. There are some people alive today who knew, at one time, that they were about to die. Then, by some accident, they didn't. Those people are never quite the same afterward, because that something has happened. With the realization of impending death, a soul gets what might be called a protective covering, though it's more like a change of form. From then on, the soul is inedible and undesirable to Them."

"What happens to a protected soul, then?"

"That I don't know. It's funny ... people have been saying for millennia that if only someone could come back from death, what strange things he could relate .. well, I did it, thanks to you. And yet I know very little more about it than you. True, I died, and my soul left my body. But then, I only went a very little way. A protected soul probably goes through stage after stage ... I don't know. Now, I'm just guessing."

"Why wasn't your soul 'protected'?"

"Because I had no warning—no realization that I was to die. It happened so quickly. And I haven't been particularly religious. Religious people, and freethinkers if they think deeply, and philosophers in general, and people whose work brings them in touch with deep and great things—these may all be immune from Them, years before they die."

"Why?"

"That should be obvious. You can't think deeply without running up against a realization of the power of death. 'Realization' is a loose term, I know. If your mind is brilliant, and you don't pursue your subject—*any* subject—deeply enough, you will never reach that realization. It's a sort of dead end to a questing mind—a *ne plus ultra*. Batter yourself against it, and it hurts. And that pain is the realization. Stupid people reach it far easier than others—it hurts more, and they are made immune easier. But at any rate, a man can live his life without it, and still have a few seconds just before he dies for his soul to undergo the immunizing change. I didn't have those few seconds."

I fumbled for my handkerchief and mopped my face. This was a little steep. "Look," I said, "this is—well, I'm more or less of a beginner. Just what *is* a soul?"

"Elementally," said the bottle, "it is matter, just like everything else in the universe. It has weight and mass, though it can't be measured by earthly standards. In the present stage of the sciences, we haven't run up against anything like it. It usually centers around the pineal gland, although it can move at will throughout the body, if there is sufficient stimulus. For example—"

He gave me the example, and it was very good. I saw his point.

"And anger, too," the bottle went on. "In a fit of fury, one's soul settles momentarily around the adrenals, and does what is necessary. See?"

I turned to Helix. "Helix," I said, "we're really learning things today." Helix extended his claws and studied them carefully. I suddenly came to my senses, realizing that I was sitting on the floor of my laboratory, holding a conversation with an empty glass bottle; that Helix was sitting in my lap, preening himself, listening without interest to my words, and *not hearing* those from the bottle. My mind reeled again. I *had* to have an answer to that.

"Bottle," I said hoarsely, "why can't Helix hear you?"

"Oh. That," said the bottle. "Because there is no sound."

"How can I hear you?"

"Direct telepathic contact. I am not speaking to you, specifically, but to your soul. Your soul transmits my message to you. It is functioning now on the nerve-centers controlling your hearing—hence you interpret it as sound. That is the most understandable way of communication."

"Then—why doesn't Helix get the same messages?"

"Because he is on a different—er—wavelength. That's one way of putting it, though thoughtwaves are not electrical. I can—that is, I believe I can—direct thoughts to him. Haven't tried. It's a matter of degree of development."

I breathed much easier. Astonishing, what difference a rational explanation will make. But there were one or two more things—

"Bottle," I said, "what's this about my saving your life? And what has my flexible glass to do with it?"

"I don't quite know," said the bottle. "But, purely by accident, I'm sure, you have stumbled on the only conceivable external substance which seems to exclude—Them. Sort of an insulator. I sensed what it was—so did They. I can tell you, it was nip and tuck for a while. They can really move, when They want to. I won, as you know. Close. Oh, yes, I was responsible for snatching the stopper out of your hand. I did it by creating a vacuum in the bottle. The stopper was the nearest thing to the mouth, and you weren't holding it very tightly."

"Vacuum?" I asked. "What became of the air?"

"That was easy. I separated the molecular structure of the glass, and passed the air out that way."

"What about Them?"

"Oh, They would have followed. But if you'll look closely, you'll see that the stopper is now fused to the bottle. That's what saved me. Whew!—Oh, by the way, if you're wondering what cooled the bottle so quickly, it was the vacuum formation. Expanding air, you know, loses heat. Vacuum creation, of course, would create intense cold. That glass is good stuff. Practically no thermal expansion."

"I'm beginning to be glad, now that it happened. Would have been bad for you . . . I suppose you'll live out the rest of your life in my bottle."

"The rest of my life, friend, is—eternity."

I blinked at that. "That's not going to be much fun," I said. "I mean—don't you ever get hungry, or—or anything?"

"No. I'm fed—I know that. From outside, somehow. There seems to be a source somewhere that radiates energy on which I feed. I wouldn't know about that. But it's going to be a bit boring. I don't know—maybe some day I'll find a way to get another body."

"What's to prevent your just going in and appropriating someone else's?"

"Can't," said the bottle. "As long as a soul is in possession of a body, it is invulnerable. The only way would be to convince some soul that it would be to its advantage to leave its body and make room for me."

"Hmm . . . say, Bottle. Seems to me that by this time you must have experienced that death-realization you spoke about a while back. Why aren't you immune from Them now?"

"That's the point. A soul must draw its immunity

from a body which it possesses at the time. If I could get into a body and possess it for just one split second, I could immunize myself and be on my way. Or I could stay in the body and enjoy myself until it died. By the way, stop calling me Bottle. My name's Gregory—Wallace Gregory."

"Oh. Okay. I'm Pete Tronti. Er—glad to have met you."

"Same here." The bottle hopped a couple of times. "That can be considered a handshake."

"How did you do that?" I asked, grinning.

"Easy. The tiniest of molecular expansion, well distributed, makes the bottle bounce."

"Neat. Well—I've got to go and get some grub. Anything I can get for you?"

"Thanks, no, Tronti. Shove along. Be seeing you."

Thus began my association with Wally Gregory, disembodied soul. I found him a very intelligent person; and though he had cramped my style in regard to the new glass—I didn't fancy collecting souls in bottles as a hobby—we became real friends. Not many people get a break like that—having a boarder who is so delightful and so little trouble. Though the initial cost had been high—after all, I'd almost gone nuts!—the upkeep was negligible. Wally never came in drunk, robbed the cash drawer, or brought his friends in. He was never late for meals, nor did he leave dirty socks around. As a roommate, he was ideal, and as a friend, he just about had Helix topped.

One evening about eight months later I was batting the wind with Wally while I worked. He'd been a great help to me—I was fooling around with artificial rubber synthesis at the time, and Wally had an uncanny ability for knowing exactly what was what in a chemical reaction—and because of that, I began to think of his present state.

"Say, Wally—don't you think it's about time that we began thinking about getting a body for you?"

Wally snorted. "That's about all we can do—think about it. How in blazes do you think we could ever get a soul's consent for that kind of a transfer?"

"I don't know—we might try kidding one of them along. You know—put one over on him."

"What—kid one along when he has the power of reading every single thought that goes through a mind? Couldn't be done."

"Now, don't tell me that every soul in the universe is incapable of being fooled. After all, a soul is a part of a human being."

"It's not that a soul is phenomenally intelligent, Pete. But a soul reasons without emotional drawbacks—he deals in elementals. Any moron is something of a genius if he can see clearly to the roots of a problem. And any soul can do just that. That is, if it's a soul as highly developed as that of a human being."

"Well, suppose that the soul isn't that highly developed? That's an idea. Couldn't you possess the body of a dog, say, or—"

"Or a cat ... ?"

I stopped stirring the beakerful of milkweed latex and came around the table, stopping in front of the bottle. "Wally—not Helix. Not that cat! Why, he's—he's a friend of mine. He trusts me. We *couldn't* do anything like that. My gosh, man—"

"You're being emotional," said Wally scornfully. "If you've got any sense of values at all, there'll be no choice. You can save my immortal soul by sacrificing the life of a cat. Not many men have that sort of an opportunity, especially at that price. It'll be a gamble. I haven't told you, but in the last couple of months I've been looking into Helix's mentality. He's got a brilliant mind for a cat. And it wouldn't do anything to him. He'd cease to exist—you can see that. But his soul is primitive, and has been protected since he was a kitten, as must be the case with any primitive mentality. Man needs some powerful impetus to protect his soul, because he has evolved away from the fear of death to a large degree—but a cat has not. His basic philosophy is little different from that of his wild forebears. He'll be okay. I'd just step in and he'd step out, and go wherever it is that good cats go when they die. You'd have him, in body, the same as you have now; but he'd be motivated by my soul instead of his own. Pete, you've *got* to do it."

"Gosh, Wally . . . look, I'll get you another cat. Or . . . say! How's about a monkey?"

"I've thought about all that. In the first place, a monkey would be too noticeable, walking around by himself. You see, my idea is to get into some sort of a body in which I can go where I please, when I please. In the second place, I have a headstart with Helix. It's going to be a long job, reconditioning that cat to my needs, but it can be done. I've been exploring his mind, and by now I know it pretty well. In the third place, you know him, and you know me—and he knows me a little now. He is the logical subject for something which, you must allow, is going to be a most engrossing experiment."

I had to admire the way Wally was putting it over. Being dissociated from emotionalism like that must be a great boon. He had caused me to start the conversation, and probably to put forward the very objections to which he had prepared answers. I began to resent

him a little—but only a little. That last point of his
told. It *would* be a most engrossing experiment—preparing a feline body and mind to bear a human soul,
in such a way that the soul could live an almost normal
life . . . "I won't say yes or no, Wally," I said. "I want
to talk it over a little . . . Just how would we go about
it, in case I said yes?"

"Well—" Wally was quiet a minute. "First we'd
have to make some minor changes in his physique, so
that I could do things that are impossible for a cat—
read, write, speak and memorize. His brain would
have to be altered so that it could comprehend an
abstraction, and his paws would have to be made a
little more manageable so that I could hold a pencil."

"Might as well forget the whole thing, then," I told
him. "I'm a chemist, not a veterinary surgeon. There
isn't a man alive who could do a job like that. Why—"

"Don't worry about that. I've learned a lot recently
about myself, too. If I can once get into Helix's brain,
I can mess around with his metabolism. I can stimulate
growth in any part of his body, in any way, to any
degree. I can, for instance, atrophy the skin between
his toes, form flesh and joints in his claws. Presto—
hands. I can—"

"Sounds swell. But how are you going to get in
there? I thought you couldn't displace his soul without
his consent. And—what about Them?"

"Oh, that will be all right. I can get in there and
work, and his soul will protect me. You see, I've been
in contact with it. As long as I am working to increase
the cat's mental and physical powers, his soul won't
object. As for getting in there, I can do it if I move
fast. There are times when none of Them are around.
If I pick one of those times, slide out of the bottle
and into the cat, I'll be perfectly safe. My one big

danger is from his soul. If it wants me out of there, it can bring a tremendous psychic force into play—throw me from here to the moon, or farther. If that happened—that will finish me. They wouldn't miss a chance like that."

"Golly ... listen, friend, you'd better not take the chance. It's a swell idea, but I don't think it's worth it. As you are now, you're safe for the rest of time. If something goes wrong—"

"Not worth it? Do you realize what you're saying, man? I have my choice between staying here in this bottle forever—and that's an awful long time, if you can't die—or fixing up Helix so that he can let me live a reasonable human existence until he dies. Then I can go, protected, into wherever it is I should go. Give me a break, Pete. I can't do it without you."

"Why not?"

"Don't you see? The cat has to be educated. Yes, and civilized. You can do it, partly because he knows you, partly because that is the best way. When we can get him speaking, you can teach him orally. That way we can keep up our mental communication, but he'll never know about it. More important, neither will his soul. Pete, can't you see what this means to me?"

"Yeah. Wally, it's a shabby trick on Helix. It's downright dirty. I don't like it—anything about it. But you've got something there ... all right. You're a rat, Wally. So am I. But I'll do it. I'd never sleep again if I didn't. How do we start?"

"Thanks, Pete. I'll never be able to thank you enough ... First, I've got to get into his brain. Here's what you do. Think you can get him to lick the side of the bottle?"

I thought a minute. "Yes. I can put a little catnip

extract—I have some around somewhere—on the bottle. He'll lick it off ... Why?"

"That'll be fine. See, it will minimize the distance. I can slip through the glass and be into his brain before one of Them has a chance at me."

I got the little bottle of extract and poured some of it on a cloth. Helix came running when he smelled it. I felt like a heel—almost tried to talk Wally out of it. But then I shrugged it off. Fond as I was of the big black cat, Wally's immortal soul was more important.

"Hold it a minute," said Wally. "One of Them is smelling around."

I waited tensely. Helix was straining toward the cloth I held in my right hand. I held him with the other, feeling smaller and smaller. He *trusted* me!

"Let 'er go!" snapped Wally. I slapped the cloth onto the side of the bottle, smeared it. Helix shot out of my grip, began licking the bottle frantically. I almost cried. I said, "May God have mercy on his soul ..." Don't know why ...

"Good lad!" said Wally. "I made it!" After a long moment, "Pete! Give him some more catnip! I've got to find out what part of his brain registers pleasure. That's where I'll start. He's going to enjoy every minute of this."

I dished up the catnip. Helix, forgive me!

Another long pause, then, "Pete! Pinch him, will you? Or stick a pin in him."

I chose the pinch, and it was a gentle one. It didn't fool Wally. "Make him holler, Pete! I want a real reaction."

I gritted my teeth and twisted the spiral tail. Helix yowled. I think his feelings were hurt more than his caudal appendage.

And so it went. I applied every possible physical

and mental stimulus to Helix—hunger, sorrow, fright, anger (that was a hard one. Old Helix just wouldn't get sore!), heat, cold, joy, disappointment, thirst and insult. Hate was impossible. And Wally, somewhere deep in the cat's mind, checked and rechecked; located, reasoned, tried and erred. Because he was tireless, and because he had no sidetracking temptations to swerve him from his purpose, he made a perfect investigator. When he finally was ready to emerge, Helix and I were half dead from fatigue. Wally was, to hear him talk, just ready to begin. I got him back into his bottle without mishap, using the same method; and so ended the first day's work, for I absolutely refused to go on until the cat and I had had some sleep. Wally grumbled a bit and then quieted down.

Thus began the most amazing experiment in the history of physiology and psychology. We made my cat over. And we made him into a—well, guess for yourself.

Inside of a week he was talking. I waited with all the impatience of an anxious father for his first word, which was, incidentally, not "Da-da" but "Catnip." I was so tickled that I fed him catnip until he was roaring drunk.

After that it was easy; nouns first, then verbs. Three hours after saying "Catnip" he was saying "How's about some more catnip?"

Wally somehow stumbled onto a "tone control" in Helix's vocal cords. We found that we could give him a loud and raucous voice, but that by sacrificing quantity to quality, something approximating Wally's voice (as I "heard" it) could be achieved. It was quiet, mellow and very expressive.

After a great deal of work in the anterior part of Helix's brain, we developed a practically perfect memory. That's one thing that the lower orders are a little short on. The average cat lives almost entirely in the present; perhaps ten minutes of the past are clear to him; and he has no conception of the future. What he learns is retained more by muscular or neural memory than by aural, oral or visual memory, as is the case with a schoolchild. We fixed that. Helix needed no drills or exercises; to be told once was enough.

We hit one snag. I'd been talking to Wally the way I'd talk to anyone. But as Helix came to understand what was said aloud, my long talks with no one began to puzzle and confuse him. I tried hard to keep my mouth shut while I talked with Wally, but it wasn't until I thought of taping my mouth that I succeeded. Helix was a little surprised at that, but he got used to it.

And we got him reading. To prove what a prodigy he was, I can say that not one month after he started on his ABC's he had read and absorbed the Bible, Frazer's *Golden Bough* in the abridged edition, *Alice in Wonderland* and four geography texts. In two months he had learned solid geometry, differential calculus, the fourteen basic theories of metempsychosis, and every song on this week's Hit Parade. Oh, yes; he had a profound sense of tone and rhythm. He used to sprawl for hours in front of the radio on Sunday afternoons, listening to the symphony broadcasts; and after a while he could identify not only the selection being played and its composer, but the conductor as well.

I began to realize that we had overdone it a bit. Being a cat, which is the most independent creature on earth, Helix was an aristocrat. He had little, if any, consideration for my comparative ignorance—yes, ignorance; for though I had given him, more or less, my own education, he had the double advantage of recent education and that perfect memory. He would openly sneer at me when I made a sweeping statement—a bad habit I have always had—and then proceed to straighten me out in snide words of one syllable. He meant me no harm; but when he would look over his whiskers and say to me, "You don't really know very much, do you?" in that condescending manner, I burned. Once I had to go so far as to threaten to put him on short rations; that was one thing that would always bring him around.

Wally would spring things on me at times. He went and gave the cat a craving for tobacco, the so-and-so. The result was that Helix smoked up every cigarette in the house. I had a brainstorm, though, and taught him to roll his own. It wasn't so bad after that. But he hadn't much conception of the difference between "mine" and "thine." My cigarettes were safe with Helix—as long as he didn't feel like smoking.

That started me thinking. Why, with his mental faculties, couldn't he learn not to smoke my last cigarette? Or, as happened once, eat everything that was on the table—my dinner as well as his—while I was phoning? I'd told him not to; he couldn't explain it himself. He simply said, "It was there, wasn't it?"

I asked Wally about it, and I think that he hit the right answer.

"I believe," he told me, "that it's because Helix has no conception of generosity. Or mercy. Or any of those qualities. He is completely without conscience."

"You mean that he's got no feeling toward me? That bringing him up, feeding him, educating him, has done nothing to—"

Wally sounded amused. "Sure, sure. He likes you—you're easy to get along with. Besides, as you just said, you're the meal ticket. You mustn't forget, Tronti, that Helix is a cat, and until I take possession, always will be. You don't get implicit obedience from any cat, no matter how erudite he may be, unless he damn well pleases to give it to you. Otherwise, he'll follow his own sweet way. This whole process has interested him—and I told you he'd enjoy it. But that's all."

"Can't we give him some of those qualities?"

"No. That's been bothering me a little. You know, Helix has a clever and devious way of his own for going about things. I'm not quite sure how he—his soul—stands on this replacement business. He might be holding out on us. I can't do much more than I've done. Every attribute we have developed in him was, at the beginning, either embryonic or vestigial. If he were a female, now, we might get an element of mercy, for instance. But there's none in this little tiger here; I have nothing to work on." He paused for a moment.

"Pete, I might as well confess to you that I'm a little worried. We've done plenty, but I don't know that it's enough. In a little while now he'll be ready for the final stage—my entrance into his psyche. As I told you, if his soul objects, he can sling mine out of the solar system. And I haven't a chance of getting back. And here's another thing. I can't be sure that he doesn't know just why we are doing this. If he does— Pete, I hate to say this, but are you on the level? Have you told Helix anything?"

"Me?" I shouted. "Why, you—you ingrate! How could I? You've heard every single word that I've said to that cat. You never sleep. You never go out. Why, you dirty—"

"All right—all right," he said soothingly. "I just asked, that's all. Take it easy. I'm sorry. But—if only

I could be sure! There's something in his mind that I can't get to ... Oh, well. We'll hope for the best. I've got a lot to lose, but plenty to gain—everything to gain. And for heaven's sake don't shout like that. You're not taped up, you know."

"Oh—sorry. I didn't give anything away, I guess," I said silently. "But watch yourself, Gregory. Don't get me roiled. Another crack like that and I throw you and your bottle into the ocean, and you can spend the rest of eternity educating the three little fishies. *Deve essere cosi.*"

"In other words, no monkey business. I took Italian in high school," sneered the voice from the bottle. "Okay, Pete. Sorry I brought it up. But put yourself in my place, and you'll see what's what."

The whole affair was making me increasingly nervous. Occasionally I'd wake up to the fact that it was a little out of the ordinary to be spending my life with a talking bottle and a feline cum laude. And now this friction between me and Wally, and the growing superciliousness of Helix—I didn't know whose side to take. Wally's, Helix's, or, by golly, my own. After all, I was in this up to my ears and over. Those days were by no means happy ones.

One evening I was sitting morosely in my easy chair, trying to inject a little rationality into my existence by means of the evening paper. Wally was sulking in his bottle, and Helix was spread out on the rug in front of the radio, in that hyperperfect relaxation that only a cat can achieve. He was smoking sullenly and making passes at an occasional fly. There was a definite tension in the air, and I didn't like it.

"Helix," I said suddenly, hurling my paper across the room, "what ails you, old feller?"

"Nothing," he lied. "And stop calling me 'old feller.' It's undignified."

"Ohh! So we have a snob in our midst! Helix, I'm getting damn sick of your attitude. Sometimes I'm sorry I ever taught you anything. You used to show me a little respect, before you had any brains."

"That remark," drawled the cat, "is typical of a human being. What does it matter where I got anything I have? As long as any talents of mine belong to me, I have every right to be proud of them, and to look down on anyone who does not possess them in such a degree. Who are you to talk? You think you're pretty good yourself, don't you? And just because you're a member of the cocky tribe of"—and here his words dripped the bitterest scorn—"Homo sapiens."

I knew it would be best to ignore him. He was indulging in the age-old pastime of the cat family—making a human being feel like a fool. Every inferiority complex is allergic to felinity. Show me a man who does not like cats and I'll show you one who is not sure of himself. The cat is a symbol of aloneness superb. And with man, he is not impressed.

"That won't do you any good, Helix," I said coldly. "Do you realize how easy it would be for me to get rid of you? I used to think I had a reason for feeding you and sheltering you. You were good company. You certainly are not now."

"You know," he said, stretching out and crushing his cigarette in the rug because he knew it annoyed me, "I have only one deep regret in my life. And that is that you knew me before my little renaissance. I remember little about it, but I have read considerably on the subject. It appears that the cat family has long misled your foolish race. And yet the whole thing is summed up in a little human doggerel:

I love my dear pussy, his coat is so warm,
And if I don't hurt him, he'll do me no harm.

"There, my friend and"—he sniffed—"benefactor, you have our basic philosophy. I find that my actions previous to your fortuitous intervention in my mental development led you to exhibit a sad lack of the respect which I deserve. If it were not for that stupidity on my part, during those blind years—and I take no responsibility on myself for that stupidity; it was unavoidable—you would now treat me more as I should be treated, as the most talented member of a superlative race.

"Don't be any more of a fool than you have to be, Pete. You think I've changed. I haven't. The sooner you realize that, the better for you. And for heaven's sake stop being emotional about me. It bores me."

"Emotional?" I yelled. "Damn it, what's the matter with a little emotion now and then? What's happening around here, anyway? Who's the boss around here? Who pays the bills?"

"You do," said Helix gently, "which makes you all the more a fool. You wouldn't catch me doing anything unless I thoroughly enjoyed it. Go away, Pete. You're being childish."

I picked up a heavy ashtray and hurled it at the cat. He ducked it gracefully. "Tsk tsk! *What* an exhibition!"

I grabbed my hat and stormed out, followed by the cat's satiric chuckle.

Never in my life have I been so completely filled with helpless anger. I start to do someone a favor, and what happens? I begin taking dictation from him. In return for that I do him an even greater favor, and what happens? He corrupts my cat. So I start taking dictation from the cat too.

It wouldn't matter so much, but I had loved that cat. Snicker if you want to, but for a man like me, who spends nine-tenths of his life tied up in test tubes and electrochemical reactions, the cat had filled a great gap. I realized that I had kidded myself—Helix was a conscienceless parasite, and always had been. But I had loved him. My error. Nothing in this world is quite as devastating as the realization of one's mistaken judgment of character. I could have loved Helix until the day he died, and then cherished his memory. The fact that I would have credited him with qualities that he did not possess wouldn't have mattered.

Well, and whose fault was it? Mine? In a way; I'd given in to Wally in his plan to remake the cat for his use. But it was more Wally's fault. Damn it, had I asked him to come into my house and bottle? Who did he think he was, messing up my easy, uncomplicated life like that? ... I had someone to hate for it all, then. Wallace Gregory, the rat.

Lord, what I would have given for some way to change everything back to where it was before Gregory came into my life! I had nothing to look forward to now. If Wally succeeded in making the change, I'd still have that insufferable cat around. In his colossal ego there was no means of expressing any of the gentler human attributes which Wally might possess. As soon as he fused himself with the cat, Helix would disappear into the cosmos, taking nothing but his life force, and leaving every detestable characteristic that he had—and he had plenty. If Wally couldn't make it, They would get him, and I'd be left with that insufferable beast. What a spot!

Suppose I killed Helix? That would be one way ...

but then what about Wally? I knew he had immense potentialities; and though that threat of mine about throwing him into the ocean had stopped him once, I wasn't so sure of myself. He had a brilliant mind, and if I incurred his hatred, there's no telling what he might do. For the first time I realized that Wally Gregory's soul was something of a menace. Imagine having to live with the idea that as soon as you died, another man's soul would be laying for you, somewhere Beyond.

I walked miles and hours that night, simmering, before I hit on the perfect solution. It meant killing my beloved Helix; but, now that would be a small loss. And it would free Wallace Gregory. Let the man's soul take possession of the cat, and then kill the cat. They would both be protected then; and I would be left alone. And, by golly, at peace.

I stumbled home after four, and slept like a dead man. I was utterly exhausted and would have slept the clock around. But that would not have suited Helix. At seven-thirty that morning he threw a glass of ice water over me. I swore violently.

"Get up, you lazy pig," he said politely. "I want my breakfast."

Blind with fury, I rolled out and stood over him. He stood quite still, grinning up at me. He was perfectly unafraid, though I saw him brace his legs, ready to move forward or back or to either side if I made a pass at him. I couldn't have touched him, and he knew it, damn him.

And then I remembered that I was going to kill him, and my throat closed up. I turned away with my eyes stinging. "Okay, Helix," I said when I could speak. "Comin' up."

He followed me into the kitchen and sat watching

me while I boiled us some eggs. I watched them carefully—Helix wouldn't eat them unless they were boiled exactly two minutes and forty-five seconds—and then took his out and cut them carefully in cubes, the way he liked them. And then I put a little shot of catnip extract over them and dished them up. Helix raised his eyebrows at that. I hadn't given him any catnip for weeks. I'd only used it as a reward when he had done especially well. Recently I hadn't felt like rewarding him.

"Well!" he said as he wiped his mouth delicately, "I see that little session of ambulating introspection in which you indulged after your outbreak last night did you good. There never need be any friction between us, Pete, if you continue to behave this way. I can overlook almost anything but familiarity."

I choked on a piece of toast. Of all the colossal gall! He thought he had taught me a lesson! For a moment I was tempted to rub him out right then and there, but managed to keep my hands off him. I didn't want him to be suspicious.

Suddenly he swept his cup off the table. "Call this coffee?" he said sharply. "Make some more immediately, and this time be a little careful."

"You better be careful yourself," I said. "I taught you to say 'please' when you asked for anything."

" 'Please' be damned," said my darling pet. "You ought to know by this time how I like my coffee. I shouldn't have to tell you about things like that." He reached across the table and sent my cup to the floor too. "Now you'll have to make more. I tell you, I won't stand for any more of your nonsense. From now on this detestable democracy is at an end. You're going to do things *my* way. I've taken too much from you. You offend me. You eat sloppily, and I never did care particularly for your odor. Hereafter keep away from me unless I call. And don't speak unless you are spoken to."

I drew a deep breath and counted to ten very, very slowly. Then I got two more cups out of the closet, made more coffee, and poured it. And while Helix was finishing his breakfast, I went out and bought a revolver.

When I got back I found Helix sleeping. I tiptoed into the kitchen to wash the dishes, but found them all broken. His idea of a final whimsical touch. I ground my teeth and cleaned up the mess. Then I went into the laboratory and locked the door. "Wally!" I called.

"Well?"

"Listen, fella, we've got to finish this up now— today. Helix has gotten it into his head that he owns the place, me included. I won't stand for it, I tell you! I almost killed him this morning, and I will yet if this nonsense keeps up. Wally, is everything ready?"

Wally sounded a little strained. "Yes ... Pete, it's going to be good! Oh, God, to be able to walk around again! Just to be able to read a comic strip, or go to a movie, or see a ball game! Well—let's get it over with. What was that about Helix? Did you say he's a little—er—intractable?"

I snorted. "That's not the word for it. He has decided that he is a big shot. Me, I only work here."

"Pete, did he say anything about—about me? Don't get sore now, but—do you think it's safe? If what you say is true, he's asserting his individuality; I wouldn't like that to go too far. You know, They have a hunch that something's up. The last time you got me into Helix's mind, there were swarms of Them around. When they sensed that I was making a change, They all drew back as if to let me get away with it. Pete, They have something up Their sleeve, too."

"What do you mean, 'too'?" I asked quickly.

"Why nothing. Helix is one, They are another. Too. What's the matter with that?"

It didn't relieve me much. Wally probably knew I was planning to kill the cat as soon as he made the change, thus doing him out of several years of fleshly enjoyment before he went on his way. He wasn't saying anything, though. He had too much to lose.

I took the bottle out of the laboratory into the kitchen and washed it, just by way of stalling for a minute. Then I set it down on the sink and went and got my gun, loaded it and dropped it into a drawer in the bench. Next I set the bottle back on the bench— I was pretty sure Wally hadn't known about the gun, and I didn't want him to—and went for Helix.

I couldn't find him.

The cushion where he had been sleeping was still warm; what was he up to now?

I hunted feverishly all through the apartment, without success. This was a fine time for him to do a black-out! With an exasperated sigh I went back into the laboratory to tell Wally.

Helix was sitting on the bench beside the bottle, twirling his whiskers with his made-over right paw and looking very amused. "Well, my good man," he greeted me, "what seems to be the trouble?"

"Damn it, cat," I said irritably, "where have you been?"

"Around," he said laconically. "You are as blind as you are stupid. And mind your tone."

I swallowed that. I had something more important to think about. How was I going to persuade him to lick the bottle? Mere catnip wouldn't do it, not in his present frame of mind. So—

"I suppose," Helix said, "that you want me to go through the old ritual of bottle-cataglottism again. Pardon the pun."

"Why, yes," I said, surprised but trying not to show it. "It's to your benefit, you know."

"Of course," said the cat. "I've always known that. If I didn't get something out of it, I'd have stopped doing it long ago."

That was logical, but I didn't like it. "All right," I said. "Let's go!"

"Pete!" Wally called. "This time, I want you to hold him very firmly, with both hands. Spread your fingers out as far as possible, and if you can get your forearms on him too, do it. I think you'll learn something—interesting."

A little puzzled, I complied. Helix didn't object, as I thought he might. Wally said, "Okay. They're drawing away now. Get him to lick the bottle."

"All right, Helix," I whispered tightly.

The pink tongue flashed out and back. The bottle tipped the tiniest bit. Then there was a tense silence.

"I ... think ... I'll ... make it ..."

We waited, Helix and I.

Suddenly something deep within me wrenched sickeningly. I almost dropped with the shock of it. And there was a piercing shriek deep within my brain— Wally's shriek, dwindling off into the distance. And faintly, then, there was a rending, tearing sound. It was horrible.

I staggered back and leaned against the lathe, gasping. Helix lay unmoving where I had left him. His sides were pumping in and out violently.

Helix shook himself and came over to me. "Well,"

he said, looking me straight in the eye, "they got your friend."

"Helix! How did you know about that?"

"Why must you be so consistently stupid, Pete? I've known about that all along. I'll give you a little explanation, if you like. It might prove to you that a human being is really a very, very dull creature."

"Go ahead," I gulped.

"You and I have just been a part of a most elaborately amusing compound double cross." He chuckled complacently. "Gregory was right in his assumption that I could not overhear his conversations with you— and a very annoying thing it was, too. I knew there was something off-color somewhere, because I didn't think that you were improving me so vastly just out of the goodness of your heart. But—someone else was listening in, and knew everything."

"Someone else?"

"Certainly. Have you forgotten Them? They were very much interested as to the possibilities of getting hold of our mutual friend Mr. Gregory. Being a lower order of spirit, They found it a simple matter to communicate with me. They asked me to toss Mr. Gregory's soul out to Them." He laughed nastily.

"But I was getting too much out of it. See what a superior creature I am! I told Them to stand by; that They would have a chance at Gregory when I was through using him, and not before. They did as I said, because it was up to me to give what They wanted. That's why They did not interfere during the transfers."

"Why, you heel!" I burst out. "After all Wally did for you, you were going to do that?"

"I wouldn't defend him, if I were you," the cat said precisely. "He was double-crossing you too. I know

all about this soul-replacement business; needn't try
to hide that from me. He was sincere, at first, about
using my body, but he couldn't help thinking that
yours would suit his purpose far better. Though why
he'd prefer it to mine—oh, well. No matter. However,
his idea was to transfer himself from the bottle to me,
and then to you. That's why he told you to hold me
firmly—he wanted a good contact."

"How—how the devil do you know that?"

"He told me himself. After I had reached a satisfac-
tory stage of development, I told him that I was wise.
Oh, yes, I fooled him into developing a communication basis in me! He thought it was a taste for alcohol
he was building up! However, he caught wise in time
to arrest it, but not before it was good enough to
communicate with him. If he'd gone a little farther,
I'd have been able to talk with you that way too. At
any rate, he was a little dampened by my attitude;
knew he'd never get a chance to occupy me. I suggested to him, though, that we join forces in having
him possess *you.*"

*"Me!"* I edged toward the drawer in the bench. "Go
on, Helix."

"You can see why I did this, can't you?" he asked
distantly. "It would have been embarrassing to have
him, a free soul, around where he might conceivably
undo some of the work he had done on me. If he
possessed you, you would be out of the way—They
would take care of that—and he would have what he
wanted. An ideal arrangement. You had no suspicion
of the plan, and he had a good chance of catching
your soul off-guard and ousting it. He knew how to
go about it. Unfortunately for him, your soul was a
little too quick. It was *you* who finally killed Wallace
Gregory, not I. Neat, eh?"

"Yes," I said slowly, pulling the gun out of the drawer and sighting down the barrel, right between his eyes. "Very neat. For a while I thought I'd be sorry to do this. Now, I'm not." I drew a deep breath; Helix did not move. I pulled the trigger four times, and then sagged back against the bench. The strain was too much.

Helix stretched himself and yawned. "I knew you'd try something like that," he said. "I took the trouble of removing the bullets from your gun before the experiment. Nice to have known you!"

I hurled the gun at him but I was too slow. In a flash he was out of the laboratory, streaking for the door. He reached for the knob, opened the door, and was gone before I could take two steps.

There was a worrisome time after that, once I had done all the hysterical things anyone might do—pound out, run left, run right, look up and back and around. But this was a *cat* I was chasing, and you don't catch even an ordinary cat that does not in some way want to be caught.

I wonder why he decided to crack a safe.

No, I don't. I know how his head works. Worked. He had plans for himself—you can be sure of that, and unless I'm completely wrong, he had plans for all of us, ultimately. There have been, in human history, a few people who had the cold, live-in-the-present, me-first attitude of a cat, and humanity has learned a lot of hard lessons from them. But none of them was a cat.

Helix may have made a try or two to get someone to front for him—I wouldn't know. But he was smart enough to know that there was one tool he could use that would work—money. Once he had that, who knows how he would have operated? He could write, he could use a telephone. He would have run a lethal and efficient organization more frightening than anything you or I could imagine.

Well—he won't do it now. As for me, I'll disappear into research again. Flexible glass would be a nice patent to own and enjoy, but thank you, I'm glad to pass on that one.

But Helix . . . damn him, I miss him.

# BETWEEN A CAT AND
# A HARD PLACE

## by Jimmy Vines

This morning, as every morning, Charlie Wainwright woke up sneezing. His swollen and irritated eyes felt like lumps of wet sand that were beginning to dry and harden around the edges. At breakfast he rubbed his itching arms and neck, and tried to taste his Cheerios.

"Now don't forget," his wife Gerta said impatiently, "today's Thursday, time for Slyboots's weekly checkup!"

She kissed the big cat's mouth, then wiped lipstick off its furry chin. "That's right, Slyboots," she said lovingly, "you're going to see nice Dr. Feemer today!" Gerta was a heavy woman of fifty-eight in a blue dress that was too tight in the bosom and too loose everywhere else. She poured the cat out of her arms gently and it nuzzled her puffy ankles. "The appointment's at one o'clock. Don't be late. I will call the vet to make sure you've been there!"

Charlie started to mumble the obligatory, "Yes, dear," around a mouthful of cereal, but a sneeze took the words and sprayed them across the table as globs of mash and milk.

Gerta slammed the door and waddled up the driveway to her car. She had a very busy schedule, forever hurrying between church functions, the bridge club, and local cultural events, so Charlie was always left to take care of her adorable little Slyboots.

The instant Gerta backed her car into the road, Charlie hurled his spoon at the cat. His aim was bad: the spoon whacked the refrigerator. Slyboots scurried away before Charlie could throw anything else. The cat might just as well have walked slowly—because for a whole minute Charlie was immobilized by a harsh sneezing fit.

Charlie was sixty-nine, and he'd had two heart attacks in recent years. A specialist had warned that a third heart attack or even a stroke was very likely, so Charlie took it easy and stayed on his diet and medication. Until fourteen months ago, in spite of his heart problem, things were going fine for Charlie; he'd planned on living a long quiet life.

The turning point came that fine spring day Gerta brought the cat home. Charlie hadn't objected at first, because he didn't think he was allergic to cats. Since he'd never owned a cat, and since friends' cats didn't bother him, the possibility of a latent allergy never crossed his mind. Yet as it happened, something about this cat made Charlie sneeze ceaselessly.

And the sneezing hadn't started the first day; it was only after a couple of weeks, once the house was thoroughly permeated with shedded cat hairs, that Charlie's sinuses awoke and began giving him fits. But by that time Gerta was so attached to her pet that she wouldn't give it up.

Charlie's specialist told him sneezing was bad on the heart, but Charlie already knew that. He felt his heart stammer every time he had a sneezing bout.

Reasoning with Gerta proved futile. She refused to believe that her dear, darling little Slyboots was to blame for Charlie's suffering. She blamed the sneezing on everything else: dust, pollen, the spray deodorant that he used. Gerta would not be coerced into giving the cat away.

But Charlie, out of extreme discomfort and fear for his weak heart, decided to take control of the situation. The cat had to go! One afternoon, after an especially tiresome and fruitless argument about the cat, Gerta left the house to attend one of her various social functions. She'd be gone a few hours, Charlie knew. He put Slyboots outdoors. There was plenty of time for the cat to wander off and never be heard from again. Charlie waited. And waited. And much to his chagrin, the fat feline stayed on the porch, howling the whole time. That evening, when Gerta's car bounced up the driveway, Charlie quickly let the cat back inside before his wife found out what he'd done.

About a week later, after another lost battle of words, when Gerta left the house, Charlie drove the cat to the outskirts of the neighborhood and remorselessly let it out of his car by a thick wooded lot. That night he told Gerta that when he was taking out the trash, Slyboots had slipped past him. He said he'd chased the cat across three neighbors' yards but that Slyboots was just too fast for him, what with his weak heart and all. Gerta scoffed at the story. She accused Charlie of being responsible for the cat's disappearance, and Charlie vehemently denied it. But the crowning hideous thing happened later in a dark hour past midnight: just like one of those famous pets in *Readers Digest,* the cat somehow found its way home and woke a teary-eyed Gerta with its wailing at the back door.

Now the possibility that the cat might "run away" was exhausted. After all, what's better proof of a pet's loyalty than its return after a twelve-hour absence? Suddenly Charlie was faced with the one alternative by which to restore an equilibrium to his life: he had to kill the cat. The way Charlie saw it, if he didn't kill the cat, the cat would kill him.

Taking a cat's life should be simple. But to keep Gerta from divorcing him, and to avoid a lawsuit from the Animal Rights people, Charlie had to make the little murder look as though his furry tormentor died of natural causes. He couldn't leave a mangled corpse. He had to do this carefully.

At ten o'clock one morning, about to take a shower, Charlie reached inside the linen closet for a big fluffy towel. He hadn't seen the cat since breakfast, and in the meantime his sneezing and itching had subsided a little.

Charlie took a towel and started to close the folding doors when a red-brown blur sprang from the shadowy depths of the closet with a *Yowwwwwl,* swiping Charlie's arm loathsomely and scampering away.

"Goddamnit!" Charlie bellowed. The cat disappeared down the hallway with a twitch of its tail. Charlie shook all over, realizing his towel was contaminated with cat hair. He flung the towel down to the floor and kicked it after the cat.

*Control,* he reminded himself. Must keep control. His heart lost its rhythm, and he leaned against the closet doors until danger passed.

Suppressing rage, Charlie grabbed a towel down deep in the stack, one that the cat couldn't possibly have touched. He sneezed violently, and had to pause for a long ten-count before proceeding to the shower.

Over the months, Charlie had thought of many different ways of killing the cat that would position him so that his own innocence could not be doubted. All the methods he devised, except one, were slightly flawed for one reason or another. The plan that he'd finally settled on seemed perfect, and he was now ready to carry it out.

Today was the day.

His plan involved the veterinarian, Nathan Feemer.

The veterinarian was an old family friend. His private office was a small cedar-paneled room with potted plants in the windows and bright prints of well-bred dogs on the walls. With the door closed, the din of the animals in the kennel across the hall quieted to muffled background noise. Behind the desk sat Dr. Nathan Feemer, a solidly built man of sixty, writing something in a file.

"Well, Charlie! I'm happy to say that Slyboots is in tiptop shape. Really," he chuckled, "you ought to tell Gerta that weekly checkups aren't necessary. Don't get me wrong, I'm not trying to turn away business—but once every two months would be more than ample."

Charlie glanced down at the Kitty Kondo which housed Slyboots. He wiped his nose with a handkerchief which he replaced in the pocket of his rumpled brown sportscoat. His silver hair hung limply over his forehead, dangling in his bloodshot eyes. He looked miserable.

Dr. Feemer closed his file and smiled at Charlie.

Charlie squirmed. It suddenly seemed impossible. How could he tell his friend the vet, a man whose life's work was healing pets, that this cat must die? He opened his mouth to speak, but no sound came out.

"I'll bill you as usual," the vet said, blinking slowly behind his thick glasses.

Last week when Charlie had taken the cat for its checkup he wanted to explain the situation and reveal his plan. But instead, he'd stalled and pushed his thoughts to the back of his mind until he was out the door, hating his silence.

Now Charlie drew a breath, gathered his resolve. "I have a problem, Nate. And you're the only one I can turn to," he said. "I mean, this falls in your field of expertise."

The vet rubbed his chin, waited for Charlie to continue. His eyes registered puzzlement, with a hint of intrigue.

Charlie plucked at the hairs on the back of his hand and then blurted: "I've got to—"

The vet's eyes narrowed.

"I've got to kill my wife's cat!" He saw that his fists were clenched.

The vet was taken by surprise. "What did you say?"

"I'VE GOT TO KILL MY WIFE'S CAT!"

Nate seemed flustered. "*Kill* the—?" His eyes ticked about the room. "Whatever for? Why—why would anyone want to kill a dear pet?"

"Dear pet!" Charlie pulled out his handkerchief just in time, and sneezed into it. His face crimsoned; he felt hot all over. Irritably swiping cat hair from his lapels, he stood up and began pacing—and the whole story tumbled out.

Afterwards, in the silence that followed, Charlie groped for his chair and sat, a bewildered expression on his face, as if he'd just woken from a nap and didn't know quite where he was.

The vet cleared his throat and took a moment, and when he spoke it was with studied patience, as if he were explaining the game of Tic-Tac-Toe to an imbecile. "I can't just haul Slyboots into the operating room and make a mistake for you. It would jeopardize my whole practice."

"I wasn't suggesting that *you* kill him, Nate!"

"I'm sorry, I won't offer any advice on how to kill him either."

"I've thought it all out," Charlie said. "I've looked at it from every angle!" Charlie shoved the plastic Kitty Kondo with his foot. His voice dropped to nearly a whisper. "I can't shoot the cat—how would I explain the bloody little corpse? And besides, the bang of the pistol, even if I was prepared for it, might be too much for my heart. Can't poison his food because Gerta opens a fresh can of cat food for each of his meals. Strangling is no good because I'd get clawed and bitten, and might end up breaking his furry neck."

There was a pause. Slyboots scratched at the walls of his Kitty Kondo.

"You're my only hope." Charlie's hands fluttered helplessly. "You put animals to sleep all the time. You do it by injection, don't you?"

"I've already said I won't be party to this."

Charlie smacked his thigh once, hard. *"Don't you give a cat an injection to put it to sleep?"*

"Yes!" Now the vet's hands were fluttering. "But that is irrelevant because I'll not—"

"Give me a hypodermic!" Charlie was wild-eyed. "I'll do it myself, at home!"

The doctor stood abruptly. "Good day, Charles." He pointed to the door.

"Please! I'll pay you! I'll—"

"I said, good day!"

The office door opened, and a pretty young red-haired nurse leaned in. "The O.R.'s ready, Doctor."

Nathan Feemer's frosty eyes thawed at the sight of the young nurse.

Charlie noticed this, and then he listened closely for subtle nuances in the doctor's vocal tones.

"Yes, Suzanne," Feemer said, "I—I'll be with you in a moment." She withdrew, closing the door quietly. A fresh tantalizing trace of perfume lingered in the office. The veterinarian stared at the door, seemingly lost in thought, his eyes blank blue orbs.

Charlie swiveled in his chair. He made some quick calculations, and what he calculated made his blood run hot. He'd thought his old friend would understand and help him. But now he saw that Nate would have to be forced. In past visits Charlie noticed the intimacy with which Nate and his nurse spoke; but now, with the scent of her perfume fresh in his nostrils, Charlie was ready to explore the issue. It was Charlie's reserve ammunition, his last resort.

He stretched out, propping his feet on the Kitty Kondo, as if to stay awhile longer. Looking at his friend Nathan Feemer, he cackled.

The glassy look in the vet's eyes shattered.

Charlie then dealt his trump card, the one he'd held so close to his vest until just the right moment. He accused Nathan Feemer of marital infidelity.

Feemer was thrown. His chin jiggled as he blubbered a flimsy denial. The vet marched around his desk, jaw clenched. He jerked the door open and demanded that Charlie leave.

But like a swordsman who has disarmed his opponent and sent him sprawling on the flagstones, Charlie chuckled victoriously. Riding a swell of bravado, the same feeling that drives a swaggering swordsman to tickle the fallen man's throat with the blade until a trace of blood seeps forth, Charlie made it clear that he was not above planting seeds of evidence that would arouse a wife's suspicions.

At that moment the men were interrupted: the nurse's voice, light and pure-sounding, floated down the hall. "You coming, Nate?"

Nate whined, *whined*, down deep in his throat; checked himself. "Yes, yes, Nurse Summerton," he said. His voice was too even. "Just a moment." He shut the door and thrust fists in his pockets. "What do you want from me?"

"I already told you, Nate. A hypo. Simple little hypo. I know you've got one around here somewhere." Charlie pitched forward and sneezed.

Dr. Feemer turned to the wall, and then to Charlie, and then turned away again. He was quietly livid. "You don't honestly think I can be bribed."

YES! Charlie wanted to say, but he did not. What he said, after pursing his lips thoughtfully, was: "*Bribed?* A bad word choice, Nate. That cancels any doubts I might have had about your illicit little tête-à-tête with Nurse—Summerton, is it? Now, I'll have that hypo."

"This is criminal!"

Charlie smiled up at the veterinarian, and snuffled. "Since when is killing a cat against the law?" He rubbed his watery eyes.

The doctor paced a moment. He looked at Charlie; looked at the door. His shoulders drooped defeatedly. Then he took a key from his desk drawer. Pulling on his white lab coat, he mumbled, "Wait here."

When the vet returned to the office, Charlie was scratching under his collar, but he was a happy man. The vet produced a small clear hypodermic from a big pocket in his lab coat. "Won't she get another cat, Charlie? To replace the first?"

"No, I've already figured that out." Charlie's red-rimmed eyes sparkled when he spoke. His voice trembled enthusiastically. "I'll remind her psychologists say it's very unhealthy to get a pet that's even remotely similar to a recently deceased pet. We'll get a canary or something. A goldfish. I don't know. But we won't have a cat!"

Feemer held the syringe up to the light and looked through it. A protective plastic cap sheathed the needle. "You've obviously thought this through in every detail."

"Oh yes. Yes." Charlie Wainwright's face was that of a child's sitting on Santa's lap the day before Christmas. "I know what I want. Give me the needle."

"You didn't get this from me. I'll deny it to my last gasp."

"I know! I know!"

The vet was tense and pale. "Sodium pentobarbital. The best place to inject is in the abdomen, and deep. Too shallow and you put the poison in the fatty areas around its stomach. Takes longer to work that way—a minute or so. Push the needle to the hilt and it'll take just seconds."

"Okay. Okay," Charlie said, pocketing the hypo.

"And don't uncap the needle until you're ready to use it. You don't want to stick yourself, you know."

"Righto," Charlie said, grabbing the handle of the Kitty Kondo and heading for the door. Slyboots growled.

"Er—one more thing, Charlie," the doctor said shamefacedly, wringing his hands. "Is it—are we, Suzanne and I—really that obvious?"

"The secret is safe with me," Charlie said with a wink.

That night Charlie was in his favorite chair, a brown vinyl recliner to which cat hair would not cling, when

Gerta came in the front door after an evening at the theater. She wore a maroon felt hat with a gigantic brim, a dark velvety dress, ropes of fake pearls, and an antique fox stole. She chattered noisily as she crossed the room. "The play was an *abomination,* Charles. Really, you should have seen it. When the poor dreadful actors weren't dropping props they were dropping lines. You ever heard anybody improvise Shakespeare?"

"Glad you had a nice time, dear," Charlie said behind his newspaper.

The cat ambled into the den from some other part of the house, fat and slow. It crossed between Gerta's ankles, rubbing against her vein-corded legs, shedding reddish brown hairs on her white stockings.

How hard it had been for Charlie not to launch the cat into eternity before Gerta got home! But if she'd come home to find the cat dead, no amount of feigned sorrow on Charlie's part would have been enough to fully convince her that he hadn't played a part in the cat's untimely demise. He'd stretched his willpower to the limit, reminding himself that it would be only a few hours. He would do the deed while Gerta—and supposedly he—was asleep.

"*Othello* was a torture! They had a Chinese woman playing the title part, of all things. Have you ever heard of such?" She flung her big hat and tiny clasp purse on the couch. "That's right, Slyboots."

Charlie grimaced at the sound of the cat's name.

Gerta buried her face in the cat's long red fur, and went to the kitchen. "Let's get you something to eat, and then you and Mommy are going beddiebye. I'll give you your dinner in bed. You like that, don't you, Slyboots? Hm?"

Charlie could picture the cat licking one of Gerta's

many chins. And even as the thought came to him, he heard Gerta giggle.

"Stop that, Sly. You know I'm ticklish!"

A minute later, Gerta came through the den with an open can of cat food and a spoon. Slyboots, in her arms, batted at the nose of the dead fox that hung around Gerta's neck. "You coming with us?" Gerta asked her husband.

"In a little while, sweets," he said, reaching out and patting the cat between the ears.

"Come on, Sly," Gerta crooned, going down the hallway. "We'll have dinner and then you and Mommy will snuggle up and go to sleep . . ."

Charlie waited until her voice died away before he allowed himself to sneeze. He sneezed three times, each more explosive than the last. After it was over, he wiped his runny eyes and nose, and sat still as his heart whacked against his ribs. Willing himself to relax, he closed his eyes until his heart slowed to its normal pace.

Everything was perfect. He'd shown no antagonism toward the shedding red beast; he'd even been kind to it. He was sure Gerta noticed the gentle pat, and would remember it. This was just the position he wanted to be in before the cat's stiffening body was found in the morning.

Earlier today he'd taken a pair of gardening gloves from the tool room and stowed them in the very back of the linen closet, under plenty of towels. The gloves would afford protection from getting scratched in the process of plunging the needle into the cat. He didn't want to have to explain scratches in the morning.

Three hours passed. It usually took Gerta a long time to fall asleep. Charlie couldn't concentrate on the newspaper, but he dared not turn on the television.

He didn't want the noise to bother Gerta or the cat and keep either from sleeping. He read the same comics page again and again, not taking in a word of it, not cracking a smile.

At two A.M. he rose slowly from the chair. His heart skipped along at a rather fast rate, but he didn't let it upset him. He simply stood in place until it slowed a fraction. Then he stepped into the dark hall and opened the doors of the linen closet.

Gloves on, hypodermic in hand, he advanced to the bedroom door. It was open, and the room was very dark. He let his eyes adjust. Blue moonlight through the gauzy drapes gave the room an otherworldly glow. Charlie stood at the foot of the bed looking at his wife, who was rolled into a comfortable ball on one side of the bed. Beside her, on the nightstand, Charlie saw the half-finished can of cat food which, as always, would be scraped down the garbage disposal in the morning. Under her arms, a lumpy form. The cat? How could he inject the cat if it was wrapped so intimately against its mother's bosom?

But on closer examination Charlie saw that Gerta was not holding the cat. It was a pillow she was suffocating in her sleep. Charlie moved around the foot of the bed, his eyes wide in search of the cat.

There, on a chair next to the bed, not a yard from the opened can of cat food, Charlie's eyes found the form they sought. The creature had assumed the pose of its mother, head tucked down, front legs wrapped under its chin, deep in a world of dreams.

Charlie's heart flopped and hung quiet for an instant too long. He shut his eyes and stood perfectly still until the moment passed. When he opened his eyes again, he checked Gerta; she was still in a knot on the bed. His victim hadn't moved either.

He went across the floor on his knees. The carpet whispered beneath him. For fear of waking the beast, he breathed shallowly. In one practiced motion he took the cap off the needle and placed it between his teeth. Now at the chair, he leaned in.

But Charlie recoiled suddenly, his back high, straight. He was going to sneeze. His free hand covered his nose, pinched it tight. The glove leather tickled his nostrils and he sneezed silently, keeping the sound deep inside his chest. Once. Twice. The needle shook in the moonlight. Had Gerta moved? Not an inch. The cat? Quiet as ever. Relieved, Charlie dropped his shoulders and hesitated, listening to his heart until it was regular, before leaning over the chair again.

Swiftly, surprising himself, Charlie clamped his hand over the cat's head to keep the mouth from opening with a screech as the hand with the needle swept into the beast from underneath—careful to avoid pinning the seat cushion by mistake—and pressed the plunger home. He shivered at the crucial moment, but he would not let himself be betrayed by his own body. He held the needle in place until he was calm again— had the cat kicked?—and froze for two minutes. Removing the drained hypo, he stood, a fine sheen of sweat on his forehead.

He backed away, glancing over his shoulder, careful not to bump into anything on his way out. Then he turned out of the room and walked down the hall, capping the needle with a trembling hand. Victory!

Charlie replaced the leather gloves in the linen closet for removal tomorrow, and went to the kitchen. In the trash can under the sink was the cardboard milk carton he'd emptied and placed there early in the evening. He dropped the syringe in the carton and closed the mouth of it. Rooting down into the mess of egg shells, coffee grinds, and cat food cans, Charlie interred the milk carton with its hidden evidence. He washed his hands under the faucet and dried them on the handtowel, making sure he left no bits of debris on the towel.

He stood at the counter awhile, quivering with an overwhelming happiness. The oven clock ticked in rhythm with his heartbeat. Though his heart had been through some terrible strains that night, Charlie wasn't going to take any more of his pills. He'd already had the prescribed daily dose, and besides, now that his work was accomplished, wouldn't he go to bed with a light heart? He already felt better than he had in a long, long time.

He took several deep relaxing breaths, and drank a glass of water. Then he went to the den and flopped down in his favorite chair to read the comics. He was sure they'd be funny this time. He'd enjoy himself a little before going to bed.

Charlie shook the paper to straighten it, and beamed at the antics of the cartoon characters. Where did those guys get their ideas? He laughed out loud, and then reminded himself to stay quiet. He'd go to bed soon.

And then suddenly the bottom edge of the newspaper crinkled, and a furry red form sprang into Charlie's lap. The cat! For a full four seconds he stared with horror and disbelief at the beast as it walked in circles looking for a place to sit. Charlie started to sneeze, but instead—he screamed.

The next day, as Gerta made her way through the group of mourners who'd assembled themselves in her living room, one of the ladies from church, a tiny twig of a woman, took Gerta aside to give her personal regards. She said how sorry she was that Charlie's heart gave out on him so suddenly, and how good Gerta looked in spite of everything.

Gerta smiled sadly, and hugged her cat Slyboots closer. "Yes," she said, "Charlie was a dear heart. We sure will miss him."

The twig woman commented on Gerta's fox stole, and wondered aloud why people didn't wear them much anymore.

Gerta said they were coming back in style, you just watch and see. Then, fingering the fox fur absently, she withdrew her hand and said, "Ugh! Looks like I've got to get this thing cleaned. Somehow the fur's gotten all damp and sticky!"

# THE EMPTY BIRDHOUSE
## by Patricia Highsmith

The first time Edith saw it she laughed, not believing her eyes.

She stepped to one side and looked again; it was still there, but a bit dimmer. A squirrel-like face—but demonic in its intensity—looked out at her from the round hole in the birdhouse. An illusion, of course, something to do with shadows, or a knot in the wood of the back wall of the birdhouse. The sunlight fell plain on the six-by-nine-inch birdhouse in the corner made by the toolshed and the brick wall of the garden. Edith went closer, until she was only ten feet away. The face disappeared.

That was funny, she thought as she went back into the cottage. She would have to tell Charles tonight.

But she forgot to tell Charles.

Three days later she saw the face again. This time she was straightening up after having set two empty milk bottles on the back doorstep. A pair of beady black eyes looked out at her, straight and level, from the birdhouse, and they appeared to be surrounded by brownish fur. Edith flinched, then stood rigid. She thought she saw two rounded ears, a mouth that was neither animal nor bird, simply grim and cruel.

But she knew that the birdhouse was empty. The bluetit family had flown away weeks ago, and it had been a narrow squeak for the baby bluetits as the Masons' cat next door had been interested; the cat could reach the hole from the toolshed roof with a paw, and Charles had made the hole a trifle too big for bluetits. But Edith and Charles had staved Jonathan off until the birds were well away. Afterward, days later, Charles had taken the birdhouse down—it hung like a picture on a wire from a nail—and shaken it to make sure no debris was inside. Bluetits might nest a second time, he said. But they hadn't as yet—Edith was sure because she had kept watching.

And squirrels never nested in birdhouses. Or did they? At any rate, there were no squirrels around. Rats? They would never choose a birdhouse for a home. How could they get in, anyway, without flying?

While these thoughts went through Edith's mind, she stared at the intense brown face, and the piercing black eyes stared back at her.

"I'll simply go and see what it is," Edith thought, and stepped onto the path that led to the toolshed. But she went only three paces and stopped. She didn't want to touch the birdhouse and get bitten—maybe by a dirty rodent's tooth. She'd tell Charles tonight. But now that she was closer, the thing was still there, clearer than ever. It wasn't an optical illusion.

Her husband Charles Beaufort, a computing engineer, worked at a plant eight miles from where they lived. He frowned slightly and smiled when Edith told him what she had seen. "Really?" he said.

"I *may* be wrong. I wish you'd shake the thing again and see if there's anything in it," Edith said, smiling herself now, though her tone was earnest.

"All right, I will," Charles said quickly, then began to talk of something else. They were then in the middle of dinner.

Edith had to remind him when they were putting the dishes into the washing machine. She wanted him to look before it became dark. So Charles went out, and Edith stood on the doorstep, watching. Charles tapped on the birdhouse, listened with one ear cocked. He took the birdhouse down from the nail, shook it, then slowly tipped it so the hole was on the bottom. He shook it again.

"Absolutely nothing," he called to Edith, "not even a piece of straw." He smiled broadly at his wife and hung the birdhouse back on the nail. "I wonder what you could've seen? You hadn't had a couple of Scotches, had you?"

"*No.* I described it to you." Edith felt suddenly blank, deprived of something. "It had a head a little larger than a squirrel's, beady black eyes, and a sort of serious mouth."

"Serious mouth!" Charles put his head back and laughed as he came back into the house.

"A tense mouth. It had a grim look," Edith said positively.

But she said nothing else about it. They sat in the living room, Charles looking over the newspaper, then opening his folder of reports from the office. Edith had a catalogue and was trying to choose a tile pattern for the kitchen wall. Blue and white, or pink and white and blue? She was not in a mood to decide, and Charles was never a help, always saying agreeably, "Whatever you like is all right with me."

Edith was thirty-four. She and Charles had been married seven years. In the second year of their marriage Edith had lost the child she was carrying. She had lost it rather deliberately, being in a panic about giving birth. That was to say, her fall down the stairs had been rather on purpose, if she were willing to admit it, but the miscarriage had been put down as the result of an accident. She had never tried to have another child, and she and Charles had never even discussed it.

She considered herself and Charles a happy couple. Charles was doing well with Pan-Com Instruments, and they had more money and more freedom than several of their neighbors who were tied down with two or more children. They both liked entertaining, Edith in their house especially, and Charles on their boat, a thirty-foot motor launch which slept four. They plied the local river and inland canals on most weekends when the weather was good. Edith could cook almost as well afloat as on shore, and Charles obliged with drinks, fishing equipment, and the record player. He would also dance a hornpipe on request.

During the week-end that followed—not a boating week-end because Charles had extra work—Edith glanced several times at the empty birdhouse, reassured now because she *knew* there was nothing in it. When the sunlight shone on it she saw nothing but a paler brown in the round hole, the back of the birdhouse; and when in shadow the hole looked black.

On Monday afternoon, as she was changing the bedsheets in time for the laundryman who came at three, she saw something slip from under a blanket that she picked up from the floor. Something ran across the floor and out the door—something brown and larger than a squirrel. Edith gasped and dropped the blanket. She tiptoed to the bedroom door, looked into the hall and on the stairs, the first five steps of which she could see.

What kind of animal made no noise at all, even on bare wooden stairs? Or had she really seen anything? But she was sure she had. She'd even had a glimpse of the small black eyes. It was the same animal she had seen looking out of the birdhouse.

The only thing to do was to find it, she told herself. She thought at once of the hammer as a weapon in case of need, but the hammer was downstairs. She took a heavy book instead and went cautiously down the stairs, alert and looking everywhere as her vision widened at the foot of the stairs.

There was nothing in sight in the living room. But it could be under the sofa or the armchair. She went into the kitchen and got the hammer from a drawer. Then she returned to the living room and shoved the armchair quickly some three feet. Nothing. She found she was afraid to bend down to look under the sofa, whose cover came almost to the floor, but she pushed it a few inches and listened. Nothing.

It *might* have been a trick of her eyes, she supposed. Something like a spot floating before the eyes, after bending over the bed. She decided not to say anything to Charles about it. Yet in a way, what she had seen in the bedroom had been more definite than what she had seen in the birdhouse.

A baby yuma, she thought an hour later as she was sprinkling flour on a joint in the kitchen. A yuma. Now, where had that come from? Did such an animal exist? Had she seen a photograph of one in a magazine, or read the word somewhere?

Edith made herself finish all she intended to do in the kitchen, then went to the big dictionary and looked up the word yuma. It was not in the dictionary. A trick of her mind, she thought. Just as the animal was probably a trick of her eyes. But it was strange how they went together, as if the name were absolutely correct for the animal.

Two days later, as she and Charles were carrying

their coffee cups into the kitchen, Edith saw it dart from under the refrigerator—or from behind the refrigerator—diagonally across the kitchen threshold and into the dining room. She almost dropped her cup and saucer, but caught them, and they chattered in her hands.

"What's the matter?" Charles asked.

"I saw it again!" Edith said. "The animal."

"What?"

"I didn't tell you," she began with a suddenly dry throat, as if she were making a painful confession. "I think I saw that thing—the thing that was in the birdhouse—upstairs in the bedroom on Monday. And I think I saw it again. Just now."

"Edith, my darling, there wasn't anything in the birdhouse."

"Not when you looked. But this animal moves quickly. It almost flies."

Charles's face grew more concerned. He looked where she was looking, at the kitchen threshold. "You saw it just now? I'll go look," he said, and walked into the dining room.

He gazed around on the floor, glanced at his wife, then rather casually bent and looked under the table among the chair legs. "Really, Edith—"

"Look in the living room," Edith said.

Charles did, for perhaps fifteen seconds, then he came back, smiling a little. "Sorry to say this, old girl, but I think you're seeing things. Unless, of course, it was a mouse. We might have mice. I hope not."

"Oh, it's much bigger. And it's brown. Mice are gray."

"Yep," Charles said vaguely. "Well, don't worry, dear, it's not going to attack you. It's running." He added in a voice quite devoid of conviction, "If necessary, we'll get an exterminator."

"Yes," she said at once.

"How big is it?"

She held her hands apart at a distance of about sixteen inches. "This big."

"Sounds like it might be a ferret," he said.

"It's even quicker. And it has black eyes. Just now it stopped just for an instant and looked straight at me. Honestly, Charles." Her voice had begun to shake. She pointed to the spot by the refrigerator. "Just there it stopped for a split second and—"

"Edith, get a grip on yourself." He pressed her arm.

"It looks so evil. I can't tell you."

Charles was silent, looking at her.

"Is there any animal called a yuma?" she asked.

"A yuma? I've never heard of it. Why?"

"Because the name came to me today out of nowhere. I thought—because I'd thought of it and I'd never seen an animal like this that maybe I'd seen it somewhere."

"Y-u-m-a?"

Edith nodded.

Charles, smiling again because it was turning into a funny game, went to the dictionary as Edith had done and looked for the word. He closed the dictionary and went to the Encyclopaedia Britannica on the bottom shelves of the bookcase. After a minute's search he said to Edith, "Not in the dictionary and not in the Britannica either. I think it's a word you made up." And he laughed. "Or maybe it's a word in *Alice in Wonderland.*"

It's a real word, Edith thought, but she didn't have the courage to say so. Charles would deny it.

Edith felt done in and went to bed around ten with

her book. But she was still reading when Charles came in just before eleven. At that moment both of them saw it: it flashed from the foot of the bed across the carpet, in plain view of Edith and Charles, went under the chest of drawers and, Edith thought, out the door. Charles must have thought so, too, as he turned quickly to look into the hall.

"You saw it!" Edith said.

Charles's face was stiff. He turned the light on in the hall, looked, then went down the stairs.

He was gone perhaps three minutes, and Edith heard him pushing furniture about. Then he came back.

"Yes, I saw it." His face looked suddenly pale and tired.

But Edith sighed and almost smiled, glad that he finally believed her. "You see what I mean now. I wasn't seeing things."

"No." Charles agreed.

Edith was sitting up in bed. "The awful thing is, it looks uncatchable."

Charles began to unbutton his shirt. "Uncatchable. What a word. Nothing's uncatchable. Maybe it's a ferret. Or a squirrel."

"Couldn't you tell? It went right by you."

"Well!" He laughed. "It *was* pretty fast. You've seen it two or three times and you can't tell what it is."

"Did it have a tail? I can't tell if it had or if that's the whole body—that length."

Charles kept silent. He reached for his dressing gown, slowly put it on "I think it's smaller than it looks. It is fast, so it seems elongated. Might be a squirrel."

"The eyes are in the front of its head. Squirrels' eyes are sort of at the side."

Charles stooped at the foot of the bed and looked under it. He ran his hand over the tucked foot of the bed underneath. Then he stood up. "Look, if we see it again—*if* we saw it—"

"What do you mean *if*? You did see it—you said so."

"I *think* so." Charles laughed. "How do I know my eyes or my mind isn't playing a trick on me? Your description was so eloquent." He sounded almost angry with her.

"Well—*if*?"

"If we see it again, we'll borrow a cat. A cat'll find it."

"Not the Masons' cat. I'd hate to ask them."

They had had to throw pebbles at the Masons' cat to keep it away when the bluetits were starting to fly. The Masons hadn't liked that. They were still on good terms with the Masons, but neither Edith nor Charles would have dreamed of asking to borrow Jonathan.

"We could call in an exterminator," Edith said.

"Ha! And what'll we ask him to look for?"

"What we saw," Edith said, annoyed because it was Charles who had suggested an exterminator just a couple of hours before. She was interested in the conversation, vitally interested, yet it depressed her. She felt it was vague and hopeless, and she wanted to lose herself in sleep.

"Let's try a cat," Charles said. "You know, Farrow has a cat. He got it from the people next door to him. You know, Farrow the accountant who lives on Shanley Road? He took the cat over when the people next door moved. But his wife doesn't like cats, he says. This one—"

"I'm not mad about cats either," Edith said. "We don't want to acquire a cat."

"No. All right. But I'm sure we could borrow this one, and the reason I thought of it is that Farrow says the cat's a marvelous hunter. It's a female nine years old, he says."

Charles came home with the cat the next evening, thirty minutes later than usual, because he had gone home with Farrow to fetch it. He and Edith closed the doors and the windows, then let the cat out of its basket in the living room. The cat was white with gray brindle markings and a black tail. She stood stiffly, looking all around her with a glum and somewhat disapproving air.

"Ther-re, Puss-Puss," Charles said, stooping but not touching her. "You're only going to be here a day or two. Have we got some milk, Edith? Or better yet, cream."

They made a bed for the cat out of a carton, put an old towel in it, then placed it in a corner of the living room, but the cat preferred the end of the sofa. She had explored the house perfunctorily and had shown no interest in the cupboards or closets, though Edith and Charles had hoped she would. Edith said she thought the cat was too old to be of much use in catching anything.

The next morning Mrs. Farrow rang up Edith and told her that they could keep Puss-Puss if they wanted to. "She's a clean cat and very healthy. I just don't happen to like cats. So if you take to her—or she takes to you—"

Edith wriggled out by an unusually fluent burst of thanks and explanations of why they had borrowed the cat, and she promised to ring Mrs. Farrow in a couple of days. Edith said she thought they had mice, but were not sure enough to call in an exterminator. This verbal effort exhausted her.

The cat spent most of her time sleeping either at the end of the sofa or on the foot of the bed upstairs, which Edith didn't care for but endured rather than alienate the cat. She even spoke affectionately to the cat and carried her to the open doors of closets, but Puss-Puss always stiffened slightly, not with fear but with boredom, and immediately turned away. Meanwhile she ate well of tuna, which the Farrows had prescribed.

Edith was polishing silver at the kitchen table on Friday afternoon when she saw the thing run straight beside her on the floor—from behind her, out the kitchen door into the dining room like a brown rocket. And she saw it turn to the right into the living room where the cat lay asleep.

Edith stood up at once and went to the living-room door. No sign of it now, and the cat's head still rested on her paws. The cat's eyes were closed. Edith's heart was beating fast. Her fear mingled with impatience and for an instant she experienced a sense of chaos and terrible disorder. The animal was in the room! And the cat was of no use at all! And the Wilsons were coming to dinner at seven o'clock. And she'd hardly have time to speak to Charles about it because he'd be washing and changing, and she couldn't, wouldn't mention it in front of the Wilsons, though they knew the Wilsons quite well. As Edith's chaos became frustration, tears burned her eyes. She imagined herself jumpy and awkward all evening, dropping things, and unable to say what was wrong.

"The yuma. The damned yuma!" she said softly and bitterly, then went back to the silver and doggedly finished polishing it and set the table.

The dinner, however, went quite well, and nothing was dropped or burned. Christopher Wilson and his

wife Frances lived on the other side of the village, and
had two boys, seven and five. Christopher was a law-
yer for Pan-Com.

"You're looking a little peaked, Charles," Christopher said. "How about you and Edith joining us on
Sunday?" He glanced at his wife. "We're going for a
swim at Hadden and then for a picnic. Just us and the
kids. Lots of fresh air."

"Oh—" Charles waited for Edith to decline, but she
was silent. "Thanks very much. As for me—well, we'd
thought of taking the boat somewhere. But we've borrowed a cat, and I don't think we should leave her
alone all day."

"A cat?" asked Frances Wilson. "Borrowed it?"

"Yes. We thought we might have mice and wanted
to find out," Edith put in with a smile.

Frances asked a question or two about the cat and
then the subject was dropped. Puss-Puss at that moment was upstairs, Edith thought. She always went
upstairs when a new person came into the house.

Later when the Wilsons had left, Edith told Charles
about seeing the animal again in the kitchen, and
about the unconcern of Puss-Puss.

"That's the trouble. It doesn't make any noise,"
Charles said. Then he frowned. "Are you *sure* you
saw it?"

"Just as sure as I am that I ever saw it," Edith said.

"Let's give the cat a couple of more days,"
Charles said.

The next morning, Saturday, Edith came downstairs
around nine to start breakfast and stopped short at
what she saw on the living-room floor. It was the
yuma, dead, mangled at head and tail and abdomen.
In fact, the tail was chewed off except for a damp stub
about two inches long. And as for the head, there was

none. But the fur was brown, almost black where it was damp with blood.

Edith turned and ran up the stairs.

"Charles!"

He was awake, but sleepy. "What?"

"The cat caught it. It's in the living room. Come down, will you?—I can't face it, I really can't."

"Certainly, dear," Charles said, throwing off the covers.

He was downstairs a few seconds later. Edith followed him.

"Um. Pretty big," he said.

"What is it?"

"I dunno. I'll get the dustpan." He went into the kitchen.

Edith hovered, watching him push it onto the dustpan with a rolled newspaper. He peered at the gore, a chewed windpipe, bones. The feet had little claws.

"What is it? A ferret?" Edith asked.

"I dunno. I really don't." Charles wrapped the thing quickly in a newspaper. "I'll get rid of it in the ashcan. Monday's garbage day, isn't it?"

Edith didn't answer.

Charles went through the kitchen and she heard the lid of the ashcan rattle outside the kitchen door.

"Where's the cat?" she asked when he came in again.

He was washing his hands at the kitchen sink. "I don't know." He got the floor mop and brought it into the living room. He scrubbed the spot where the animal had lain. "Not much blood. I don't see any here, in fact."

While they were having breakfast, the cat came in through the front door, which Edith had opened to air the living room—although she had not noticed any smell. The cat looked at them in a tired way, barely raised her head, and said, "Mi-o-ow," the first sound she had uttered since her arrival.

"Good pussy!" Charles said with enthusiasm. "Good Puss-Puss!"

But the cat ducked from under his congratulatory hand that would have stroked her back and went on slowly into the kitchen for her breakfast of tuna.

Charles glanced at Edith with a smile which she tried to return. She had barely finished her egg, but could not eat a bite more of her toast.

She took the car and did her shopping in a fog, greeting familiar faces as she always did, yet she felt no contact between herself and other people When she came home, Charles was lying on the bed, fully dressed, his hands behind his head.

"I wondered where you were," Edith said.

"I felt drowsy. Sorry." He sat up.

"Don't be sorry. If you want a nap, take one."

"I was going to get the cobwebs out of the garage and give it a good sweeping." He got to his feet. "But aren't you glad it's gone, dear—whatever it was?" he asked, forcing a laugh.

"Of course. Yes, God knows." But she still felt depressed, and she sensed that Charlie did, too. She stood hesitantly in the doorway. "I just wonder what it was." If we'd only seen the head, she thought, but couldn't say it. Wouldn't the head turn up, inside or outside the house? The cat couldn't have eaten the skull.

"Something like a ferret," Charles said. "We can give the cat back now, if you like."

But they decided to wait till tomorrow to ring the Farrows.

Now Puss-Puss seemed to smile when Edith looked

at her. It was a weary smile, or was the weariness only in the eyes? After all, the cat was nine. Edith glanced at the cat many times as she went about her chores that week-end. The cat had a different air, as if she had done her duty and knew it, but took no particular pride in it.

In a curious way Edith felt that the cat was in alliance with the yuma, or whatever animal it had been—was or had been in alliance. They were both animals and had understood each other, one the enemy and stronger, the other the prey. And the cat had been able to see it, perhaps hear it too, and had been able to get her claws into it. Above all, the cat was not afraid as she was and even Charles was, Edith felt. At the same time she was thinking this, Edith realized that she disliked the cat. It had a gloomy, secretive look. The cat didn't really like them, either.

Edith had intended to phone the Farrows around three on Sunday afternoon, but Charles went to the telephone himself and told Edith he was going to call them. Edith dreaded hearing even Charles's part of the conversation, but she sat on with the Sunday papers on the sofa, listening.

Charles thanked them profusely and said the cat had caught something like a large squirrel or a ferret. But they really didn't want to keep the cat, nice as she was, and could they bring her over, say around six? "But—well, the job's done, you see, and we're awfully grateful .. I'll definitely ask at the plant if there's anyone who'd like a nice cat."

Charles loosened his collar after he put the telephone down. "Whew! That was tough—I felt like a heel! But after all, there's no use saying we want the cat when we don't. Is there?"

"Certainly not. But we ought to take them a bottle of wine or something, don't you think?"

"Oh, definitely. What a good idea! Have we got any?"

They hadn't any. There was nothing in the way of unopened drink but a bottle of whiskey, which Edith proposed cheerfully.

"They did do us a big favor," Edith said.

Charles smiled. "That they did!" He wrapped the bottle in one of the green tissues in which their liquor store delivered bottles and set out with Puss-Puss in her basket.

Edith had said she did not care to go, but to be sure to give her thanks to the Farrows. Then Edith sat down on the sofa and tried to read the newspapers, but found her thoughts wandering. She looked around the empty, silent room, looked at the foot of the stairs and through the dining-room door.

It was gone now, the yuma baby. Why she thought it was a baby, she didn't know. A baby *what*? But she had always thought of it as young—and at the same time as cruel, and knowing about all the cruelty and evil in the world, the animal world and the human world. And its neck had been severed by a cat. They had not found the head.

She was still sitting on the sofa when Charles came back.

He came into the living room with a slow step and slumped into the armchair. "Well—they didn't exactly want to take her back."

"What do you mean?"

"It isn't their cat, you know. They only took her on out of kindness—or something—when the people next door left. They were going to Australia and couldn't take the cat with them. The cat sort of hangs around the two houses there, but the Farrows feed her. It's sad."

Edith shook her head involuntarily. "I really didn't like the cat. It's too old for a new home, isn't it?"

"I suppose so. Well, at least she isn't going to starve with the Farrows. Can we have a cup of tea, do you think? I'd rather have that than a drink."

And Charles went to bed early, after rubbing his right shoulder with liniment. Edith knew he was afraid of his bursitis or rheumatism starting.

"I'm getting old," Charles said to her. "Anyway, I feel old tonight."

So did Edith. She also felt melancholy. Standing at the bathroom mirror, she thought the little lines under her eyes looked deeper. The day had been a strain, for a Sunday. But the horror was out of the house. That was something. She had lived under it for nearly a fortnight.

Now that the yuma was dead, she realized what the trouble had been, or she could now admit it. The yuma had opened up the past, and it had been like a dark and frightening gorge. It had brought back the time when she had lost her child—on purpose—and it had recalled Charles's bitter chagrin then, his pretended indifference later. It had brought back her guilt. And she wondered if the animal had done the same thing to Charles? He hadn't been entirely noble in his early days at Pan-Com. He had told the truth about a man to a superior, the man had been dismissed—Charles had got his job—and the man had later committed suicide. Simpson. Charles had shrugged at the time. But had the yuma reminded him of Simpson? No person, no adult in the world, had a perfectly honorable past, a past without some crime in it . . .

Less than a week later, Charles was watering the

roses one evening when he saw an animal's face in the hole of the birdhouse. It was the same face as the other animal's, or the face Edith had described to him, though he had never had such a good look at it as this.

There were the bright, fixed black eyes, the grim little mouth, the terrible alertness of which Edith had told him. The hose, forgotten in his hands, shot water straight out against the brick wall. He dropped the hose, and turned toward the house to cut the water off, intending to take the birdhouse down at once and see what was in it; but, he thought at the same time, the birdhouse wasn't big enough to hold such an animal as Puss-Puss had caught. That was certain.

Charles was almost at the house, running, when he saw Edith standing in the doorway.

She was looking at the birdhouse. "There it is *again*!"

"Yes." Charles turned off the water. "This time I'll see what it is."

He started for the birdhouse at a trot, but midway he stopped, staring toward the gate.

Through the open iron gate came Puss-Puss, looking bedraggled and exhausted, even apologetic. She had been walking, but now she trotted in an elderly way toward Charles, her head hanging.

"She's back," Charles said.

A fearful gloom settled on Edith. It was all so ordained, so terribly predictable. There would be more and more yumas. When Charles shook the birdhouse in a moment, there wouldn't be anything in it, and then she would see the animal in the house, and Puss-Puss would again catch it. She and Charles, together, were stuck with it.

"She found her way all the way back here, I'm sure. Two miles," Charles said to Edith, smiling.

But Edith clamped her teeth to repress a scream.

# MRRRAR!

## by Edgar Pangborn

Timmy ate his field mouse, washed, and climbed on a log for a cat's midsummer-night thoughts; black, ten pounds of readiness, no longer young.

Above the house beyond the hayfield a night hawk was rasping. A swaying of trees now and then released the brilliance of village lights a mile away. Down the blind thread of a nearby road swept a noise, with blazing eyes; Timmy ignored it, but tense at something else appearing on the road—human, it was moving with unhuman quiet, slinking to Timmy's house, crouching at the back door.

Timmy had left through that door two hours ago, by request. Returning, he need only jump on the box outside it and rattle the knob. There would be delays, creaks, moanings—but The Friend would come; it was rarely necessary to wail. The Friend would open up, and say: "Well, damn it ..."

That human shadow entered the woodshed. Nothing of importance. Timmy relaxed, yawned, and stretched ...

The Friend used little of the house except the kitchen. His musty cot was there, and a rocking chair where Timmy could sprawl in his lap accepting the caress of crinkled hands, responding with his own bari-

tone purr. It was a good life: Timmy could take it on
his own terms.

The shadow was at the door again. A hint of smell
with evil association reached Timmy, but it was too
faint for complete recognition, and the memory was
many days old ...

A good life. Compatibility; a supply of milk and
mixed-up meat that wasn't bad, and sometimes a sardine; mutual concessions and forbearance. Periodically
one of those road-monsters stopped, with one who
clattered in to spread mysteries on the table and exchange with Timmy's associate a harmless barking;
after this episode something of value usually appeared
in Timmy's dish. Few others ever came; when they did
Timmy retired under The Friend's cot—except for
The Friend he distrusted the tribe.

For one, a slab-faced roarer, he had loathing. Not
long ago, The Friend had been engaged in one of his
peculiar activities—prying up a floor board, lifting a
black box, waving away Timmy's nose while the box
rustled and jingled. The roarer had arrived during the
operation, with uncharacteristic quiet. The Friend had
jumped up; the atmosphere was stiff with alarm; Timmy
had gone under the cot. But then the intruder had made
peaceful sounds, while Timmy studied barnyard-smelling
feet and a furry something dangling at the roarer's
middle—a rabbit's foot, its odor not quite gone. In
time, Timmy had emerged. And without warning the
roarer had grabbed his tail, a wet mouth letting off a
blast of noise. Timmy had gashed a thick arm and
fled in swollen rage while the kitchen boiled, shrillness
mingling with the roaring and a slam of the back door.
Timmy had not seen the roarer again; once or twice
he had caught a whiff of the same stench outdoors,
and had hidden in the grass.

The shadow was of no importance. It was only making noiseless motions at the window, lifting it, climbing inside. Timmy stretched again, and wandered into the woods, the best part of the world, his feet touching leaf-mold as an owl's wing touches air.

In a moonless clearing he played make-believe with a pine cone, falling on his side to kick at it, having fun ...

His ears warned him in time to whirl on his back— hell was loose, on an owl's down-padded wings. Timmy strove, with teeth and slashing legs—no such rabbit as the owl may have imagined. A hook stabbed; Timmy yelled, and raked a wild tufted face. The horror let go and vanished in the night.

One talon had bared a rib, going no deeper, but the gash was painful. Recovering from shock in the safety of thick brush, Timmy licked it. In due time he crept slowly home, watchful of the sky. A new thing—trouble had never before come at Timmy out of the sky. But in his careful passage he had no traffic with imaginary dangers. Timmy met danger as he should: readiness was all.

He jumped to his box. Near the house that faint Bad Smell now identified itself—slab-faced roarer and no mistake. But pain and the desire for known shelter were strongest: the door-knob had to be rattled. Here was a difficulty: normally the right paw was the knob-rattling paw, and the wound was on Timmy's right side. But he made it.

There had been dim sounds of motion in the house; instead of answering Timmy's application, they ceased. A dead moment; then a pounding of heavy steps— away. The front door banged open; feet thudded up the road. Though alarming, that was all of secondary importance.

What mattered was that The Friend had to come. Timmy rattled again; after a decent interval he wailed. The front door squealed in rising wind, but that was all ... Timmy tried the woodshed: no good.

He considered a window-sill, but his side hurt too much when he bunched for a leap. At last his forlorn prowling brought him to the open front door; he trotted through to the kitchen, tail up, calling inquiry. He sniffed at torn-up floor boards, an empty black box, and hurried to his dish. It was overturned, but he licked some comfort from a milk puddle.

The bulk on the cot was the right size for The Friend. A dangling hand smelled almost right; Timmy saw it twitch, and arched his neck to rub against it. No answering caress, but something tumbled—a rabbit's foot on a bit of cord, fastened in some substance with marks on it that clicked as Timmy pushed it. But the atmosphere was wrong for play. Timmy batted the thing idly under the cot, and climbed up.

The bumps and hollows were wrong, unresponsive. Any position troubled the smarting side; Timmy whimpered in exasperation. The Friend was not quite there. Only a pillow at the head end—some spread of white hair above it, but the pillow had the Bad Smell. Timmy returned to his milk puddle: dried up. The front door continued its noise, squeaking and pounding ...

A road-master hummed slowly past, stopped, and returned. Brisk footsteps, noise of a voice. Timmy went under the cot.

Below a round white glare in the kitchen doorway Timmy saw legs in a dark shining of leather. These hurried to the cot; the pillow hit the floor. A hand came into Timmy's line of vision, feeling The Friend's fingers, lifting them out of sight. The Leather Legs ran out shouting, returning with another like himself. A spitting flare bloomed into white steady light on the table—The Friend had done that every evening. The object hanging near the back door was jangled: Timmy was used to that—The Friend had often wound the crank as Leather Legs did now, and made his noises into it.

One Leather Legs peered under the cot—usual arrangements of pale skin, mouth, nose. He said; "Here, kitty, kitty!" Timmy spat.

The milk dish was righted and filled. A Leather Legs was busy at the table, but his companion stood too near the hall door—no chance to make a break for it yet. Timmy nosed the rabbit's foot, bored.

The table noises were tearing clashes and a moderate "Damn!"—as if The Friend himself were doing the miracle, a miracle now confirmed by the celestial odor and substance of sardine. Beyond the cot Timmy thrust an inquiring face like a black moon. Leather Legs retired. Watching the two with readiness, Timmy accepted ... Then the milk. A Leather Legs reached; Timmy went under the cot. But pain was easing; thirst was appeased; he could wait it out. If The Friend had come back, Timmy might even have made overtures, to the extent of sniffing a shoe-tip. But The Friend did not come back.

Fine night odors were pouring in; the Bad Smell was almost cleaned away. A fox barked, answered by the passion of a dog-voice in the village; the night hawk grated. Timmy worried the rabbit's foot to pass the time.

Poor stuff—no wiggle. A casual flirt of his paw sent it out into lamplight. A hand swooped down for it with a lively "Hey!"

Timmy didn't mind. What interested him was that

now the doorway was clear. A Leather Legs was again booming into the jangling thing.

Timmy ran.

A shout followed him. Actually a human expression of gratitude and esteem, offering an option on a second sardine.

But to Timmy it was only a type of barking. The Friend had gone away.

He watched the sky, traveling slowly but with lessening pain. Trouble, of course, can come from any quarter of the universe: readiness is all. The forest was the best part of the world—there you sometimes even met your own kind. Timmy said: "Mrrrar. Mrrraraorrh?"

# MYSTERY FAVORITES